FIREPLAY

In the armoury sat Makarov, behind a chess board, his elbow upon a small table, chin resting in his left hand. A studious set to his face, plastic chess pieces and a Russian chess magazine completed the tableau.

Six magazines of another kind – for use in a sub-machine gun – lay on the table. The sound of footsteps on the marble outside the armoury brought Makarov to his feet. The armourer wanted another signature from his caller, and he slipped carbon between the leaves of his requisition book.

Makarov bent over his receipts and, if he noticed Yazov raise his right hand, he paid no special attention. The flattened hand came down with chop to snap Makarov's spinal cord in three places.

William Wingate

FIREPLAY

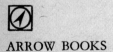

ARROW BOOKS

Arrow Books Ltd
3 Fitzroy Square, London WIP 6JD

An imprint of the Hutchinson Publishing Group

London Melbourne Sydney Auckland
Wellington Johannesburg and agencies
throughout the world

First published by Hutchinson & Co. (Publishers) Ltd 1977
Arrow edition 1979
© William Wingate 1977

Made and printed in Great Britain
by The Anchor Press Ltd
Tiptree, Essex

ISBN 0 09 917830 3

*For Robin
and Julian*

I

April 1973 was a hot and sticky month in the mid-Pacific, noted for a hurricane called Clarissa. While Clarissa raged above the surface, the Soviet submarine *Doneska* sank to the sea bottom some 950 miles north-east of Midway atoll. Her plunge to disaster set in train the decade's most elaborate intelligence project, unleashing forces which were to go unpredictably out of control.

Twenty-two months earlier, in June 1971, a Sikorsky Sea Horse helicopter of the United States Navy had been engaged in a routine task in the same area of the ocean. It had lowered into the sea a cage looking like a baby's big rattle and containing a device which would monitor undersea sounds for many years to come.

This was just one among hundreds of rugged self-mooring sonar buoys which the navy had lowered into 20000 feet of water near naval bases and in narrow straits where Russian submarines patrolled. The buoys crossed the Pacific, stretching from the equator to the polar seas, and received sounds that travelled long distances through the water's cold deeper depths. How far and how well the sensitive hydrophones eavesdropped was limited only by changes in sea pressures and the variety of sounds in the Pacific itself; in fact, the acoustic receivers could even pick up the quick snap of a shark's jaw.

Sonar buoy 1321A guarded some of the approaches to the strategic US naval and air bases at Midway atoll. It easily monitored the big sounds of the submarine as it sank in

April 1973, recording the rumbles made by its engines and propeller shaft before the explosions.

As it was programmed to do, sonar buoy 1321A automatically re-transmitted, above hurricane Clarissa's fury, all the noise it had collected to the US Navy's Ocean Surveillance System. It was then forwarded 1350 miles to the navy's SOSUS shore receiving station at Pearl Harbor, where the bleeps and squawks were analysed by computers.

On surface or under water, every diesel submarine engine has its own rumble; every propeller shaft has its own distinctive whirr; every shape of hull creates a special turbulence of wake; every steel hull generates a definable magnetic field. All these physical effects combine to give a submarine its own distinctive clank.

The US Navy relies on clank for its underwater sonar network, storing these electronic signatures in computer libraries of magnetic tapes. Within sixty-three days of *Doneska*'s maiden run her signature had been on tape at all major US naval bases. From that time on she was classified, computerized, tracked and plotted wherever she patrolled. If her clank changed slightly, so did the electronic squiggles on her tapes.

Shortly after the noise from sonar buoy 1321A was processed at Pearl Harbor, United States Naval Intelligence knew – even before the Russian navy at Vladivostok – that a first-generation, *Golf*-class submarine had probably sunk to the sea floor some fifty miles off this buoy, and that it was the diesel-powered Russian ballistic missile submarine *Doneska*.

The computers had even deciphered the noise of *Doneska*'s disaster buoy, which had inexplicably broken from an aft mounting to drift erratically in undersea currents.

By that time a series of hard facts about the vessel, its description and history had already clattered on to the printouts at Pearl Harbor. The commander in chief of the Soviet Pacific Fleet at Vladivostok knew most of what was printed and much more; information still secret from the US Navy. What he did not know was that *Doneska* had gone down at a point 39°17'N and 165°13'W as defined by the IBM computers. For the Russian navy, in April 1973, possessed no comparable Suspended Array Surveillance System in the Pacific.

One hour after the *Doneska* had failed to transmit her coded call sign to Vladivostok, a search-and-rescue operation began. Ships of the Pacific Fleet mounted watches around the clock to listen for distress calls and report any unusual undersea noises.

As Vice-Admiral V. I. Yashin – short, square-shouldered, taciturn – drove in a staff car to the docks of Vladivostok, squadrons of long-range reconnaissance aircraft operated by the Russian navy were already flying over wide areas of the Pacific, using electronic equipment that included top secret magnetic anomaly booms and anti-submarine detectors housed in extended radomes.

By the time Yashin climbed aboard his flagship, *Kresta*, the navy's land-based Bears and Turboprop Mail flying boats had radioed in the first coded, negative reports. Ships of the Soviet Navy were under full steam in the Pacific towards a staging area 1000 kilometres off the central, western seaboard of the United States. A formidable fleet was gathering: fighting, merchant, trawler and hydrographic ships which Yashin commanded through very high and low radio frequencies.

After he had read the reports, Yashin stood peering through binoculars as *Kresta* steamed steadily through a channel broken by ice-breakers in Golden Horn Bay, to enter the Sea of Japan at 1203 hours. Then there was nothing more to see, even with binoculars.

Sergei Rudnev, captain of the *Kresta* and related by marriage to Yashin, stood beside him on the bridge. He asked, 'What do you think of this mission, sir?'

'Hopeless.' Yashin lowered his binoculars. 'Absolutely hopeless – which doesn't mean that we fail to go through the motions, do what we can. We have to keep them happy, our submarine crews. The navy has to keep morale up in a special key area. It wouldn't do, would it Sergei, if *Doneska* were simply written off. All our submarines must know that, whatever the chances, we will do what we can.'

Rudnev nodded. 'Yes, sir.'

'Unfortunately the whole complicated costly business will fail. Our submarine crews are too well trained. They would survive most emergencies. But this silence . . . ' Yashin shrugged.

As if to emphasize his words, a klaxon hooted. *Kresta*'s crewmen ran efficiently through a standard drill, checking that she was safe and sea-worthy, that all her systems were working.

'Yes, I suppose her silence is bad.'

'Bad, Sergei? Fatal. There must have been a major electrical or mechanical failure. Her oxygen reserves will have gone in three, maybe four days. They are all dead. And even if we found her now, you know as well as I do that no recoveries are possible beyond a few fathoms.'

'Yes, of course.' Rudnev began to regret that he had started Yashin off on a lecture, but it was too late.

'There are other things, too. We should try and find the missiles. Maybe recover them, maybe destroy them. That would be a hell of a business, I don't mind telling you. But I'm confident we'll not find a damn thing, not even the ship, so I'll not worry about that question,' Yashin smiled grimly.

Kresta's captain looked up at the array of the guided missile cruiser's electronic gear, which even from the bridge was impressive. Back-to-back search radar; surveillance radar; surface-to-surface missile radar; all of which could spot ships and aircraft from afar. She also carried two anti-submarine helicopters that could be launched off the flush decks of her stern.

'Useless, Sergei. Useless,' Yashin read Rudnev's thoughts. 'All of it very wonderful but only useful for operational depths. If *Doneska*'s down deep, what then? The same goes for all the other ships and aircraft. None of this wonderful stuff is designed to work at thousands of metres in depth. Not effectively, anyhow.'

'What about our trawlers and hydrographic craft?'

'Well, what about our trawlers? They are crammed with electronic gadgetry, but that will only help if *Doneska* is transmitting radio signals. And that's not likely.'

'And *Zaytiv* and the other hydrographics?' Rudnev asked, persisting only because he was married to Yashin's niece. Perhaps that was why he commanded *Kresta*, he sometimes thought.

Zaytiv was a 5700-ton oceanographic survey ship which had completed sea trials in the northern Pacific, with a crew of 137 officers and men, and 73 scientists on board.

'*Zaytiv* is only one ship,' Yashin said. 'She can never cover the whole vast area of water where *Doneska* may have sunk.'

Yashin was right. Rudnev knew that the vice-admiral had left unsaid the fact that the cold-war code for a Russian ballistic missile submarine required *Doneska* to sail silently and hide in the sea; radio signals would have alerted ships of the US Navy on Pacific patrol.

'And she was on a KGB mission,' Yashin told Rudnev for the first time. 'Oh, our security friends in Moscow have been about as helpful as ever. Nothing in her secret mission, apart from the usual patrol, could have been dangerous, they assure me. No details, as usual. Only, don't worry, it's not our fault. What's more, *Doneska* was to have sailed for the KGB into waters off Chile after the cold-war patrol. After some kind of Chilean contact, she would have refuelled from a fleet tanker about 1500 kilometres south-west of Santiago. Anyway, so they tell me. She never made it. Never made the Chilean contact, never refuelled.'

'A little depressing with the KGB involved too, sir.'

'Not all that depressing, Sergei. Even the KGB can have its brighter side. Frankly, without them, I'd not have known where to begin this search. Fortunately, it's not my responsibility because they've given the general guidelines and told me how to start and finish. It's nice to feel a pawn occasionally, particularly when the mission's fairly hopeless anyway.'

Captain Rudnev saluted as Yashin left the bridge for the operations room.

Mechanically, Yashin plotted on a chart the route *Doneska* had filed with Vladivostok. It was the usual cold-war patrol for a ballistic missile submarine of the Soviet Pacific Fleet save for one difference: *Doneska*'s route took her south of the Aleutian Islands to sail a constant course about 1000 miles off the Alaskan, Canadian and United States coast-lines down to the Mexican border; but instead of patrolling back to the Aleutians, *Doneska* would have sailed on to Chile for the KGB.

What depressed the admiral was that *Doneska* could have foundered anywhere from her last radioed position off Los Angeles to close by Valparaiso. Without refuelling, *Doneska* had a range of about 22000 miles, which meant that the submarine could have gone down anywhere thousands of miles south of California.

Yashin reckoned the likeliest theory was that *Doneska* had sailed the shortest line along this route. Still, the area of Pacific to be covered was too vast for success without a great slice of pure luck.

Working hours without rest, Yashin dutifully made intelligent assumptions and did calculations. Alone and undisturbed, he pored for hours over charts and maps which gathered thickly on the table. His collar hung loosely about his neck. Dozens of cigarette ends littered three large ash-trays.

Nevertheless, the search pattern he eventually worked out would take his task force thousands of miles from where *Doneska* lay on the Pacific bottom. . . . For three weeks, the Russian task force searched the area just south of where *Doneska* filed her last movement report to a point slightly south of Valparaiso. When the search was most intense, in the second week, sixty-three ships and fifty-four aircraft were engaged, criss-crossing the well-planned grid. Fast fighting ships sailed up and down grid lines, more than double the distances of the slower trawler and survey ships. Hydrographic ships worked underwater television cameras, electrodes to detect currents generated by metals in sea water, Geiger counters that picked up radiation from nuclear materials, and magnetometers for recording differences in magnetic fields. *Zaytiv* snapped thousands of underwater photographs of every kind of debris.

Above the task force flitted submarine hunting helicopters, launched from *Kresta*-class cruisers and *Krupny*-class guided missile destroyers. Crammed with electronic gadgets, they criss-crossed the wakes of fighting ships, and were themselves overflown by long-range aircraft.

Yashin's huge search revealed nothing of *Doneska*. Every bump in normal instrument readings, every oil slick, every photograph and every piece of marine debris was either negative or too inconclusive. The closest the task force ever got to any sunken submarine was when a dragline in shallow water along the Nazca Ridge 600 miles south-west of San Juan, Peru, brought to surface pieces of submarine battery plates which had not been made in Russia.

Doneska had disappeared for ever, Yashin was convinced. When the task force had completed its sweep past Valparaiso, he decided to call a halt. 'I don't know what more we can do,' he told the advisory committee at the last meeting he chaired in *Kresta*'s operations room. 'There is just nothing there at all.'

'I agree, sir.' Rudnev nodded.

'What do they expect, though?'

Yashin signalled the office of the commander in chief of the Soviet Navy of their failure, but he need not have worried. The vast search had satisfied Department A of the First Chief Directorate of the KGB – the department which specialized in demoralizing foreign governments and covering up KGB bungles around the world. And the search had undoubtedly buoyed the morale of the men that mattered – the submarine fleet of Russia's nuclear deterrent. They could not but be impressed by their navy's dogged determination. The way Yashin had smoothly co-ordinated the task force's team work was not wasted either, for the whole exercise had impressively tested the Pacific Fleet under emergency conditions.

The office of the commander in chief radioed back sympathy, adding congratulations. Though *Doneska* had not been found, the search had proceeded with praiseworthy efficiency and a grateful office of the commander in chief permitted Yashin to stop the search. It radioed also his promotion to Admiral of the Fleet and an official commendation from Department A of the First Directorate.

On the high seas, members of the small committee raised vodka glasses to a tired, smiling Yashin. Somebody produced a balalaika. Before the music started, Yashin completed orders to disperse the task force. He would not call off the search entirely since *Zaytiv* and other hydrographic ships still needed a couple of weeks to investigate fully all the task force's underwater contacts. For the rest, the task force would disband and slot into new missions. But until further notice, all ships would keep a routine watch for any signs of the lost submarine; in fact the lookout for *Doneska* would last indefinitely.

Only then did Yashin relax. With a hand pushed deep into the pocket of his naval jacket, he emptied three glasses of vodka and thought well of his nephew-by-marriage for arranging the small celebration.

The closest *Kresta* had been to *Doneska* was when she sailed her thirty-fifth day out of Vladivostok in choppy water, 1800 miles due west of Albion, California. At 1408 hours, *Kresta* was 430 miles east and 70 miles north of the sunken submarine. By then, *Doneska*'s shattered stern had settled into the first layer of Pacific ooze.

2

Even before Yashin boarded *Kresta* there was a report for Lieutenant Peter William Morrows, United States Naval Intelligence, Pearl Harbor. The report was typed on twenty-three pages and neatly bound between white covers. It was marked top secret and for Morrows's attention.

Morrows flicked open the first page. *SB1321A signals destruction through on-board explosions of Soviet Golf-class submarine in Pacific within ten miles square of 39°16′N and 165°14′W. Submarine identified as* Doneska *(No. 782) ten days from Vladivostok.*

According to *Doneska*'s sonar log, she had sailed out of the Sea of Japan through the Straits of Perouse, then the usual cold-war patrol south of the Aleutians, down past the seaboards of Alaska, Canada and the western United States. From far south in Chilean waters the submarine had swung north-west of the Marquesas in a straight course to disaster north-east of Midway.

There was a sketch of *Doneska*'s route: the lines were in red and dotted where sonar buoys had not picked her up and an analyst had made skilful guesses. Morrows glanced briefly at the solid and broken red lines before turning the page.

782 believed launched Komsomolsk 1963 with prototype Sark missiles. Converted to carry Serb missiles Vladivostok 1969. A brief description of *Doneska*'s major characteristics – *very large fin to house Serb missiles* – history and presumed cold-war mission completed the first half of the report.

Serb missiles only reckoned by naval intelligence to carry 500-kiloton hydrogen warheads in two stages with inertial guidance. No US intelligence agency has ever handled a Serb missile. The report reminded Morrows of something he well knew.

Doneska probably carried six bow and four stern torpedo tubes. *All torpedoes possibly tipped with nuclear warheads.* The latest Russian torpedoes, Morrows knew too, were reckoned by naval intelligence to be armed with atomic devices and sensitive acoustic receivers which homed in on sounds emitted by enemy ships. The torpedoes were believed to emit exploratory sound waves and to hunt their targets, circling around them in some way.

Morrows, who had graduated tenth in his class at the Annapolis, was a keen officer. Within thirty-five minutes of opening the report he had fully briefed his superior, Rear Admiral John P. Shilling, in Shilling's large, airy office overlooking the harbour.

Now and then, Morrows stopped reading directly from the report to add his own commentary. He finished and handed Shilling the slim volume without comment.

'That sub must have been on cold-war patrol, sir. She was probably on surface recharging her batteries. Trapped gases in the hull somewhere. A spark, then boom.'

'So simple? Don't they have too many safeguards these days for that kind of thing to happen?'

'Hydrogen may have built up off the battery anodes, hung around in some faulty corner and mixed with the sub's oxygen. Then a spark, maybe from a badly wired generator. Who knows? Maybe somebody got careless. All we know is it happened.'

'It's happened all right,' Shilling agreed. 'What about the crew?'

'I've already sent a reconnaissance flight off Midway without saying too much. Hope I did the right thing, sir.' Morrows said it more as a statement than anything else and was relieved to see Shilling nod almost imperceptibly.

'They'll be reporting soon but it'll probably be negative.

When something like this hits, things happen too fast. Sonar buoy 1321A got a few very big bangs. The guys in there probably didn't know a thing when it happened. Many would have gone with the blasts, the rest once the sub headed for the bottom. The buoy got the sound of her crashing into the sea bed.'

'There's not going to be anybody alive after all that. Still, let's wait for the reports. You've thought it out well, Morrows.'

The younger man smiled his thanks, and said, 'Sir, we know that she had ballistic missiles with nuclear warheads, maybe atomic torpedoes. She must have carried code books, her cipher. Could be big. That's just a hunch.'

'My feeling too. That'll be what everybody's after. Lots will depend on how deep she's gone.'

'It's pretty deep out there, sir.' Morrows shook his head. 'The IBMs have put her at about 15 000 feet.'

'That's a lot of water. Yes, it's going to be a problem. But right now we have another. The Russians will be out in force soon, no doubt about that. Will they find her?'

Two hours later there were reports from the reconnaissance jets off Midway atoll. Nothing. And then the first reports of a large task force preparing to leave Vladivostok.

This large Russian task force that 'exercised' in the eastern Pacific gave US Naval Intelligence no illusions. Yashin's ships were after *Doneska*. The size and scale of the search confirmed their belief that *Doneska* carried secret weaponry covered by Russia's latest advances in submarine warfare. The thought excited them: to recover a Russian missile-carrying submarine with armaments intact would be a major cold-war coup.

The Russian search expanded, and the Americans waited anxiously for the task force to move into the area where *Doneska* had gone down. When with each day Yashin's ships sailed further away from the key point Morrows had plotted on a Pacific chart, they were relieved and puzzled. How could Yashin be so far off the mark?

At last, Yashin's search was over. Gratefully, they monitored the dispersal of fighting ships, intelligence trawlers, hydrographic craft and merchantmen. It was May 1973 and Shilling and Morrows were ready; their chance had come.

Even before the Russians broke formation, Shilling had ordered into the Pacific USS *Mary Jane*, a sophisticated naval research vessel. Now, in Pearl Harbor, he stood at a window of the large white office that overlooked the port. Below the window there was a hive of activity as warships were loaded and unloaded. High cranes swung around and fork-lift trucks moved along the wharves.

Shilling had been tremendously impressed by the Russian naval machine rolling over the Pacific. Yet the search was over areas thousands of miles from where *Doneska* had exploded. How had Yashin gone wrong so badly? Perhaps there was no sunken Russian submarine. Maybe the sonar device was faulty in reporting the catastrophic noise course at 39°16′N and 165°14′W. Sometimes, Shilling knew, the sonars blinked.

USS *Mary Jane* was already in the Gulf of Panama, and Shilling did not intend to countermand anything. What was done was done. Even so, if *Doneska* had sunk at all, she had sunk in up to 20000 feet of water. *Mary Jane* had to be given a grid over ten square miles of Pacific surface, and that was still a lot of water for one hydrographic ship to cover.

A possibly faulty signal from a defective sonar; a signal that did not pinpoint *Doneska*'s location but only gave a general area; one hydrographic ship to search the whole area down to 20000 feet. . . .

Shilling did not pretend to understand *Mary Jane*'s technology in detail, but he did understand the hazards. Morrows was more confident. Geophysics had been his major at Annapolis. He knew about the technology of this kind of ship manned by technicians and scientists: almost everybody on board had some kind of degree or special training.

He gave his superior a smile of encouragement. 'Hell, you never know. When these guys get after something, there's no stopping them.'

Fully loaded, *Mary Jane* displaced 5000 tons. She was 260 feet long and her large Westinghouse electric motors drove diesels that allowed her to cruise at a steady twelve knots. Among her complement, there were twelve officers, thirty-one enlisted men with technical training and seventeen highly-skilled scientists.

Her captain was Robert H. Conrad, and if any combination could find *Doneska* it was geophysicist Conrad and his ultra-sophisticated ship. A computer enabled her to map and produce finished charts of forty square miles of ocean bottom every two days, and her underwater systems were specially designed to locate wrecks and disabled submarines.

Captain Conrad was an MIT graduate and a methodical man. Once he had Shilling's orders, before Yashin's task force gave up looking, and prior even to *Mary Jane*'s passage through the Panama Canal, he had planned, plotted and charted every detail of a two-month search along a finely spaced grid ten miles square. Inside the 100 square miles of ocean floor, Conrad would seek a target that was only 320 feet by 25 feet at its greatest width. Precision navigation was crucial. In the calm weather of the first day, Conrad began the search at the north-eastern corner of his imaginary grid.

Instruments dominated the search too much to excite the crew's imagination. They knew *Mary Jane* was searching for some kind of submarine wreck, that was all. There had been previous searches for all kinds of wrecks and the men had been none the wiser. Security was tight on *Mary Jane* and men were not expected to be curious.

Instead, they stood, sat and waited in expensively paid boredom while the sun burned. Most had stripped to white shorts, all wore protective sunglasses, and those who had used sun lotions shone in the heat.

On the ninth day of the search, *Mary Jane* bore due south along the thirty-first line of Conrad's grid. The ship streamed fishing lines astern and Conrad fished for amberjack and sea bass from the rail. A few feet from him an amberjack flopped weakly on the deck. Close to the amberjack lay the head and gaping jaws of a big barracuda – its body snapped clean away by a shark's single bite.

Conrad was adjusting his soft canvas hat when a crewman in crisp white linen called him to the sonar and radar laboratory. Wishing somebody else better luck, Conrad gave up his fishing pole to go below deck.

Inside the cool laboratory, the small room smelt strongly of ozone – the trivalent form of oxygen found around electronic gadgetry. A radar and sonar operator pointed to electronic squiggles that came and went on a large screen, while a device emitted sharp, echoing 'pings'.

Knobs were twiddled, the screen's image brightened, the pings got sharper and louder. Conrad left to check the magnetometer: weak as the signals were, they indicated an anomaly. Far below, Conrad guessed, there was probably a large mass of metal.

He returned thoughtfully to the sonar and radar laboratory. 'Well,' he said quietly to the operator, 'that's the fish.'

A triumphant blast on the ship's klaxon signalled success for the first part of *Mary Jane*'s mission. The ship's engines had already been reversed by the time a group of scientists and crewmen gathered on the stern deck. They could not see anything and knew they never would, but there was nothing better to do than stare into the deep, blue water.

To naval intelligence in Pearl Harbor, Conrad radioed a one-word code that signalled first-phase success: 'WINDY'.

Mary Jane's naval scientists had begun to work her electronic gear. 'Depth sounded at sixteen five on five,' an operator reported unemotionally. Seconds later, *Mary Jane*'s precision depth-sounder had positioned the metal 'anomaly' at 39°15′42″N and 165°14′33″W.

Mary Jane reversed, and propellers were moved cycloidally fore and aft to hold the ship still, making her hover within a foot of where Conrad wanted.

'Side-scanner ready.'

Scientists operated a super-sensitive, side-scan sonar to try and confirm what Conrad and others already thought they knew. Whatever the anomaly was thousands of feet below *Mary Jane*, side-scan sonar would trace its outline electronically for all to see. There was a low murmur of excitement as Conrad and scientists crowded round a sonar screen to watch darting flecks of neon scatter and regroup.

For a moment Conrad worried about whether he had been too quick to signal finding *Doneska*. So far he was only certain of an anomaly 16515 feet down on the Pacific bottom. Perhaps the wreck of a freighter? Another fighting ship, possibly not even Russian?

'Getting a better fix, picture emerging.'

On the screen, the sonar traced a fuzzy outline. A technician fiddled with knobs and to Conrad's relief there appeared the sharp outline of a G-class submarine. Etched clearly in neon against the screen's grey-black background was *Doneska*'s large fin. The picture was so good Conrad could even see the rounding of hatches that topped her missile tubes.

A little rashly, he had radioed Pearl Harbor his intuition rather than hard fact. Now he was relieved that he had guessed correctly. The odds were overwhelming that the typical, distinctive *Golf*-class silhouette on the screen was *Doneska*.

In the short, tropical twilight, *Mary Jane*'s crew lowered two strands of drilling pipe through the spy ship's internal well into the inky, deep waters. Pods were attached to the pipe, and television and still cameras and strong, underwater lights hung from each pod.

Shortly after dawn on the tenth day of the mission, propellers churning fore and aft, *Mary Jane* was finally ready. At 0607 hours technicians began still-photographing and video-taping *Doneska* repeatedly from bow to stern.

By evening of the thirteenth day, *Mary Jane*'s team had a series of mosaics from thousands of photographs. The calm weather changed and gusting winds showered *Mary Jane* with spray, and heavy rain slatted down. With the mission completed, she set out for Pearl Harbor, sailing a shade under her maximum of 13.5 knots.

Conrad radioed Shilling a new signal. It was *Mary Jane*'s success in two coded words: 'WINDY ANGEL'.

In that large, brightly lit office in Pearl Harbor, Rear Admiral Shilling and Lieutenant Morrows combed through thousands of photographs neatly stacked in classified piles along a rectangular conference table. The prints were sharp and clear and the photographs had a pungent fresh smell.

'Just like the IBMs said, sir. They'd widened the fin for the bigger, long-range Serbs.'

'There's no damage to the fin area,' Shilling added. 'That's lucky, Morrows. Missiles probably intact safely sealed in some kind of reinforced tower. It's all there, 16000 feet down, ready for anybody who can reach that far below.'

Morrows fingered another photograph that showed how *Doneska*'s stern had dug slightly in the bottom ooze, her bow jutting gently towards the surface. There was shattering of the stern but *Doneska*'s bow was wholly intact.

'I got it from Research this morning that she seems to be fitted in the bow with six torpedo tubes. They agree that she's probably got them hotted up with nuclear warheads. She'll be carrying anything from ten to twenty-one torpedoes.'

'And with no damage to the fin area,' Shilling concentrated again on the area around *Doneska*'s conning tower, 'the radio room may have come through the blast without too much lost. The ciphers, codes, they're probably intact, Morrows.'

'I agree, sir. And you know my feelings right now.'

Shilling put down the photographs. In a large, leather armchair, he sat a long time in silence, knowing all the while what Morrows felt. The more he pored over the photographs, the stronger those feelings grew.

He was reluctant to forsake *Doneska*, but both men knew instinctively and without discussion that *Doneska* was too big for naval intelligence. She lay inaccessibly deep, and naval intelligence had neither men, nor money, nor means to carry out such a complex technological operation in great secrecy.

The aim was straightforward: somehow to raise *Doneska* from the sea bed, 16000 feet down, to learn her secrets of nuclear weaponry, targeting and codes. They both knew there was only one agency for such a large, costly espionage effort: the Central Intelligence Agency. It was the ultimate in frustration, yet there was no alternative. They had to pass on their intelligence to the CIA and let *Doneska* slip out of their hands.

With the decision made, Morrows could not resist one sour grapes comment. 'Well, this job will sure as hell give even those hot shots something to sweat about.' Shilling grunted in sympathy.

Morrows looked at a photograph of *Doneska*'s stern held firmly in sand.

'Looks like they'll need a sandwedge to get her out,' he said idly.

So Project Sandwedge was born – and Sandwedge, they were sure, would grow very big. . . .

It was late in June 1973, when Morrows personally handed the Sandwedge report to the CIA. He entered the lobby of the CIA building in Langley, Virginia, and crossed the floor with its large, circular inset of the spy agency's coat-of-arms: a compass rose topped by an eagle's head.

3

Four copies of the navy's Sandwedge report lay upon a beech-wood table in room 551 of the CIA's Langley headquarters. The reports came in neat, blue folders that were spaced equidistantly around the circular table top in front of agents of the Department of Operations: Mallory from Operational Services, Harper of Missions and Programs, Carson from Technical Services. They waited for McLaren, one of the highest ranking members of the CIA.

So far, James Joseph McLaren had kept them waiting in his office for over fifteen minutes. That was nothing un-usual: just the expression of seniority and authority he en-joyed making. It gave time for the younger agents to look around the room and be confronted on all sides with sym-bols of McLaren's dominance: relics from his past. And that past, they had to admit, was impressive. . . .

The young McLaren had begun quietly, conventionally enough; a student at Whittier College, a Quaker institution in California: a class photograph of 1934 showed him, slim and white-faced, in a row behind Richard M. Nixon, who had gone on to become president of the United States.

After winning a scholarship to Duke University in Durham, North Carolina, McLaren displayed a liking and aptitude for being where the action was. During the Second World War he had joined OSS; after that organization's disbandment, the CIA. In 1956 he parachuted into Buda-pest, at the outbreak of the Hungarian Revolution; on his present office wall hung the photograph of a girl not more than fifteen, with a 7.62 calibre Simonov as tall as herself, a twelve-year-old boy with a sub-machine gun slung about his shoulder, McLaren himself, and the grimly smiling man who had punched the final teleprinter messages from the main Budapest news agency:

'RUSSIAN GANGSTERS HAVE BETRAYED US. A FEW HUNDRED TANKS ATTACKED BUDAPEST . . . A THOUSAND . . . THERE IS HEAVY FIGHTING . . . I STAY OPEN AND CONTINUE WITH THE NEWS . . . WE SHALL INFORM THE WORLD . . .' And, finally: 'GOODBYE, FRIENDS . . . GOD SAVE OUR SOULS. THE RUSSIANS ARE TOO NEAR.'

These messages, too, hung on a framed strip of telex paper on McLaren's office wall. He was a confirmed collector of mementoes. The small chunk of concrete and jagged glass which served as a paper-weight which Mallory was now nervously fingering was once part of the Berlin Wall – for McLaren, after escaping from Budapest and briefing Freedom Fighters in Vienna, had progressed to Germany in time for the sealing-off of East Berlin.

His colleagues ruefully agreed, that for all their conscientious labours, not one of them had ever fired a shot in anger. For all their intelligence and skill, James Joseph McLaren had the confidence of an old professional who had not got it all out of books . . . which was why, whenever it came to debates over project evaluations, he would win the arguments.

After all, what had the younger agents been doing in the fifties? Harper, the youngest, had been at Notre Dame, worrying about bed checks, fussing over midnight curfews, Mass every day, the Angelus, rosaries, benedictions and the Nine Fridays. While Harper was fearing expulsion for driving a car in South Bend, McLaren was fighting Russian tanks in Budapest. Now Harper lived with a girl, a legacy perhaps of staying too long in an all-male institution: anyway, it was something of which McLaren disapproved.

Harper and Carson had met at officers' candidate school at an Air Force Base in Colorado. That was after Harper had got his M A from Penn and Carson was already married. The hardest task given them in training was a six-day trek in the December snows on the mountains; this at a time when McLaren was in the midst of the Hungarian Freedom struggle.

And now, in 1973, McLaren was nearing retirement, one of the last of the old guard. Bespectacled and meticulous, he still worked long days and late nights. He remained, by nature, a risk-taker and relaxed by playing poker, winning most of the time. Trout-fishing was his only other recreation; he had a little fishing cabin in Vermont. Mounted on the office wall was yet another trophy: a large prize trout.

The CIA had given McLaren Project Sandwedge to evaluate. His job was to analyse and separate good from bad, to report and recommend.

The office door opened and McLaren walked in, characteristically, without any apology for his delay.

'Well,' he asked Harper, 'have you come up with any definite thoughts yet?'

'Nothing definite yet,' Harper replied after a moment's hesitation. 'It's certainly big, important; but, of course, it does need thinking through . . . discussing in depth.'

McLaren's eyes lingered a few moments on Harper before he turned to Carson. 'You?'

'Oh, it's big all right, I agree. Big, very expensive; needs a careful weighing-up of the pros and cons before any decision, I should say.'

McLaren compressed his lips slightly, allowed himself a pause, then glanced at the third agent.

'All these things: big, expensive, dangerous,' confirmed John Mallory. 'I think we require time, clear discussion, calm judgment.'

McLaren remained silent for several minutes; the others looked down at the table. At last he spoke, heavily. 'Here, gentlemen, is probably the most important, certainly the most challenging project yet to have dropped into our laps: maybe the most significant task in the agency's history. I handed it to you, I confess, with a feeling of excitement, even elation. However, what do I hear from you? *Costly, dangerous, needs careful weighing-up, pros and cons, time and calm judgment* . . .

'Do you know what I had hoped as I entered this room? That you'd be waiting, each of you, to say: "Mac, we've read and studied the papers; here is our report assessing all the facts. Now you have to take action, and we mean now." '

This was Carson's cue. He looked directly at McLaren. 'I suppose you're right,' he said. 'But before we *can* say go ahead, we have to collate our appraisals and work out the agreed report you'd like; it *must* be agreed. I'll sit down this evening and start work on it.'

McLaren glanced at Mallory before he addressed Carson again. 'I might want John and myself to get together with you, just so we keep in agreement. That's what we'll do.' He smiled and walked out of the office.

The preliminary analysis by McLaren, Mallory and Carson was short and simple. Though ostensibly the work of Carson, it had been drafted by McLaren himself, and their appraisal would now be reviewed by Harper. McLaren liked this method – a joint effort with Harper cast in the role of independent assessor, to criticize if he saw fit.

The CIA, the analysis noted, knew about Soviet nuclear missiles mostly through pictures taken by spy satellites or from aerial reconnaissance films of re-entries by warheads test-fired by the Russians. What the agency had not yet managed was to capture intact a fully armed, Russian ballistic missile.

If *Doneska* was raised, apart from dating and analysing Russian nuclear technology, CIA electronics experts would gain their best impressions ever of how accurate were Russian guidance systems. Nuclear scientists could also check how reliably the Russians were able to trigger the nuclear matter of their missiles. Such knowledge would give the United States a small but important edge.

The advantage could be exploited in several ways, most of them obvious and needing no comment. Two special benefits were, however, emphasized by McLaren. In anything short of all-out nuclear war, he stressed, missile accuracy was critical. The agency believed that the United States had a big technological lead over Russia. Better missile guidance systems got American warheads to within 500 yards of target; by contrast, Russian missiles could reliably strike no nearer than one and a half miles from their mark. If the agency's belief were proved correct by actual analysis of a Serb missile, McLaren, emphasized, the agency could advise giving a little more away at the Strategic Arms Limitation Talks to gain greater political leverage.

The second point related to the way in which the Russians might use nuclear weapons in war. American thinking had become more and more speculative on this vital question.

'They may have a policy of devastating big areas or only specific targets,' McLaren wrote. 'A policy of destroying only special targets will keep casualties down – and may mean invasion. An overkill policy would mean no invasion: possible recovery by the United States would be remote and major fallout would hamper troop landings.

'Analysis of Serb warheads to determine whether they are triggered to burst in the air or on the ground will give clues to Russian policy.'

Guidance systems and the technology of nuclear-tipped torpedoes would also provide valuable information to military scientists for countering attacks.

'Metallurgical tests of *Doneska*'s hull and various internal sections,' the report went on, 'will give vital information in planning undersea warfare.' Tests would reveal how deep Russian submarines dived.

None of the agency's cryptographers had ever examined the insides of a Russian cipher machine, nobody had ever read a Russian code book. Such inspections might lead to breaking Russian codes at last. And besides providing clues to Russian cryptographic techniques, the codes and cipher would enable deciphering of tapes stored by the National Security Agency at Fort Mead, where a library existed of thousands upon thousands of messages radioed from Soviet submarines: messages intercepted by spy ships down the years. Analysis would give the navy details of how the all-important Soviet submarine deterrent worked from day to day.

Such were the advantages listed in McLaren's preliminary draft. On the debit side were listed some of the contrary factors: neither the CIA nor the navy possessed technology to lift a wrecked submarine from 16000 feet down on the ocean floor. To develop the technology, virtually from the sea floor up, would be a long, costly job. But at McLaren's insistence, the draft report recorded a small potential profit: any system developed to salvage *Doneska* would be available to recover Russian aircraft which crashed at sea, as well as other sunken Russian or American ships.

Nor could McLaren's report deny a major hazard that would constantly overhang the secret operation. The salvage would be executed without naval escort or protection for obvious reasons of secrecy and non-confrontation. Yet the Russians might learn of Sandwedge. If they did, serious trouble of some sort was likely.

Undeniably, read the report, 'the Soviets can justify firing on people interfering with their dead'. Apart from such military hazards, knowledge of the project would be likely to harm Soviet–American détente.

In the end, McLaren gave the superficially unbiased written report his personal stamp. The way he put the advantages, they clearly outweighed any drawbacks. To Mallory, it seemed that McLaren wanted the project so badly that the evaluation was a little unbalanced. And at some stages not even McLaren could stop him from speaking his mind.

'You know, Mac, let's face it. By the time we get her up, most of that hardware is going to be obsolete.'

'Anything atomic is important,' McLaren retorted. 'Anything – ever since we exploded the first bomb off a steel tower in the desert.'

He read from the pencilled draft: 'Previous estimates of an attack on Minutemen ACBMs deployed near Whiteman Air Base near Sedalia, Missouri, indicated killing up to 26 000 people. Revised estimates, based on fallout spread by fall winds through this area – depending on type of trigger and height of fire-ball – are two to ten million killed.

'A Soviet attack on all 1054 land-based ACBM silos in the United States is now estimated to kill from 3.4 to 21.7 million people, depending on warhead size . . .' McLaren paused for emphasis, '. . . type of trigger and whether warheads are exploded in the air or on the ground. Previous estimates were only 800 000 dead.'

McLaren got together all his loose leaves of paper and tood up to go. 'Think about it, John,' he said quietly. 'That's how important it is.'

Then he was gone and Mallory sat alone with Carson. It had not escaped them that McLaren had personally written the draft that Carson was supposed to have completed.

'You have to admit he's a kind of super patriot, apart from any ego hang-ups he may have,' Mallory said.

4

John Mallory would always remember how McLaren knifed through the Tuesday meeting. Three of them were already formally on record with the joint draft report. All McLaren needed was Harper to make it unanimous.

They met around the beechwood table. McLaren sat with clasped hands, peering over his spectacles, kindly, reasonable. 'Let's think clearly,' he said. His gaze flicked to Harper, who had read the draft four times.

McLaren rose and walked to the wall graced by the large stuffed trout mounted on wood. Gently running a finger over the fish's rigid and brittle dorsal fin, he shrugged his shoulders to relax the muscles. His tie hung loose as he paced around, hands clasping and unclasping.

He spoke again. 'The way I see it, the weaponry and cryptographic stuff are vital. We need them. That's the main point of this report.'

'How does that help us if it's going to be out of date by the time –' Harper began.

'How does it *help* us?' McLaren asked incredulously. He went over the arguments he had already put to Mallory. When Harper changed tactics and mentioned money, McLaren nodded equably. 'As I have always said, in this kind of project, money is in fact the cheapest thing available.'

'What about risk? The Russians could intervene. It would be a ready made, simple pretext – even though they may not care a damn about their dead. The navy's report says that under international law, a fighting ship like a sub can only be salvaged by the mother country.'

'Harper's right, Mac,' said Mallory quietly. 'The risk is there. If the Russians get to hear about the salvage . . .'

McLaren pursed his lips. 'I was the guy who put precisely that in the report,' he said. 'Remember? Here it is: "Undeniably, the Russians can justify firing on people interfering with their dead." Also, undeniably, if we're never going to take risks we may as well pack up covert operations, and I'll tell the director that maybe the CIA ought to disband and everybody can go home.'

Harper suddenly started to feel foolish when, angrily, he knew he had no cause.

'Of course, it will cost money. Of course, it's dangerous,' McLaren went on, 'but don't you realize? We people here are seasoned pros in just this field. It's exactly the sort of thing CIA people can do.'

'It still scares me,' said Harper. 'It's such a mixed bag.'

The poker player knew he was winning. 'Who the hell can do it if we don't?' he demanded.

'Probably no one,' Harper conceded reluctantly.

'That's right – and that's our problem.' And he added, 'Remember, money is always cheaper than American lives.'

No one answered. It had come more easily than McLaren thought possible. He did not bother to look up, knowing he had his consensus.

Mallory wanted to speak, but McLaren anticipated him. 'About the Russian dead,' he said, 'and the legalities of it all. Let me say the agency's General Council thinks the navy is wrong under International Law. Anyway, when it comes to the dead we'll protect everybody's right to a proper burial under the Geneva Convention.'

McLaren continued. 'I can see it clearly: we'll play a recording of the Soviet national anthem at a burial service read in Russian by pastor-for-the-day Dick Carson.' Carson grinned a little uneasily.

McLaren said he would write the definitive report and

recommendations himself, based on the committee's unanimous findings. 'It will go down with the Forty Committee if it's put correctly,' he said. 'And I'll see it *is* correct. So now I want you all to think about how to get that sub up. Let's start working on ways and means.'

The Forty Committee, a group of influential politicians and Department of State officials, had to approve every major CIA covert operation. McLaren had known it under other names, when it was called the 303 Committee, the 54–12 Group and the Special Group, names which changed with new presidents or too much publicity.

'I can get twenty-five million dollars out of the committee for a black operation quicker than I can get fifty dollars out of Management and Services for a new coffee machine,' was McLaren's private boast. He was apt to treat the overseeing Forty Committee as an amateurish bunch of schoolboys who were hooked on the mystique of secret spy operations and a little overawed by the professional spymaster.

'They listened wide-eyed,' he told Mallory after his brief session before the committee. 'They liked it, all right. The operation has too much glamour to turn down.'

Even though Mallory felt he should have been harder on McLaren's original draft, he consoled himself with the thought that there was more going for the mission than against it.

Nine days after McLaren submitted his report, he received the Forty Committee's assent. They also appointed him to direct the project.

They would have to get outside help. Even the vast resources of the Central Intelligence Agency were too limited. After writing the report, McLaren had gone fishing near Norton, Vermont, just south of the Canadian border. Waist-deep in the icy water of a stream off the Coaticook, in between casting with easy grace, he had pondered. Finally, he decided to use Trans Acme Corporation for Sandwedge. . . .

Operating from a steel and glass skyscraper in New York, the vast, multi-national conglomerate had money in everything from tele-communications to face powders, from hire cars to curing fried chicken. Trans Acme controlled fifty-nine major companies, employed over 430000 workers and grossed forty-three billion dollars in sales. Trans Acme built warships and tanks, brewed beer and mass-produced vacuum cleaners. It owned a merchant bank in London; sold cars, machinery and appliances in Bangkok; was building an iron-and-steel mill in Seoul. A sure-footed giant, the corporation had survived wars, expropriations, competition, press attacks and anti-trust laws. It had bested everything done by foreign governments to break, stop or at least slow it: taxes, quotes, money laws, customs, tariffs, subsidies, and even nationalization.

Something that was particularly important to McLaren was the fact that Trans Acme was research oriented, employing scientists who made major discoveries in electronics, satellite communications and warhead guidance systems. Its staff included stress analysts, aerothermodynamicists, flutter and vibration specialists. Trans Acme not only had the technical know-how, it also operated smoothly and in secrecy.

Felix Townsend, a billionaire eccentric, controlled the corporation. A man with piercing eyes who talked quickly in a high voice, he often wore an old raincoat to official receptions to emphasize his disregard of convention. For all his wealth, he insisted on driving a small Datsun. Rumour had it that he started off each day by lying in bed and thinking for two hours before plunging into exercises which consisted of precisely thirty pushups and thirty-one knee bends. 'The ultimate sophistication is simplicity', was his favourite adage.

Townsend had a mania for secrecy and detail, so much so that to prevent even the possibility of his phone conversations being bugged, Trans Acme electronics engineers had developed for him a miniature telephone scrambler which he always carried in his pocket.

It was September 1973 when McLaren decided Trans Acme and Townsend were just right for Sandwedge. All he had to do was obtain the committee's consent. There would be no trouble about calling in outside civilian assistance, for while the CIA had great expertise, the committee's members would know that it could never alone undertake salvaging *Doneska* from 16000 feet. Whatever was involved, it would include a major construction job – and the agency was not in the construction business.

As soon as McLaren returned from his fishing trip, he set up a meeting with Harper, Mallory, Carson and Grantly from the Directorate of Science and Technology's Office of Special Projects. Grantly briefly admired the stuffed trout trophy before emphasizing limitations in the Directorate of Science and Technology. In short, they would have to go outside the agency.

McLaren never mentioned Townsend or Trans Acme, sitting quietly while the others named names: Tristar, TTI, Gulf Instruments . . . It was Carson who mentioned Trans Acme.

'Trans Acme is very big, into everything. Does a lot of research for us and the military. Hardly a thing goes into the air these days without something from Trans Acme aboard. Townsend can keep a thousand secrets.'

'They're already into deep-sea mining,' said Grantly. 'Would that give us a little bit of cover?'

Mallory was cautious. 'Let's face it, Townsend is a little erratic.'

'I have never met the man,' said Grantly.

'In his bizarre way, he's a big patriot and very anti the Russians,' said Carson.

To McLaren, timing was always important. Now he mentioned that Townsend had previously done good work for the CIA, and even on occasions for the Pentagon.

'He sounds exactly the kind of guy we need,' Harper said, 'especially as he's already in ocean mining.'

'There may even be a little technology there that he's already developed.' Even Mallory had come around. Sandwedge would go to Townsend and Trans Acme.

Next Carson wanted to know what naval intelligence's place was in the project. This was Harper's cue. 'Look, what shall I say to Morrows on Thursday?' he asked.

'Naval intelligence leaks too much,' McLaren replied. 'I like naval intelligence, but I don't want them in on this.'

Harper stroked his face thoughtfully while he thought up a good lie for Morrows. 'I can say the whole thing looks like it's going to be too complicated . . .'

'That's right,' McLaren asserted. 'Nothing specific.'

Next Harper asked about the code name.

'Don't worry about that,' said McLaren. 'Sandwedge is fine. We have to keep very quiet about it, that's all.'

Mallory disagreed. 'If naval intelligence ever heard it, they'd put the operation together very fast. We can't keep "Sandwedge". Anyway, sounds too much like "Sandwich". We could all get confused ordering lunch.'

There was some laughter, but everybody realized Mallory was right and McLaren asked Harper to use a little imagination.

'How about Fairway?' Harper suggested. 'Ties in with *Golf* subs and a Sandwedge.' But it still didn't seem right.

'Okay, I've got it: Fairplay.'

'Fireplay,' Mallory said.

'Project Fireplay.' McLaren savoured it. 'That's nice, I really like it better than Sandwedge. Works out even better, John. You've found it.'

5

McLaren himself composed the carefully worded memorandum for Trans Acme. It ran to four closely typed pages on the CIA's letter-head. He chose Harper as courier to take the letter by plane to New York and Felix Townsend.

In 1944 Felix Townsend had designed a 200-ton, 350-foot plywood flying boat which he called *Alvin*. The flying boat had ten engines, seated 750 fully-armed troops, flew precisely 2020 yards at exactly seventy-two feet and never flew again.

Still, Townsend never regretted *Alvin*: the flying boat was still kept under guard in a large hangar off Long Island, at a storage cost of $50000 a year, and sometimes he rambled alone through the dusty fuselage. He was just the kind of eccentric genius to whom the project of raising a wrecked Soviet submarine from 16000 feet on the Pacific sea floor would appeal.

Harper arrived late at night, on the fifty-ninth floor of Trans Acme Center. There in Townsend's thickly carpeted penthouse, Harper handed him a thin, manilla envelope and then left. In his study Townsend slipped a paper knife under the manilla flap, slid the memorandum out and read it. By the time he had paged through three of McLaren's four pages, Townsend already knew which Trans Acme undertaking would be responsible for Fireplay.

Omega Corporation was a wholly owned, Los Angeles based, Trans Acme subsidiary which had done heavily classified work and large-scale construction. It was Omega which was exploring a new and potentially rich industry: ocean mining. Through its Los Angeles subsidiary, Trans Acme was even then ahead of a hundred other companies working on undersea mining technology.

Deep-sea miners were already dredging tin off the shores of Indonesia and Thailand, diamonds off South-West Africa. But the biggest potential was in manganese nodules which littered vast belts of the ocean floor with encrustations of valuable metals like manganese, copper, nickel and cobalt.

Research done by Omega suggested that the Pacific alone was littered with 1.5 trillion tons of manganese nodules that would command up to $200 a ton. They were located in a single rich Pacific belt that ran east–west and slightly north of Midway. Omega believed there was enough valuable metal to supply all the world's needs for 300 years.

Since Trans Acme was in yet another anti-trust battle and the time was fast coming when Townsend would want a little help from the CIA, even if it were only a good word, he quickly decided not to inflate Omega's asking price for Fireplay equipment. In any event, the technology developed in salvaging *Doneska* would not go to waste. The government would be virtually sponsoring a free ride for Trans Acme into practical ocean mining.

Senior men who worked for Trans Acme were on call all the time, any time. It was past midnight when Townsend summoned Pat Garrity, a top executive, who arrived a little dazed after being awoken in bed. In Townsend's study the cool air-conditioning revived him.

As Townsend explained, Fireplay could not have come at a better time. Were Omega only to break even on the project, it would retain a multi-million dollar technology that could easily be applied to undersea mining. And by keeping the price down, Trans Acme would earn the agency's thanks.

Townsend and Garrity completed their positive responses to McLaren's memorandum as dawn broke. Their activities were unobserved since heavy curtains always guarded the penthouse against daylight, while an electric alarm system guarded it against other unspecified dangers.

When the reply was written, McLaren's secret memorandum was locked into a specially hardened steel safe in Felix Townsend's study. Garrity walked out of the fifty-ninth floor suite past closed-circuit television cameras which projected from walls to spy on callers; uniformed guards, emblazoned with the sign of the Three Circles, stood by the elevators.

Garrity flew that day in Trans Acme's executive jet to the agency's Langley headquarters. From the air, he could see the vast complex of flat dark roofs, the major part of it shaped like a huge H with a double cross bar, with part of the middle of one side missing. There were two vast areas with hundreds of cars parked in neat, double rows. Neat, tarred roads wound around the buildings and car park. Beyond the building areas was a security fence manned by marines with dogs and past the fence stretched thick woods. The jet banked steeply and came in to land at the agency's nearby airfield.

Garrity personally delivered to McLaren Trans Acme's response. He restricted himself to a few words, then left. The jet returned direct to New York, and Garrity was at his desk in the early evening to find fresh papers stacked on the dark, shiny hardwood. Riffling through Townsend's messages, all scribbled 'urgent' in the billionaire's familiar scrawl, Garrity sat with a sandwich, hot milk and a packet of fast-acting antacid tablets. With one tablet pressed into the middle of his bacon-and-tomato, Garrity bit into the bread. His front teeth crushed into the antacid, which tasted of chalk. Townsend's top executive pressed loose another tablet and dropped it into his milk.

Working at Trans Acme exacted a price. In human terms it was very high, and senior Trans Acme men were always under strain. Many drank too much, broke with their families, broke down mentally. No senior dared make a mistake; but sometimes Townsend fired an executive anyway, in accordance with his policy that nobody should stay with the same job too long after mastering it. . . .

Within three weeks of Trans Acme's response, a select committee met at Omega Corporation's Greek Street laboratories. The first meeting was chaired by Carson, assisted by Mallory, who was to report progress to McLaren, and by two of the brightest agents of the CIA's special projects office, Peter Barroso and Lloyd Williams, both of whom were PhDs. Robin D. Baker represented Trans Acme. More of an executive than a scientist, he was nevertheless an applied physicist who headed many of Trans Acme's classified projects. He had a reputation for aggressively attacking any problems that arose.

Baker kept control of his projects by an elaborate system of reports, checks and cross-checks through which he monitored every detail of the research developments. The intricate and rigorous system got results that in turn had pushed Baker's salary to $250000 a year.

Under his leadership, Project Fireplay quickly assembled a formidable spread of scientific and engineering specialists numbering twenty men and four women: physicists, chemists, metallurgists, oceanographers and mechanical, electronic, marine and naval engineers. They met secretly in a large airy room on the second floor of Omega's two-storey communications and storage centre.

Carson outlined the mission, talking for three hours, referring copiously to notes and photographs. He used a large blackboard, chalk and duster.

Nobody had ever raised a submarine from 16000 feet down on the ocean floor. The depth, pressures, temperatures and darkness presented unique problems, so the think-tank would need to start from scratch. Carson stressed the need for speed and secrecy. As he sat down Baker asked for the first suggestion.

Divers were so obviously impossible at *Doneska*'s great depth that nobody even discussed this as a possible technique. Instead, the first proposal was to use pontoons, inflatable at depth, after somehow being secured around *Doneska* – a method that was quickly discarded: should *Doneska*'s hull become over-buoyant, she would pop to the surface with ever-increasing speed, smash the pontoons on surface and then sink back into the Pacific.

By the second week the panel had divided into two schools – bathyscaphes and mechanicals. Bathyscaphe enthusiasts argued that the device had been used beyond 20000 feet. It was simple enough – essentially a free-diving vessel for exploring the ocean depths. Most bathyscaphes were comprised of a spherical cabin topped by a large buoyancy tank filled with gasoline and ballast compartments which used lead or iron shot.

The bathyscaphe would carry electronic equipment and a crew of two or three who would operate mechanical arms and tools for salvage work. Perhaps it could somehow be made to settle on and connect with *Doneska*'s escape hatch and remain water-tight, allowing one or two men to enter the hull.

This concept raised several problems. *Doneska* was shattered in the stern and probably water-logged in most of her compartments, so that to seal and re-seal any connection between the bathyscaphe and wreck at 16000 feet was highly dangerous. Anyway, one or two men alone could effectively remove very little from inside *Doneska*'s hull. Possibly the code books and cipher machine might be recovered, but it was unlikely that the men could remove any torpedoes and impossible for them to free any ballistic missile.

The bathyscaphe was clearly too limited for recovery of all the weapons, and it would also leave *Doneska* under the sea. To overcome these disadvantages, an unmanned, mechanical way of raising the entire submarine from off the bottom was proposed.

Somehow, mechanically, hundreds of steel cables might

be looped around *Doneska* from a surface salvage ship, enabling the entire submarine to be recovered without serious danger to human life. An obvious problem was the method's technical unfeasibility: how was it possible to loop so many cables around *Doneska* when she had already sunk into the ocean bed? And too, each cable would stretch over three miles from surface to sea bottom and strong undersea currents would blow such long strings of cable in every direction.

By the end of the second week, the 'mechanicals' had arrived at more sophisticated concepts. Instead of looping cables around *Doneska* – something that was almost technically impossible – they proposed to lower a series of grabs from a surface salvage vessel on to the vessel. These giant pincers, under electric power, would grab *Doneska*'s $8\frac{1}{2}$-metre-wide hull. The water-logged submarine, weighing possibly thousands of tons, would slowly be eased out of the ooze and lifted off the sea bed.

It was the turn of the bathyscaphe school to attack. Lowering grabs on to the submarine from the salvage vessel seemed an insuperable task. The technique was roughly comparable to a man in a balloon, floating three miles above the earth, uncertain of his own precise position, attempting to drop fishing lines accurately through a blizzard on to a trout in a pool. Unavoidably, the Pacific's currents would push the cables holding the grabs in every direction before they reached *Doneska*. Too much unmanned mechanical control would be essential.

The two schools demolished their opponents' solutions unmercifully and on the Sunday of the second week, a depressed Mallory phoned McLaren.

'It will take four or five years at this rate,' he said.

McLaren cursed. 'They better watch their damned cotton-picking faces,' he snapped. 'I have broken my ass to try to get Fireplay. The important thing is for you and Dick Carson to keep the momentum going. Do you want me to come?'

'We could send a chopper up to LA for you,' Mallory said, relieved.

McLaren put the phone down without saying goodbye and left Mallory unsure whether he was in fact coming to Los Angeles. So Mallory spent a disconsolate weekend playing gin rummy with Dick Carson. He tried to fathom the technical problems. Once he tried to phone Baker. Baker was out.

Nevertheless, it was Dr Baker who, on the Monday of the third week, solved the impasse and provided Fireplay's basic salvage philosophy. During the previous sessions, he had sat quietly, saying little, except to make peace when the debate got too heated. 'You've got a problem,' he drawled once. 'You won't solve it by making it worse.' Otherwise, he allowed the think-tank full freedom to range anywhere and everywhere.

At the start of the Monday session, he proposed his simple, even obvious solution. They must compromise, by mating the manned and unmanned ideas. There would be a manned bathyscaphe and an unmanned mechanical grab; men in the bathyscaphe would go down and guide the grabs on to *Doneska*.

The two methods meshed precisely where they were weakest. Men in the bathyscaphe could not raise the submarine; unmanned mechanical grabs could not efficiently manoeuvre on to *Doneska*'s hull; together they would succeed.

Mallory sighed his relief – and left the meeting immediately to speak long-distance to McLaren and report progress at last.

Once Baker had fixed the strategy, the think-tank proceeded smoothly with the tactical details. They would construct the bathyscaphe out of light but resistent material – probably titanium. In theory, a titanium vessel could reach 25 000 feet.

Metallurgists would work the metal into pieces large enough for a vessel to contain two men who would

43

manoeuvre the bathyscaphe around the sea bottom, using mechanical arms to work the grabs on to *Doneska*. This crew would also steer the strings of steel pipes connected to each grab. Aided by television cameras – on the spot, at the sea bottom – and equipped with tools and electronic controls, they should be able to drop the grabs over *Doneska* and grasp her hull.

On surface, a ship would serve as a floating, stable platform; cycloidal propellers would hold her in place; amidships there would be a well and high derrick through which steel piping and grabs would pass.

A giant submersible barge, built like a floating aircraft hangar and working in tandem with the main vessel, would be towed by her to the recovery site and sunk below the water to float directly below the mother ship. The gigantic lifting claws needed to grab *Doneska* would be carried inside the barge. Once *Doneska* was retrieved, she would be stored in the barge under a huge oval roof that would conceal her from Russian reconnaissance satellites, aircraft or trawlers.

The Baker committee, in its report, estimated that the bathyscaphe, main ship and barge would cost the CIA $300000000 in money and two years in time.

When Mallory phoned McLaren long-distance, the reaction was simple. 'Good, that means we'd better get going today.'

Within a couple of weeks, Trans Acme and Omega were tied by the CIA into Project Fireplay under a series of complex trust agreements. The agency, encouraged by McLaren's latest appraisals, allocated $350000000 for the project.

When Mallory asked McLaren how the final recommendations went down with the Forty Committee, McLaren smiled a little mysteriously. 'Basically it was a PR job,' he said. 'I got them excited all over again with big blow-ups of the stuff from naval intelligence, all kinds of nuclear equations and mystique. That's what gets them. And I made it sound very forbidden and sexy, like we were raping the Russians in their sleep.'

6

Omega Corporation built *Pacific Klondike* at the Los Angeles yards of the Mars Shipbuilding and Drydocks Company, working in the strictest secrecy. Sightseers were barred and surveillance television cameras tracked anyone who approached the dock. Armed guards wearing the Three Circle insignia patrolled wharves and ship. Nobody familiar with Trans Acme and Townsend – and Townsend's mania for secrecy – was surprised.

Trans Acme and CIA agents made full use of the cover provided by Omega's known interest in ocean mining research. From time to time, news of *Pacific Klondike*'s construction surfaced.

'If all goes well,' the *Los Angeles Herald* reported, 'the mystery ship may be at work next year scooping such metals as titanium, manganese, uranium, copper and nickel from the sea floor to fatten the fortune of the world's wealthiest tycoon.'

Omega completed *Pacific Klondike* inside eighteen months by working three shifts, all at time-and-a-half. When finished, she was 36000 tons, 618 feet long and 120 feet wide. Her maximum speed was twelve knots and six diesel-electric motors gave her 12000 horsepower.

A forest of deck-mounted cranes worked off a 12000 lb. hydraulic lifting system. She was fitted amidships with internal wells for lowering, through sliding doors, sections of oil-drilling pipe that would connect to gigantic lifting claws. The claws, similar to finger-like prongs, were driven by powerful electric motors sealed tightly against water.

The ship carried special sonar, inertial and Doppler instruments. A built-up superstructure and foremast supported sensitive radio communications discs and antennae. In the stern a square helicopter pad was built for a twin-jet Sikorsky Sea King, and a stern-mounted 250-horsepower skiff provided surface communication between *Pacific Klondike* and her bathyscaphe.

Below deck, the ship carried photographic facilities, hydrophone systems and a computer for sea-floor navigation. Above deck, she bristled with masts and booms that made her look bulky, even awkward. Prominent was a 200-foot derrick for lowering sixteen-inch diameter pipe; the derrick could lift 800 tons and *Pacific Klondike* would use three other lifts too. A pair of 150-foot docking legs was also housed on deck to hold the submerged barge in place under the main ship.

The barge was called *Omega 1*, a craft still uglier and more ungainly than *Pacific Klondike* herself, 106 feet wide with thick, fifteen-foot walls to help provide ballast. Tarpaulins completely shrouded the huge grabs nestling in her interior. *Omega 1* was designed to carry in one piece the grabs and *Doneska*. She was also designed to submerge down to 150 feet immediately under *Pacific Klondike* – the length of the docking legs – and could slide open her roof to receive sections of oil-drilling pipe.

Omega 1 and the bathyscaphe, named *Explorer*, were also built at the Mars yards in secret. *Explorer* looked like a stubby airship fitted with a spherical gondola. A series of thick-skinned cylindrical tanks that overhung the man-carrying bathysphere was all there was to her. Aviation gasoline in her tanks buoyed the sphere, which could withstand a pressure of more than two tons to every square inch. A small conning tower connected *Explorer*'s deck to the observation sphere and the craft was driven by propellers fore and aft. Attached to the underside of the cylinders were still and television cameras, floodlights, acoustic probe measurers, and echo sounders. Magnesium anodes protected her steel surfaces from corroding too rapidly. Forward of the sphere's main plexiglass viewing port were fixed a couple of mechanical arms, complete with claws, wrist, elbow and shoulder joints. Small, powerful and separate electric motors controlled each arm. *Explorer*'s cramped working area was jammed with electronic and other equipment: magneto-meters, radiation sensors, and undersea telephone, sonars, closed-circuit television consoles and controls.

While *Pacific Klondike* was in construction, a significant episode at Trans Acme Corporation headquarters was to raise serious complications for Project Fireplay. The episode in itself was not a chance one, despite its disastrous conse-quences. It was the nature of the main defect in Felix Townsend's complex, quirky character: a constant need to bolster his ego by the exercise of ruthless power.

. For years Townsend had accumulated more wealth than he could enjoy for its own sake; ambition was a word which had lost its meaning. He sought to maintain his reputation as the world's most idiosyncratic, ruthless tycoon. Occasion-al references to himself as a latter-day Hearst or a new Howard Hughes fed his egotism – but this was not enough. Where Hearst and Hughes had blazed and excited, Towns-end found himself acting the tycoon's role but leading an ever-greyer life. The social activities and popularity high-paid executives were enjoying (in the free hours he allowed them) were denied him by a reticence, an insularity he could not conquer. He was becoming especially aware of his chief executive, Pat Garrity, as an irritant, a day-to-day reminder of what he himself was missing out on in all but power.

Garrity, married and divorced, still enjoyed the occasional company of his ex-wife and son, seldom lacked other female company, worked hard and played the social round just as hard. Possessed of an extrovert personality and a position of prestige, he was in frequent demand socially.

Townsend's creation of the Trans Acme conglomerate left him little time, or inclination, for marriage. For him the only reality, the only permanence was his own place at the summit of TA. A minority of militant shareholders, striving constantly to remove him on the grounds of his eccentric mis-management, served only to confirm the tycoon in his creed that everybody at Trans Acme was dispensible but himself. According to this creed, no other man should stay in any job for long, since he was likely to slow down and rest on his past achievements – or become a threat to Townsend's own position.

Pat Garrity was a prime case in point – and Townsend half-persuaded himself that personal resentment did not influence his wish to fire his chief executive. True, he had changed jobs several times during his thirteen years with the company, but he was completing his third year as next-to-the-top at the time of the Fireplay contracts – a long time, in Townsend's book, to harbour any immediate deputy to his own post.

The pretext occurred seventeen months after the Fireplay memorandum arrived – and it was slim enough: just an incautious step by Garrity, who knew his chief's working rules well. Pat took his wife on a three-week boat-trip down the Amazon, writing Townsend a long memorandum with regard to his work in progress after being unable to phone him three times in California. It was Garrity's first real vacation for five years and he believed he had earned it – even though there were no facilities in the Brazilian jungle to maintain contact with New York.

Townsend had deliberately not taken Garrity's calls, having learned from his private secretary of the reason for them. And so, when Pat returned, he found his name-plate removed from his office door and an intimation that he was out of his $400000-a-year job.

The recent second-in-command of Trans Acme Corporation had himself fired many an executive in pursuance of Townsend's all-change policy. If he had made any other mistake, it was to assume that this policy did not apply to himself.

'You don't think thirteen years' service counts against one small mistake?' Pat asked, standing in the thickly-carpeted penthouse for the last time.

'No.' Townsend lowered the *New York Times* to look steadily at his ex-deputy. 'Nobody, especially a top executive, loses contact with head office, even on vacation. You knew that very well, Pat. I needed you urgently once last week – but it was as if the world had swallowed you up.'

'You agreed in principle months ago that a vacation was due to me.'

Townsend half-rose from his desk in a gesture to close the final interview. 'The fact is you've been with us too long, Pat. Maybe we all need a change: try to see it as a gift, a new challenge. We'll negotiate your golden handshake, of course, and you already enjoy an active, and full life outside this building.' The older man's lips twitched slightly.

'I'm not thinking about handshakes, golden or otherwise. What I cannot credit is you firing your top executive on the spot for taking his first vacation in five years. Do *you* think this will sound good for you outside this building?'

Townsend laughed briefly. 'You kidding? Everybody knows I'm a mean son-of-a-bitch: that *is* my image. Too late to change now.'

As he opened the door, Garrity heard a softly spoken 'Pat.' He turned.

'You have a dental appointment. Give him my warm regards.'

Pat flushed in anger and humiliation. They had used the same dentist for years; he had made this appointment before the Amazon trip. How typical of Townsend, who spied on all his employees, to know even about such a trivial detail as a gold filling that needed re-packing – and to add his knowledge as a final taunt.

More than anything else, perhaps, it was this revelation that was responsible for a resolve forming in Pat Garrity's mind. It was high time for Townsend to pay in kind, not merely in money. Garrity, for all his extrovert charm, had always possessed some of the ruthlessness needed for a successful career at Trans Acme. Now he had suddenly become dangerous. What he wanted, more than anything else, was revenge. Just possibly he could dislodge Townsend and secure the top job for himself: to whom could the other major shareholders turn? But that was just a thought, a bonus. The main thing was revenge, plain and satisfying, however much it might cost him.

Pat Garrity knew every detail of the penthouse's fifty-ninth-floor layout, down to the make of the safe and how the electronic monitors operated. In the safe were stored a series of highly sensitive documents which, if made available, were likely to induce the Justice Department's Anti-Trust lawyers, always alert about Trans Acme, to sit up and restart action in earnest. Such action might even land the head of TA in prison.

To obtain these documents, Garrity needed help of a very specialized kind – and it happened that he knew precisely where it could be found. Like so many large companies and corporations, Trans Acme had indulged occasionally in what was delicately termed 'industrial espionage': in other words, stealing technical secrets from their competitors. Expert thieves were available, at a price, for this work – ranging from the mere rifling of office desks and filing cabinets to cracking the most intricate safes.

Some time previously, when TA needed badly to acquire details of technology from an unsuspecting rival, Garrity had employed the services of the most skilful practitioner in this field; Bernard Hofman.

Hofman's successes added up to an impressive collection for his various clients: confidential blue-prints, price-fixing agreements, chemical formulae. For Trans Acme he had 'lifted' a computer programme, the chemical formula for

plastic beads used in the insulation of cryogenic tanks –
plus the shape of a nose-cone being developed for the
Skybolt missile. What Trans Acme's chiefs did *not* know
was that the enterprising Mr Hofman had also, through a
contact at the United Nations, sold the nose-cone's shape
and a paint-mix for cold climates to the Russians. . . .

Like most professional thieves, Hofman had his cover:
he played the saxophone in a nightclub. It was there that
Garrity had first met him, and it was the club which now gave
him their player's home address. There was the sound of
saxophone practice as Garrity knocked at the door. The
music stopped abruptly and the peephole in the door went
dark behind the small round glass. Three chains slid back
and two locks turned before the door was cautiously opened.

'Bernard Hofman – we meet again,' Garrity greeted him
with a smile. 'Remember me, from Trans Acme?'

'I remember,' replied Hofman. 'What do you want?'

What Garrity now wanted of Hofman was to outwit five
Three Circle guards, closed circuit television cameras in
certain strategic parts of the building, an electronic alarm
system – and Felix Townsend's supposedly impregnable
safe. The two men talked quietly for half an hour, drinking
instant coffee in chipped cups. By the end of their talk,
Hofman had accepted the Townsend assignment. This was
April 1975.

Next day Hofman changed flats, left his club band (saying
he had to spend some time away from New York), shaved
off his moustache and, under an assumed name, obtained a
job with C.C. Cooling Corporation, air-conditioning specialists who regularly serviced Townsend's penthouse.

He worked with them for more than four months
before he was sent in on routine service to Trans Acme
Center.

It took three months to train Peter Barroso and Lloyd
Williams, the two-man crew of *Explorer*. The CIA also

chose with the utmost care 180 sailors and scientists to man *Pacific Klondike* and *Omega 1*.

The crew of the *Pacific Klondike* were told little; but the thirty-six trained to man *Explorer* and *Omega 1* were CIA agents who knew almost everything. Everybody signed secrecy papers, promising not to talk to newspaper men or outsiders except to corroborate the cover story that they were on a secret mining mission.

The overall salvage operation was commanded by Dick Carson. Without having to go into too many details with the navy, McLaren had Robert H. Conrad of the *Mary Jane* seconded to captain *Pacific Klondike*. He sailed her out of Los Angeles harbour twenty-seven months and ten days after *Doneska* sank. She carried *Explorer* in a specially-constructed bay on deck and, behind her, she slowly towed *Omega 1*: a strange group on a curious voyage.

To further mask their mission, Conrad navigated a slow, erratic course to Honolulu. Sometimes he stopped the ship and pretended to prospect the Pacific floor. He sailed southwest in open seas where the maps were quite bare – between Los Angeles and Honolulu there was only blue water. The Tropic of Cancer was crossed twelve days out from Los Angeles and all the while Conrad was testing *Pacific Klondike*'s systems.

So far, Project Fireplay had cost the CIA $296000000. *Financial Mail*, a weekly magazine, published the most extensive press report.

Last week, a ship filled with bizarre equipment sailed out of Los Angeles harbor. Built at the yards of the Mars Shipbuilding and Drydock Company, it is sailing into a new, potentially rich industry: ocean mining.

A spokesman for Omega Corporation, a holding company for several Felix Townsend and Trans Acme Corporation enterprises, would say nothing more about the super-secret mission other than that the project will be run by Omega Corporation and that *Pacific Klondike* will complete several months of trials in the Pacific before starting mining operations.

Mining people have a good idea about what Townsend wants: he is investing $300000000 in *Pacific Klondike* and her big barge so he can exploit manganese nodules that geologists say lie in profusion across the sea floor. If they can be mined, the nodules will provide much copper, nickel, molybdenum and cobalt, as well as manganese.

The cover story was standing up so successfully, McLaren learned, that other ocean mining consultants had computer analysed a false Omega plan publicized by the CIA. These experts found that Omega Corporation's deep sea mining venture was well worth the big financial risk.

7

Wearing a C.C. Cooling uniform with an alligator marking on the overall left pocket, Bernard Hofman took a lift to the fifty-ninth floor of Trans Acme Center. With him he had an identity card, a box of tools, an oxy-acetylene torch and gas bottles.

Hofman was expected and walked without hindrance past four Three Circle guards. Two were smoking and looked bored, while another read an old copy of *Playboy* magazine. A fifth unlocked the penthouse door and helped Hofman into Townsend's study with the bottles; the rules required him to remain inside throughout the servicing.

As the guard put down the bottles, Hofman pulled out a small pen and, squeezing the cap, poured a heavy gas over the Three Circle man's nose and mouth. His mouth dropped, his eyes widened, and he sagged over the bottles on to the thick Persian carpet. Outside the sound-proofed door the other guards heard nothing.

Hofman pulled on Playtex rubber gloves and slipped a nylon cord around the guard's wrists, tying them behind his back, and then around his ankles. Next a thick, sticky piece of adhesive was taped over the unconscious man's mouth. Then Hofman got to work. . . .

The electronic alarms were disconnected in less than three minutes. The safe's intricate mechanism may have been proof against a safe-cracker's sensitive ears and fingers, but it withstood Hofman's powerful oxy-acetylene torch for no more than half an hour: about the time the cooling service would have taken.

He removed all the documents, took a swiftly appraising glance at a memorandum headed 'FIREPLAY', abstracted also some jewellery and $3800 in cash. Leaving behind a smoking safe, burn marks on the carpet, and the insensible Three Circle guard, the thief climbed out to the penthouse roof, walked down a fire escape to the fifty-seventh floor and calmly completed his exit by the lift.

By this time the four bored guards, belatedly alert, had begun hammering at the penthouse's locked door. Police later confiscated a box full of burglary tools and a second-hand oxy-acetylene kit. . . .

Safe in his flat, Hofman checked the number of an account Garrity had opened for him at a Zürich bank, making a special flight for the purpose. It had meant Garrity had to take his thief on trust, but he had no choice: Hofman demanded it this way. The number duly checked, he placed all the stolen documents – except McLaren's Fireplay memorandum – in a large, waterproof envelope, which he sealed with his hand in the Playtex glove. Everything except the Fireplay document was then mailed to a box number in San Francisco.

A cab took Hofman to an all-night safe-deposit vault, where he showed the first guard a false identity card and signed matching initials into the book. The guard pressed a button to swing open a door, and Hofman walked down a short flight of stairs to the vault. A second security man escorted him through a maze of safe-deposit boxes which lined the walls and aisles before he got to No. 1188.

Hofman fitted his key, the guard another, and they turned the locks together. The man walked away – and into a narrow steel box Hofman stuffed an envelope which contained the Fireplay memorandum.

He flew to Chicago that same night. Next morning, from a phone box in the Loop, he called the Federal Bureau of Investigation's Houston office to tell an agent that he wanted a million dollars for special information with documentary backing.

The FBI's Houston agent flew to Langley with the first full report. The caller had identified himself as Manton. He had a document called Fireplay in his possession and advised the Bureau to call the CIA. He wanted a million dollars for the return of the document, $120000 down and $72000 for personal expenses. The CIA would know what to do.

The FBI had already traced Manton's false name as belonging to a baby who died sixty-three days after birth. It was an old deception; American birth and death records were badly co-ordinated and 'Manton' had simply applied for a duplicate birth certificate in the baby's name, saying he had lost the original. The certificate was a good enough identification to get most things: from a social security number to a passport.

Nobody at C.C. Cooling knew much about Manton, merely that he was a good worker who had kept mostly to himself. The home address he had given the firm also proved false. The FBI thought Manton had already lost the first identity and had acquired a new, false one. Credentials were easily stolen, forged or even bought in the open market. Advertisements in the underground press offered for $25 ID kits that contained five birth certificates, five baptismal records and five military-discharge papers.

Two days after the break-in, Mallory and Harper sat with McLaren around the beechwood desk. Harper railed against the easy way people could acquire false identities. 'Well, there isn't a damn thing you can do about that,' McLaren said evenly.

The immediate fear was that the Russians might now learn of Fireplay. 'That's our main hazard,' McLaren said.

'The Russians could sink *Klondike* and the barge,' said

Mallory, 'just like we discussed. It's all very real now. And even if they decided not to take it that far, the alternative for us is likely to be another U-2. And nobody will love the agency for that either.'

The man calling himself 'Manton', it was clear, now had the power to imperil the biggest, costliest project yet undertaken by the CIA. McLaren looked at his colleagues, slowly emphasizing his next words.

'There is no point in our talking around the clock about this problem: the sensible, the only thing to do is to face facts. The Fireplay budget is likely to top $350000000 by the time we're finished; do we risk that kind of money for virtually nothing – if Manton goes to the Russians – or do we ensure he doesn't by paying him off? It seems plain to me that we have no choice.'

The others gloomily nodded. 'How much money – more money – would we need?' Harper asked.

'With each new call to the bureau, Manton will raise the stakes. He's now asked a million dollars – and will demand more with every delay.'

Mallory said, 'That means an extra million to protect the original 350 million investment. It's all relative, I suppose, and we should be able to raise the sum.'

'What we must do right away is to buy time,' McLaren proposed. 'Manton knows very well the bureau isn't going to cough up a cool million in one lump, without guarantees. The Fireplay memorandum has got to be produced before he sees the full amont; meanwhile, it seems to me we shall have to hand over his down payment, $120000, to keep him sweet – and silent.'

Once again, McLaren had obtained his colleagues' agreement before writing a recommendation to the CIA committee. Payment would be made through the FBI. Manton wished it to be done that way.

The FBI began with a text-book investigation which scored a routine success. Federal agents in Palm Springs interviewed Townsend for four hours, taking down notes of all the people he had fired, undercut, pressured or other-wise made into potential enemies. High on the long list was Pat Garrity, who was at once taken in for questioning.

When Garrity learned that Hofman had exceeded his brief and lifted the Fireplay memorandum, he knew he was at a cross-roads. He could lie and trust they would never find Hofman, or he could tell all and so hope to mitigate his part in the burglary. Garrity decided that a desire to avenge himself on Townsend was much easier to explain than being party to blackmailing the FBI, the CIA and the US government.

Two days after Hofman's Chicago call, the FBI had all the salient facts: including the blackmailer's identity. McLaren, Mallory and Harper were impressed.

'Well, Hoover always performed when he was chief,' McLaren said. 'They have a file on everybody.'

'Garrity says he is sorry he ever sent that burglar in there – that helps a lot,' Harper remarked drily.

'What would you do if you were in his place?' McLaren asked.

'Poison,' said Harper.

McLaren's pleasure was premature. He had reckoned without the FBI's Houston agent, Charles Gates. Gates, appointed Hofman's contact, saw a way to promotion. He was against paying any blackmail money. Hofman, Gates argued, would probably photocopy the memorandum for future blackmail or resale. Not only was he against paying Hofman; he wanted to capture him.

Bernard Hofman had made five calls in four days to Houston: the first call from Chicago, two calls from New York, and one each from Boston and Philadelphia. Gates reasoned that if Hofman was going to move from city to city, the FBI could find him through cross-checking airline passenger lists. All they needed was a few more cities, a little more time.

'He's not really smart,' Gates persuaded his Washington superiors.

The blackmailer made his sixth call from a New York coin box within twenty paces of an Orange Julius stand on Times Square. A federal agent in Houston told him that Gates was out; in fact, Gates sat next to the phone without speaking, and Hofman hung up.

Later the same day, he made a seventh call from near the Metropolitan Museum in New York. This time Gates answered. Hofman wanted to know about the money. 'Is something wrong?' he asked.

'Yeah, well there is something wrong. . . .' Gates said. 'We have to wash the money. We get a hundred thousand dollars out of a bank, and it all comes in serialized bills.'

'I understand.'

'And that means going to Vegas with it or a bookmaker in New York City.'

'Okay. Go ahead,' Hofman replied. But a red warning was by now alerting his mind. He made no further calls to Gates, or anyone else at the bureau.

After six days' silence, McLaren sardonically recalled his earlier misgivings about the heavy-handed methods of the FBI.

8

Hofman's guess that federal agents were by now checking all the internal arteries was correct. He now knew the bureau was close to him, but no doubt existed in his mind that the Fireplay memorandum was worth big money in the right market place. He had tried the FBI and CIA; only the Russians remained. The *Pacific Klondike* was somewhere on the high seas and this meant he would have to act with reasonable speed.

Hofman's first priority, however, was his own personal safety. He stayed a night in a student boarding house in Greenwich Village, moving the next day to a quieter place in the back streets. There, behind a securely locked door, he stared up at the fly-blown ceiling and thought hard and long.

If there was no other way, he would contact the Russians through their Washington embassy, despite the obvious dangers. But first he would use his earlier contact, Vasili Novikov; that was how he had effected his first secrets sale to the Soviet Union some years ago. The two men had met shortly after Hofman left Columbia University, and the acquaintance developed significantly along with Hofman's industrial espionage activities. When they had first met, Novikov was posing as a Yugoslav immigrant seeking a job. Hofman soon learned that, in fact, he acted as part-time interpreter at the UN – and correctly guessed him to be using this job as a cover. Soviet intelligence agents, Hofman read often enough in the newspapers, were forever posing as embassy officials, diplomats, newsmen, scientists and even immigrants, as they conducted unceasing efforts to obtain all kinds of useful information.

Novikov had given him a way of making contact: a phone number, a simple code. It was time to use it again.

From a call box near the Port Authority Bus terminal, Hofman rang the special number. Immediately the receiver was lifted, Hofman set his down. The same number was once more dialled by the blackmailer. This time he carefully counted the number of rings up to five. Five rings indicated that Novikov was to proceed to a public call box near General Theological Seminary on West 23rd Street.

Hofman himself moved to a call box in the Pennsylvania railway station. Precisely forty minutes later the phone rang for Novikov at the appointed call box.

The Russian and Hofman went through a simple, brief, coded identification: it was some years since they last met. While Novikov listened intently, Hofman guardedly outlined what he had to sell. They arranged to meet at precisely ten o'clock the next evening, by which time Novikov hoped to have obtained instructions from his superiors. If he did not come, Hofman was to take it that any deal was off.

While Hofman walked off to see a porno movie at a Times Square theatre, the KGB agent made haste to report in code to the Soviet Embassy in Washington. In his turn, the KGB duty officer in the embassy beamed the message to the senior department of the information service of the KGB's First Directorate in Moscow. A few hours later, from Moscow Centre, the KGB's Executive Action Department relayed a message to the Washington embassy for Mikhail Petrovich Ivanov, the KGB resident director in New York.

A few blocks from the White House, a large rambling four-storey building serves as the Soviet Embassy. A building with balconies on the first and fourth floors, its ill-kept façade is sometimes cause for unfavourable comment. A much greater sore point is the embassy's roof, which sprouts clumps of sensitive antennae and radio dishes to serve powerful radio receivers and transmitters stored safely inside: sophisticated equipment that is technically on Soviet territory and beyond the laws of the United States.

From this somewhat grim-looking building the Russians make the most of their diplomatic immunities to pick up from Moscow Centre the KGB's coded instructions, which are re-transmitted via the embassy and received by KGB agents in all parts of the United States. In turn, the signals are monitored around the clock by the National Security Agency, which is fully aware of the embassy's activities. Unfortunately, any encoded KGB message is virtually crack-proof, and all that the NSA can do is store in Fort Meade tapes of the embassy broadcasts against the day that any code booklets might somehow come into their possession.

It was with one of these code booklets that Mikhail Petrovich Ivanov sat in a Brooklyn storeroom, only hours after Novikov's contact with Hofman. Headphones to his ears, Ivanov twisted the knobs to a powerful radio set kept in his dingy, musty hideaway. Upon the table rested the small booklet consisting of fifty once-only codes which were printed on cellulose nitrate pages.

Ivanov's codes were printed in black; the keys to coded messages received by him came in red. As soon as he had used the code he would tear the page free and destroy it. The resident director of the KGB's New York network posed successfully as an erratic Village artist, a cover that had held up very well since the spring of 1971. In that year he had boarded a Soviet freighter bound to collect wheat from Ontario, Canada. Two months later, after illegally crossing the border into the United States, he had settled down to directing the network.

At precisely 1803 hours, Ivanov identified his call sign, and depressed the button of a small tape recorder. Steady signals streamed in for a few minutes before the coded message finished. Ivanov replayed the tape to decode his orders. Then a page was carefully torn from the tiny code booklet. Ivanov struck a match and held it to the cellulose nitrate, which burst briefly into a bright light before trailing smoke off his fingers.

The orders were to kidnap Bernard Hofman who was already very much wanted by the FBI. It would be done through Novikov, Hofman's contact man, and there was not much time. Novikov would furnish Hofman's address, allay any suspicions prior to the kidnapping – and then accompany the victim, who would be smuggled aboard *Byelostroov*, a Russian freighter, a grain carrier out of Murmansk, at present berthed in New York harbour.

The operation was to take place inside twelve hours, the count starting at midnight following the day of the coded transmission.

The KGB had trained Ivanov to cope with most emergencies. After some consideration he went to a call box and rang Dmitri Kiselev, a well-disciplined professional killer with big, bushy eyebrows, who had been long enough with the Executive Action Department of the KGB to have known it under its old title: the Thirteenth Department of Line F. Novikov, who himself had undergone routine training in Moscow, would assist if it became necessary. But Dmitri Kiselev was probably enough.

In the phone booth Ivanov waited, noting that the headset was badly chipped. In Moscow such vandalism was not known.

As Ivanov put the finishing touches to his plan for kidnapping Bernard Hofman, the industrial spy lay worrying on a narrow bed in his 'safe place' on West 12th Street. He was wondering if he ought to move; there were probably hundreds of federal agents out with faded photographs of him, taken from the Columbia University records. Still, that was a long time ago and he'd looked very different, with a beard and long hair. The main thing was to remember that the photographs existed and not to underestimate the FBI.

For hours Hofman stared up at the ceiling. Would Novikov be under surveillance? Most Eastern bloc diplomats and officials were watched by the FBI. Obviously, Novikov would know that too and make every effort to shake free of anybody who might be trailing him. He should know well enough how to do it.

Then again, dealing with Novikov was not going to be easy. What he had to sell was a straight piece of news; the Fireplay memorandum itself was only corroboration of the valuable facts he had deduced from it. He had told Novikov about the importance of the information in a guarded manner, without making any material disclosure. But when he met the Russian again, he would have to be more explicit. Yet what guarantees did he have that Novikov would not breach any bargain?

Selling the news was a once-only affair, and Hofman had still not quite decided in his own mind how best to go about it when there was a soft rap on the door. Three short raps, a pause, two others. Warily, he got off the bed and approached the door. He himself rapped twice on the wood and to his relief there were three soft raps in reply.

Hofman slipped the latches, turned a heavy key and held in place the last chain before opening the door a few inches. Outside, Novikov smiled. Another rattle and the door swung open to let the Russian in. For a split second Hofman was distracted by Novikov's hand, thrust forward in greeting. It was then that Kiselev sprang through the doorway, his right hand chopping into the base of Hofman's neck, crumpling him to the floor without any sound except that of a small table overturning as Hofman fell against it.

'You've killed him!' Alarm flared in Novikov's face.

'*Nyet*,' the trained assassin replied, smiling.

Unconvinced, Novikov felt for the unconscious man's heart-beat and was reassured to feel it flutter under his palm. Together they carried Hofman down the narrow stairs. A pretty blonde girl swinging three bottles of Coca-Cola in a plastic net bag walked into the small apartment house. She started up the stairs and stopped. Above her the wood creaked, feet thudded and she heard men breathing hard.

At the top of the stairs, Novikov and Kiselev appeared lugging Hofman's limp body. They swayed down the wooden steps, causing old paint to flake off the walls where they rubbed.

'What's the matter?' the girl asked.

Kiselev put his finger to his lips. 'We have to get him to Bellevue,' the famous New York hospital. 'And we have to hurry.'

The blonde girl stepped aside to let them pass, watching them load Hofman into a station wagon parked right outside. Kiselev turned left into West Houston Street, turned right up Broadway, drove past City Hall, turned left again down Fulton Street and nosed into the South Street seaport area just south of Brooklyn Bridge. Novikov had already drugged Hofman, checked his pulse again and pushed him on to a makeshift bed of pillows.

The station wagon moved along the river front, under the East River drive. Up ahead, off the dock, Kiselev recognized the *Byelostroov*. Someone, he had been told, would have bribed the guard, and when he drove slowly on to the dock past a smiling official, he knew someone had.

Kiselev parked, hopped out and moved to the rear of the car. *Byelostroov*'s funnel was smoking hard, and he guessed that she was preparing to sail. As he and Novikov eased Hofman out of the back of the station wagon, three of *Byelostroov*'s crew came down the gangway to help. Hofman was quickly aboard. Even as Kiselev got behind the wheel and turned the car's starter, the gangway was being stowed.

The freighter captain came out on deck to meet Novikov and exchange coded greetings. Like many Russian freighter captains, he was loosely attached to the communications division of the KGB's First Directorate, the division that provided escape routes. *Byelostroov* sailed within the hour, against the tide, only half laden and without the clearance of the Port Authority.

Novikov watched the lights of the Woolworth building and the twin towers of the World Trade Center to the north. The buildings blurred to merge with the dark; lights winked, twinkled and faded. Only as *Byelostroov* sailed through the Upper Bay and under the Verranzano Narrows bridge did he at last feel able to relax.

While the captain moved out of his own cabin, Novikov set to work using codes given him in the United Nations building. A detailed report to Moscow Centre was transmitted under the respectful gaze of the radio operator. Moscow would get the signals through the Washington embassy.

Once the freighter was safely out on the open Atlantic, Novikov went out on deck to tear a page from the tiny, one-time code booklet. Rolling the cellulose nitrate page into a small ball, he flicked it into the water. Now there was nothing to do but wait. *Byelostroov* rolled a little and his stomach felt queasy.

Three days later, code instructions streamed in. *Byelostroov* would change course and make for Odessa on the Black Sea; a military Ilyushin would fly Novikov and Hofman from Odessa to Sofia, Bulgaria.

The Russian considered the implications. KGB operatives from the First Directorate's 11th Department controlled the spy and counter-spy services of Romania, Bulgaria, Hungary, Poland, Czechoslovakia and East Germany, and most intelligence collected by these services went directly to Moscow. Evidently the KGB was taking Hofman to Sofia because they wanted him to be interrogated there.

At first Novikov was puzzled. Why Sofia rather than Moscow? There was no shortage of space in the KGB's notorious Lubianka Prison. He speculated for a short time and decided that the Centre was trying to avoid direct implication if anything went wrong. If the interrogation were to be conducted by the Bulgarian MGB, it would lessen the chances of a direct KGB–CIA confrontation.

The last decoded sentences of Moscow's instructions confirmed that Sofia it was to be, Novikov was to accompany Hofman to MGB headquarters in Brzina Street and hand him to Colonel Ivan Yazov. Hofman, he thought, must be very important, for Ivan Yazov was a merciless man, word of whom had passed far beyond Brzina Street. The orders had come from Special Service II, with approval from Department V and Department A. Counter-intelligence, investigations, treason, satellite spying, Executive Action and Disinformation were all interested.

Whatever it was, Novikov concluded, it was big and he had better finish his part without hitch. In spite of the cold wind he left the warmth and comfort of his cabin and walked across the deck to check yet again that Hofman was alive, well and safely under guard.

9

When all seemed bleakest to Mallory, there came a fortuitous stroke of fortune: Colonel Anatoli Sedlacek, a highly-placed colonel of the KGB, defected to the United States ten days after Hofman's last call to the FBI.

Sedlacek walked off an Aeroflot flight from Moscow to Copenhagen and having passed through customs and passport control, he stepped briskly out of the airport building into a taxi which took him straight to the United States Embassy in Dag Hammerskjöld Alle. 'I wish to go to the United States of America,' the first major defector to that country for fourteen years told a startled marine.

CIA agents at the embassy stopped a US military transport warming up on runway seven at Copenhagen airport. Within ninety minutes of entering the embassy, Sedlacek was safely aboard, unworried by the frantic search launched by the Soviet Embassy, after his failure to arrive there. While the Russians checked vainly with the Danish police, hospitals, morgues, hotels, railway station, airports and border outposts, Sedlacek flew to Kennedy airport and on to the CIA's Langley headquarters. After resting for twenty-four hours, he underwent tiring de-briefing sessions – careful, skilful, CIA mixtures of friendliness and disbelief.

Tall, powerfully-built and bald, Sedlacek chain-smoked badly-smelling Balkan or French cigarettes. With a hand around a slim, blue pack of Gitanes, ever fidgeting with the pack's flap, he eventually proved his importance. His interrogators laughed when he perfectly mimicked the voices of high-ranking NATO officials and officers. The defector had heard dozens of recorded telephone calls between senior officials and generals in the North Atlantic Treaty Organisation and Supreme Headquarters, Allied Powers in Europe because the KGB had monitored and taped all such calls. More important to the Fireplay team, he had brought with him dozens of coded booklets issued to part of the KGB's network in the United States, taken with a miniature KGB roll-over camera.

The CIA immediately passed processed copies of Sedlacek's photographs to the National Security Agency. Working urgently, the NSA ran the reconstructed code books through computers, starting with tapes of the latest signals radioed (and monitored) from the Soviet Embassy in Washington. Working back in time, the computers matched signals and codes in micro-seconds and printed out, on long rolls of paper, messages which had been intercepted by the NSA listening posts located in suburban Maryland and Virginia.

Sedlacek's code books enabled the NSA to decipher dozens of tapes stored in Fort Meade and precipitated the quiet arrest by the FBI of the KGB's resident director in the mid-west. In a covert negotiation this agent was 'traded' for a CIA man, apprehended in East Germany.

It was the defector who provided the booklet to match Novikov's. At last, McLaren, Mallory and Harper learned of Hofman's kidnapping, where he was, and where he was being taken. The messages beamed by the KGB from their Washington embassy to *Byelostroov* now lay decoded on McLaren's beechwood desk.

It was past midnight. McLaren leaned back in his chair with hands behind his head and stared past Mallory and Harper. A glass of milk made a paperweight for the NSA's decoded messages.

'You've got to hand it to the NSA,' McLaren said, 'They're unbelievable.'

'With all those computers they've got in their concrete basements, it's not so hard to credit,' Mallory remarked.

'And more people and a bigger budget than we have,' Harper added. 'Mathematicians. They told me that they had two thousand monitoring stations all over the world.'

'You know, I heard not so long ago that they can even bug typewriters these days,' McLaren shook his head. 'They pick up the feeblest electronic pulses coming from typewriters and then hook on to a standard electric typewriter and translate the impulses into words. It's getting crazy.'

'Sure,' Mallory replied, hoping McLaren would now get down to the business of what to do about Hofman. 'Well, we're certainly not in the jam that we were last night. At least we know where Hofman is and where he's being taken.'

'He can be a complete disaster for us,' said Harper. 'He's going to do everything he can to save his ass.'

'Sure, I think you're both right,' McLaren said. 'We've got to put that fire out, and we've got to do it fast.'

'Have you got the stuff on Yazov, John?' Harper asked Mallory.

'It's all here, everything the agency has,' Mallory tapped files he had got from the Director of Operations' top-secret Central Reference Service. 'The MGB in Sofia are well penetrated, it seems. We hooked into Yazov through a guy named Kovaliov, their head of Department Three. A matter of evaluation. Seems we got them both in the usual way.'

'Money?' McLaren asked.

Mallory nodded. 'The dollar is mightier than the ruble.'

'Let's try and keep it that way,' McLaren said – and they all laughed.

'Yazov's a regular son-of-a-bitch,' Mallory flipped again through the file. 'He does their interrogations. Before we bought him, he killed a few guys, a couple of our own too.'

'What's it look like to you, John?'

'We'll have to hurry. There's a report that the KGB

are already investigating Kovaliov. They're on to something, and the whole penetration looks like coming apart.'

'The top guy there is Zerov. General Zerov, isn't that the fellow?' McLaren referred to the chief of the Bulgarian Secret Service.

'Yes, Zerov. Looks like he wasn't minding the store and the KGB are getting around to purging the service.'

'Why the hell couldn't the FBI have paid Hofman?' McLaren demanded for the fifth time. 'Gates had to be a hero. The trouble with the bureau is that it's full of heroes. Nobody can make an arrest without powdering his face in case he has to do it on TV.'

Mallory returned to the subject. 'We've got to work through Yazov,' he said. 'Hofman will be taken to the maximum security part of the building, under guard twenty-four hours a day. It can only be done by somebody trusted to enter any part of the building, someone who can escort him out – in fact, someone like Yazov.'

Suddenly McLaren knew it was going to be easy. He made a brief review. They could not hijack *Byelostroov* without risking war; the CIA did not want direct involvement; so Yazov, the double agent, would have to break cover.

'We'll have to use him,' McLaren continued. 'A pity, but Fireplay is bigger than Yazov. I'll get the authority for it, that'll be no sweat, and our Sofia Station chief can work out the details.'

Mallory and Harper nodded their agreement. Nobody wanted to break a major agent's cover, but Fireplay was too important. McLaren went on. 'We'll have to re-kidnap Hofman. We could get Yazov to kill him, if we have to, but let's find out what he's given away. He may have sold Fireplay on *Byelostroov*. I don't think so, but he just might have done.'

'I don't think that either,' Mallory said. 'All he's got to sell is Fireplay – his life depends on that. The news means more than the memorandum. The paper only proves it. I think we can gamble on his not talking before they get him under some strong lights in a small room.'

McLaren agreed. 'But let's make certain. We need to know for sure. So we need him alive, if we can, dead only if necessary. I want to get the Fireplay memorandum back too.'

'There are more risks that way,' Harper spoke up again. 'But I think it has to be right. Hofman told something to someone, that's why he's on that freighter. And he hasn't told everything, that's why he's going to Yazov.'

'So we'll fetch him right out of Brzina Street and see,' McLaren summed up. 'Of course, it's going to cost plenty. I know money is hard, but I've got a feeling that it could be even harder to get a new typewriter out of General Services.'

McLaren patted his battered Olivetti Lettera 22, his thumb prints dirtying the fading blue-green paintwork. It was two in the morning; he was about to start a very secret memorandum that would be encoded for transmission to the station chief in Sofia.

When he had finished that, he would start work on another report – this one on *Pacific Klondike*'s progress. Teams in Honolulu harbour had worked days and nights to repair the cracked shaft; still some time had been lost. Defective refrigeration components had already been replaced. Tests on most of the other equipment had thrown up minor faults which Conrad had solved by making adjustments on board. Towing *Omega 1* was slow but easy, morale was high despite delays.

And the cover story was holding up well. A Honolulu newspaper had reported 'the mystery ship's surprise visit' and rewritten all the old deep-sea mining copy.

Pacific Klondike had sailed out of Honolulu harbour, her secrets safe. Carson's latest report was that the only sign of anything Russian had been a long-range Tupolev 95 reconnaissance aircraft which had flown over *Pacific Klondike* very high without circling. Her radars showed she was free of surface or underwater surveillance. Carson estimated they would reach *Doneska*'s site within thirty-six hours.

Two of McLaren's fingers tapped on the Lettera's worn plastic keys, a signal for Mallory and Harper to stretch themselves and go home. Down the passage they could still hear the intermittent clatter of McLaren's keys, and Harper stifled a big yawn.

10

Pacific Klondike stopped under hot sun directly over a pre-determined point, 39°15′42″ north and 165°14′33″ west, cycloidal propellers churning, as she hovered gently in five-foot waves. Peter Barroso and Lloyd Williams, who had been part of Fireplay since the first Greek Street think sessions, were among the scientists gathered below deck to scan positive readings on an array of instruments. One of the instruments, side-scan sonar, had printed on a screen the wreck's ghostly outline.

Conrad's crew worked all night lowering still and tele-vision cameras. In the morning, the television camera's floodlights illuminated *Doneska*'s conning tower. A different type of picture of the wreck swam steadily on the cathode ray tube and the large white numbers 782 on the tower's starboard side rippled.

The objective was a close-up of *Doneska* on the sea floor. In the water, Barroso and Williams, both of them seasoned by months of training, readied *Explorer* for her first opera-tional dive. Scuba divers, who had rigged underwater cameras to *Explorer*, surfaced and climbed into *Pacific Klondike*'s skiff. At 2036 hours Carson himself inspected the sphere's 400-pound steel door. 'OK, down you go – and good luck,' he said to the two scientists before the door swung shut behind them.

Barroso snapped into place a single bolt along the inside of *Explorer*'s heavy steel hatch. Inside the air was fresh and dry, cleaned by a silica gel. Barroso and Williams sat on small stools in a sphere seven feet in diameter.

The dive began at 2100 hours with *Explorer* going down like a slow, old lift. By 2500 feet it was dark and through the plexiglass Barroso and Williams saw the first traces of phosphorescent plankton. All the while Williams busied himself with measuring and adjusting the speed of *Explorer*'s descent, constantly checking water and gasoline temperature, water pressure, how much ballast he had released and what was available. A small cabin lamp provided just enough light for reading instruments. The water temperature steadily fell, the cabin cooled, Barroso and Williams pulled on warm sweaters.

Readings on the magnetometer and radiation sensors grew stronger. Steadily, the scanning sonar's echoes pinged more sharply while an on-board computer kept *Explorer* automatically on course. At 8000 feet Barroso used the under-sea telephone to report to Carson in *Pacific Klondike* that there were no problems. The dive speeded up as the more compressible gasoline allowed sea water to enter freely and increase the bathyscaphe's weight. At 16000 feet the depth finder recorded the sea bottom 505 feet below *Explorer*.

Fifty minutes later, *Explorer*'s mercury floodlights swept across the sunken submarine as the bathyscaphe hovered 30 feet above *Doneska*'s conning tower, with the submarine extending 160 feet on either side.

'Beautiful, kids.' Barroso spoke laconically into the telephone. 'She's really here, she really exists.'

'A little weird.' Williams was slightly awed. 'She's a ghost more than anything.'

'Take a ride over her, from stem to stern,' Carson instructed.

'Cameras ready,' Barroso intoned as he flicked on four automatic cameras. Large, red shrimps and sole-like fish danced under the floodlights reflecting off the submarine's fin and hull. *Doneska*'s rivets were clearly visible, red rust spots dotted her steel hull. Her bow hung a few feet above a uniformly sandy floor which the sea had laid down over thousands of years.

Explorer's battery-powered electric motors spun her shafts and the bathyscaphe moved slowly forward. Williams glided the craft over the stern area where *Doneska* stuck in the ooze, and then moved her off line, to the side of the wrecked submarine. A push of the switch released gasoline, and *Explorer* gently dropped another fifteen feet to traverse the side of *Doneska*'s hull.

'Transponders going down,' Williams talked into the undersea telephone.

While automatic cameras clicked photograph after photograph, Williams released seven transponders around *Doneska*. Each transponder was tied to a fifty-foot plastic cable tethered to the sea floor and was immediately activated to receive and transmit sonic pulses. From that time on, as *Explorer* emitted sound pulses every thirty seconds, her pings and echoes were programmed into computers. On board the mother ship a computer printed out a thin, wavy line that was *Explorer*'s course in a navigation grid around *Doneska* accurate within five feet.

'She's waterlogged. Holed badly in three places.' Barroso confirmed *Mary Jane*'s photographs. 'I've got one of the holes in the lights.' *Explorer* floodlit a jagged hole in *Doneska*'s stern.

'In three places?' Carson asked.

'Yes, sir.'

'That may be a problem.'

'It may be a real problem.'

Until *Explorer*'s positive confirmation, CIA scientists had hoped that *Doneska* had not been damaged too badly. Now it was finally known that the raising would tax all *Pacific Klondike*'s lifting equipment because the waterlogged submarine would be that much heavier. The problem was that the strain could stall *Pacific Klondike*'s lifts, powerful as they were.

'It's going to be slow. We'll have to distribute the strains very accurately, Pete.' Carson's voice crackled into the bathyscaphe. 'How difficult are the grabs going to be?'

'Easy to grab forward of the tower, not too easy behind.' Barroso informed the mother ship that he could easily fix two grabs forward of *Doneska*'s conning tower and that a third directly aft of the tower was feasible. 'She's stuck in the mud at the stern and that's going to be trouble. She's about ten degrees to the sea floor along her length, but the lift operators won't have too much trouble spreading the load over all four grabs.' While Williams drove *Explorer* around the submarine for two-and-a-half hours, Barroso kept up a marathon commentary, automatically tape-recorded, on every detail of *Doneska*'s disposition. Carson and *Pacific Klondike*'s scientists carefully studied every detail thrown on to television screens. A mass of still photographs taken by *Explorer* was to come and the films would be processed overnight.

The strong click of *Explorer*'s Geiger alongside *Doneska*'s conning tower brought Carson back on the undersea telephone.

'Pay dirt, Pete?' Carson asked.

Peter Barroso confirmed Carson's impression that the Geiger had located radioactive emissions in *Doneska*'s missile stowage areas. Helpfully, Williams stationed *Explorer* a few feet above the rounded hatches to *Doneska*'s ballistic missile bays and the Geiger-Muller tube rattled hard as it counted electrically charged alpha-particles escaping from radioactive materials.

As the bathyscaphe floated around *Doneska*'s stern and bow, the Geiger rattled again over the suspected torpedo tubes and stowages.

'Atomic everything,' came Carson's voice. 'I like it.'

At last, with *Explorer*'s battery voltage running dangerously low, Williams pulled an electric switch, and a simple electro-magnet poured a stream of steel pellets from *Explorer*'s ballast silos. The pellets fell to the sea floor and a lightened *Explorer* soared towards the surface at six feet a second.

The bathyscaphe burst into sunshine and a sea rougher than earlier that day. Barroso and Williams climbed up the conning tower, on to a deck awash with sea water. Their muscles were cramped and soon they were drenched in spray. *Pacific Klondike*'s skiff sped towards them while scuba divers swam around the bathyscaphe to check her external equipment.

Carson radioed McLaren a long, quietly optimistic report. Work would go on around the clock to recharge and re-ballast *Explorer* and check out *Pacific Klondike*'s vital equipment.

Weather reports were favourable. If the weather held, they would lower the grabs at 0600 hours the next day.

Five hours before McLaren got the message, *Byelostroov* docked in Odessa. Novikov and Hofman were taken to the airport in a fast, black Russian Fiat.

Details of Colonel Yazov's plan were forwarded to the CIA by Dick Salisbury, their station chief in Sofia. Harper took the decoded message directly to McLaren, who was talking to Mallory. The latter was McLaren's natural deputy. He was quiet and cautious and, without anything being formally agreed, had come to control things when McLaren was away. He could quite understand that McLaren wanted to be on *Pacific Klondike* for the raising of *Doneska*; Mallory would remain at Langley to co-ordinate all Fireplay's varied aspects.

Harper walked in with the message and waved it around excitedly. 'Yazov has given Dick a $2000000 plan that is really incredible,' he said. 'It involves killing everybody in Brzina Street headquarters and blowing up the whole building.'

'He sounds crazy.' Mallory shook his head with alarm.

'Now take it easy, kids,' McLaren said, making Mallory

wince. He was thirty-nine years old, nobody's kid, and he also knew McLaren was signalling a major policy difference. 'You have to learn not to go off at the deep end without looking.'

Then McLaren sat back in his leather chair, shut his eyes and laughed, which alarmed Mallory even more.

'Why kill everybody, Mac? Why blow up the building? It is something with big risks and small gains.'

McLaren stopped laughing and spoke across the table to Harper without looking at Mallory. 'What did Dick tell Yazov?' he asked.

'He avoided any commitment. He said Yazov did all the talking; he just listened.'

'Good, I like that. We don't want to scare Yazov off, and I'm glad Dick didn't turn him down flat.' McLaren removed his glasses and sucked on the plastic tip of one arm. 'You know, we're in this guy Yazov's hands. And if he wants to do it his way, I don't care as long as it's done. We're concerned here with results, not methods.'

'I can see that. But that way, it's much harder for Yazov, don't you think?'

'He probably wants to justify the two million. He thought up a plan he could sell for two million.'

Mallory was increasingly alarmed at McLaren's apparent acceptance of Yazov's proposals. 'Jim, this could be a disaster. The agency has to stay out of this . . .'

McLaren smiled a little impatiently. 'The agency is out of it. Yazov's supposed to be *their* man, not ours. I don't see how we can be implicated. I'm not about to order him to blow up anything. But what he decides is his business and I can't really stop that, can I?'

'I guess you can't,' Harper replied. 'I guess nobody can.'

'We have to pay the two million without haggling too much, and I'm alarmed that Dick haggled. He's starting to sound more and more like Gates. I don't intend to do another economy run on a 350-million operation.'

'But what about the risks? It still sounds crazy to me,' Harper asked.

'Why don't you think for five seconds?' McLaren said. 'It's not that bad. I see he wants to start at four in the morning. Probably no more than a dozen people in the building. With surprise working for him, he could take them easily.'

'And blowing up the building afterwards?'

'A massive diversion. Once the building goes up there's going to be chaos and confusion. The lines will be buzzing with panic. Makes it easier to get Hofman out before the enemy thinks about plugging holes in the nets around the airports, railway stations and border posts.'

'Frankly, I don't like it.' Mallory refused to conceal his misgivings.

McLaren said coolly, 'Then stay out of it, kid.'

But Mallory was in it, whether he liked it or not and Harper was not wholly convinced either. 'Would you reply to Dick?' he asked McLaren.

'Sure,' McLaren said. 'I know exactly what I'll say. And I don't want any mistakes.'

There was an uneasy quiet in the room.

'You know, you have to remember something else too,' McLaren said. 'Yazov knows that the KGB is getting closer to him and that he has to get out anyway. So he's getting out and trying to take a bundle of money with him. He doesn't know how important Hofman is to us. So for two million he has to start thinking big. And big to Yazov means killing people and blowing the building.'

Mallory took his leave a little coldly but in the blue-carpeted passage, walking to his own office, he said to Harper: 'I have to admit, the way that twister puts it, the whole thing may not be so wild after all. Mac has a way of arguing that makes it all seem possible.'

'He can make a cesspool sound clean when it suits his purpose,' Harper replied shortly.

Mallory closed his door and went to sit behind a pile of

accumulated paperwork. He ran his eyes over scores of print-outs, telexes, reports and books that flowed over his desk and shelves on to the floor. Someday soon, he thought, he would have to clean up and stuff it all into burn-bags. The job had begun to grow sour on him. . . .

11

The man to whom the CIA was prepared to pay so much money for freeing Hofman lived outside Sofia in a cottage built of stone and rigged with floodlights on every side. Three Alsatian watchdogs romped in the garden. Ivan Yazov always slept within easy reach of a rifle in an airy bedroom that opened through french doors on to a small brick patio. The patio was kept cool and green by a large syringa that grew there.

During the afternoon before the day fixed for the killings, Yazov had been taking a nap and was awakened just after four o'clock by the singing of small birds in this tree. The Bulgarian lay in his big brass bed, yawning and clearing his mind, and went through his plans for killing everybody in the MGB's Brzina Street headquarters in the dark, early morning of the next day.

Work would be slowest in the hour before dawn, and the tired workers on late-night duty most off their guard. Yazov would have to kill about fourteen people, mostly agents of Departments One, Two, Three and Four. Ordinarily, there would be nobody from Department Four on the late stint but, at a guess, Mikozev's lawyers would still be with Mikhail Kovaliov of Department Three.

Kovaliov was being interrogated because the Bulgarian Secret Service was under pressure. Rumours abounded of CIA infiltrations and some of the badly-paid agents were under suspicion. 'You are heavily infiltrated by the CIA,' the KGB had told General Zerov. The spymaster had been worried enough to call a meeting of department heads which ordered Colonel Mikozev, head of Department Four, to start with Kovaliov and obtain a confession. Kovaliov had held out for over twenty-four hours, Yazov reflected.

Though Yazov was in charge of Department Five, the section that interrogated Western agents, General Zerov had decided to use Department Four for Kovaliov. Or was it *because* he was in charge of Department Five?

Yazov would do most of his killing with a fast, light, accurate and silenced sub-machine gun. It had special features of its own which he proceeded to recheck. Unscrewing the top of a tube, Yazov carefully poured on to the white sheets of his bed a series of parts precision-machined from fine steel. A few pieces screwed together, snapped into alignment, and, when it was done, he held a slim, spidery sub-machine gun.

The stock was a metal A-frame that screwed into the back of the barrel. On the front of the gun's barrel Yazov carefully wound a silencer that fitted like a very long, fat sausage. On the barrel, with another snap, went a telescopic sight of Zeiss lenses. Finally, there were grub screws, which controlled the telescopic sight to line up for the range of fifty metres. He would use explosive bullets from the basement armoury. Satisfied, the Bulgarian cautiously broke the gun into its components and slipped them back into the thin tube.

He would kill Makarov, the MGB armourer, he thought, with a chop to the neck or maybe a silenced Lüger. Hofman would be taken by Novikov to Department Five's interrogation room. Novikov with the Lüger, and the tape recordist, Parkomov, too. Lock Hofman in the interrogation room, kill Yakolev, the guard, with the sub-machine gun, then through the old three-storey headquarters, from room to room with the gun. . . . He planned to start killing from the third floor and work down. Galena Romanova, the receptionist, would be last.

Enough high explosives were stored in the armoury.

Plastic explosives, small mines, delayed charges, time bombs and incendiaries. After the killings, he would mine the building with explosives.

Yazov walked naked into the bathroom. He washed his face with cold water, brushed his teeth twice and pulled his lips off his teeth to examine how white they were.

Once, long ago, he had been interested in becoming an actor. He had even played a few small parts in Bulgarian plays and had said a dozen words in a propaganda film about Bulgaria's anti-colonialism. Now he was a colonel in the MGB, which was very different, and what lay ahead would be very different too. A new life was starting in the early morning and he was lucky to be starting it.

Yazov drove to headquarters in a medium-sized Russian-made Fiat. There were so few cars on the road that he seldom dipped his headlamps. The Fiat entered a small car park in front of a squat building and stopped in a free space with a clear way out.

Brzina Street headquarters was a famous Sofia landmark, having been constructed in the sixth century to serve as a monastery for the Knights of the Cross. Six hundred and fifty years later its huge cupola was destroyed, and in the eighteenth century the building was renovated to house the Sofia Supreme Court. Where monks had once meditated in sunlight filtering through stained glass windows, lawyers had come to argue heatedly. In their turn, the black-gowned lawyers had made way for agents of subversion and sabotage.

Situated diagonally opposite the Bulgarian National Bank off Graf Ignatiev, the stone construction was topped by a red-tiled roof. In its big windows lights shone dimly. The centre of Bulgaria's spying network consisted of wide corridors, a double staircase from the ground floor and dozens of old arches between walls painted light cream and green. Departments One and Two were housed on the first floor. Most of the agents and laboratory technicians of those departments worked in large, old courtrooms: the MGB used an open-plan system wherever it could, despite a degree of insecurity which came with such a system.

Yazov climbed twenty-six stone steps to the entrance into a small rotunda. His feet clicked on a floor of black and white marble. In his right hand he held his official identification card for scrutiny by an MGB guard. The guard had strapped to his shoulder an old Russian-made PPS sub-machine gun with a curved box of a magazine and wooden stock.

At the switchboard, amid a carefree clutter of make-up, white tissues, books and two empty coffee-cups, sat Galena Romonova.

'Anything I need to know?' Yazov greeted her amiably.

'Your package comes in at three hundred hours,' Galena Romanova's message referred to Hofman.

'Anything else?'

'No, sir,' she answered, 'except that I'm not feeling too well and we're having trouble again. The sections upstairs are still behind.'

'They're months behind.'

'Yes, and General Z is thinking of trebling the night staff to get through all the paper.'

'You mean tonight . . .?'

'No, not tonight, thank God. Maybe next week. But General Z is worried about falling behind in evaluation work.'

'Yes, I know.'

'General Z told Colonel Mikozev that he had more trouble from the KGB. He said that Special Investigation were on to him again.' Galena Romanova gossiped in her indiscreet way.

'Bye, I have to go.' Yazov slipped away down marble steps into the basement armoury where he found Makarov reading a newspaper. Makarov got up.

'Evening, Colonel, anything you want?' Makarov asked wearily.

Yazov, who wanted 120 explosive bullets, tapped on the

sealed steel tube. Makarov nodded, knowing what was wanted. Into the blunt ends of bullets were drilled thin holes for carefully poured droplets of mercury. After that, into tiny spaces between the mercury droplets and blunt tips of the bullets, would go molten lead. Once the lead hardened, Makarov would file the tops into the old cupro-nickel tipped shapes. On impact, the bullets exploded like small grenades.

The armourer pushed a pad of forms toward Yazov, who filled in specifications and signed with a flourish. While Makarov checked the form, Yazov peered into the armoury. Crate was stacked upon crate, box sat on box. Yazov saw loose bombs, grenades, pistols, rifles and pieces of rifle. In an armoury, so untidy that he understood again why General Zerov was in trouble, sufficient explosives were stored to blow up the building.

'I'll pick it all up later,' Yazov told Makarov casually, then turned for the stairs and walked to Department One.

Department One gathered intelligence. It had desks for the Middle East, Far East, Africa, Latin America, Western Europe, Southern Europe and North America. Each desk was controlled by an officer who supervised the relevant military, political, economic, armament, technical and counter-espionage aspects of each geographical area. Most of the agents worked at desks in the large open room. Yazov found only Kobolov on duty under a slowly moving, single-bladed fan that hung from the old courtroom's high ceiling. The heavy, carved wooden door closed silently and Yazov went to Department Two, which was down a wide corridor.

This department did technical work and was like a large laboratory. While the work benches were filled by day, there were usually few workers at night. To confirm that, Yazov opened another heavy, carved door to see a solitary laboratory assistant in a white coat, half-hidden behind bubbling chemical jars, retorts, test tubes, wiring. He was probably processing urgent photographs. Department Two also ran the armoury and telex room on the second floor; a walk up carpeted steps took Yazov to the communications centre. He turned an ornate, brass door knob and the clatter from four rows of teleprinter machines suddenly increased in volume. Inside Tanya Posanska, wearing the pink smock in which she was soon to die, bent low over a row of keys. She neither saw nor heard Yazov open and close the door.

The hardest part was going to Department Three, also on the second floor. It analysed raw intelligence gathered by Department One, a task in which it had fallen far behind – and Lieutenant Colonel Mikhail Kovaliov was being asked why. Under General Zerov's prodding, Pavlov, Kovaliov's deputy, was working hard to catch up, with the help of a few men who worked long hours into the night. They would still be in their large room when the time came. But how many?

To check, Yazov opened the door to Department Three's main workroom and counted men at the desks for North America and Africa. At a large desk in the middle, Pavlov smoked a cigar and blue smoke drifted into the single-bladed fan above him and dispersed. On seeing Yazov enter, Pavlov drew on the cigar, pulled it to the side of his mouth, clamped his teeth over it and smiled.

'Colonel Yazov, nice to see you. Anything I can do?'

'Nothing really,' Yazov replied. 'What's new?'

'Portugal is active but our agents there are filing rubbish,' Pavlov waved at a pile of spiked and discarded paper. Yazov smiled but his eyes were expressionless. He decided against firing from Pavlov's desk: he would never get that far without losing surprise. From the door Barolski and Vassilovich were the furthest off with the angles most acute. He would shoot them through the Zeiss. Pavlov would then, of course, get under cover. What happened thereafter was less predictable.

With a wave to Pavlov, he went up the stairs to Department Four, the administration section which did accounting, finances, legal work, recruitments, training and internal investigations. Lawyers from this department were investigating Kovaliov, preparing for his trial.

Beyond an arch there was a smaller courtroom on the door of which Yazov knocked politely before trying the handle. The fact that it opened made Yazov realize again why the Secret Service was in trouble.

Kovaliov sat under a white light, his face pale, lined and very tired. There were two lawyers in uniform and Yazov's impression was that they were etched in black outside a circle of light around Kovaliov. Quietly Yazov re-closed the door and walked back through the arch down a green carpeted corridor past the central library; the document centre also came under Department Four and its doors were reassuringly locked.

His reconnaissance done, the assassin passed through a short tunnel to salute Ivan Yakolev, who guarded the double doors into Yazov's own interrogation room. Yakolev was armed with a PPS sub-machine gun whose black barrel shone.

A blind over the peep-window of the inner door enabled Yazov to sit unobserved at his deak. He unscrewed the hollow tube to pour out the gun before clicking and screwing metal pieces into a slim, spidery weapon. The telescopic sight went home with a snap, the silencer wound slowly about threads on the barrel. From inside a drawer Yazov took four thirty-round magazines of mercury-tipped 9 mm. bullets, one of which he clipped into the barrel.

The weapon weighed two kilograms and developed a muzzle velocity of 500 metres a second; it could fire single shots or, with the flick of a catch, 900 bullets a minute.

Yazov placed the gun in a large desk drawer from which he had removed an old Lüger pistol loaded with a magazine of eight explosive 9 mm. bullets. Flipping the safety catch, he placed the Lüger on his desk's green blotter.

The phone rang. Galena Romanova.

'Your package has just landed at the military airport.'

'Yes?'

'He'll be here in thirty minutes.'

'Thank you. When they get here, let them come straight through to me.'

'Very good, sir.'

Yazov waited ten minutes. Then he pushed the Lüger into the top of his trousers and went to kill Makarov.

12

In the armoury sat Makarov, behind a chess board, his elbow upon a small table, chin resting in his left hand. A studious set to his face, plastic chess pieces and a Russian chess magazine completed the tableau.

Six magazines of another kind – for use in a sub-machine gun – lay on the table. The sound of footsteps on the marble outside the armoury brought Makarov to his feet. The armourer wanted another signature from his caller, and he slipped carbon between the leaves of his requisition book.

Makarov bent over his receipts and, if he noticed Yazov raise his right hand, he paid no special attention. The flattened hand came down with a chop to snap Makarov's spinal cord in three places where it entered the cranium and disappeared past the clavicles, killing the armourer outright. Yazov left him behind the small table, scooped up the machine gun magazines, locked the steel armoury doors and slipped the large key into his pocket. As he walked back through the marble rotunda, Galena Romanova made signs with her raised right hand and pointed up the stairs. Hofman was in the building.

The lobby guard turned at the sound of Yazov's heels to nod in the direction of the stairs. Because he took the steps two at a time, Yazov was slightly winded by the third floor. He saluted Yakolev before pulling the soundproof double doors shut behind him. Inside he found Novikov, Hofman and Parkomov. A tape recorder was being plugged in by Parkomov, who flipped switches and pressed flat, plastic buttons. Hofman sat with his head in his hands. Someone had removed his jacket and tie; his shirt sleeves and collar hung loosely around his wrists and neck.

Yazov shook Novikov's hand limply.

'Was it a good journey?'

'It was long.'

Extracting the Lüger from out of the top of his trousers, Yazov took a few seconds to wind on a thick, round silencer, while Novikov stood placidly, content that he had safely completed his long mission from New York. What he wanted now was a cup of coffee and, maybe, a kind word or two to mark his success. He wore on his face a look of confidence, the smile of a job well done.

'You must be tired?'

'Not specially, but I'm glad it's all over for me.'

Yazov nodded and checked the safety catch before lifting the Lüger. Parkomov looked up casually. Then the tape recordist's face tensed with curiosity, growing comprehension, disbelief, and, finally, alarm.

The still unsuspecting Novikov took Yazov's 9 mm. slug in his chest from three paces. The bullet sliced through fabric to hit a space between the fifth and sixth ribs. Explosive pressure-energy expanded through Novikov's chest cavity, carrying flesh and bone. It knocked him off his feet and blew out half his spine.

Parkomov remained with ear-phones in place, the microphone leads in mid-air, his mouth flopping open absurdly. He had one moment to realize he was being killed. Yazov shot Parkomov in the temple from one-and-a-half paces. His skull exploded and he went over backwards, breaking the wooden chair and pulling the tape recorder with him. The ear-phones were blown off his blond head

Hofman was gasping with total incomprehension. Then, instinctively, he dived off the chair and lay abjectly against a wall, his wide eyes reflecting blank terror.

'You are Hofman.' Yazov stated more a fact than a question.

The thief tried to speak, could not manage it. Instead, he nodded blankly.

'That's fine, then. Your people are paying me to get you out of here, you understand that?' Again, a blank nod.

'I'm going to do it, that's all,' Yazov said simply.

It was three minutes and ten seconds since he had killed Makarov. Yazov put down the Lüger and pulled out the flat drawer in the middle of his desk to retrieve the machine gun. Then he took a green canvas bag and strapped it to his chest, the straps being looped around his back and neck. Inside the bag were packed nine thirty-bullet magazines of 9 mm. exploding ammunition, together with the Lüger and a spare eight-bullet magazine. Moving his arms in small circles, Yazov tested the straps to see how free they were. He slipped the left strap a couple of holes, tried again, and his arms moved easily. Then he turned to Hofman, who was crouching in a corner, his eyes averted, as far away as possible from Novikov's and Parkomov's bodies.

'Take it easy; get yourself under control,' Yazov said.

In response, the prisoner stood up and leaned against the wall. He still looked blank

'I'll come back quite soon. Don't panic.'

'Okay,' was all Hofman could manage as Yazov picked up the gun, unlocked the door and walked out to Yakolev.

The guard stood resting the sole of his boot against a panel wall. The key's rattle in the last of the double doors made him straighten smartly. Yakolev had just eaten a bar of chocolate, and he worried about what to do with the wrapper. Should he pocket it or go down the corridor to the waste basket?

A burst from Yakov's gun sent Yakolev crashing against the wall. A button flew where a bullet snapped it off the uniform. The guard slid down the wall, smoking.

Yazov dragged Yakolev behind the first of the double doors, locked Hofman into the room and moved down the corridor past the library, under several cream-coloured arches, to where Kovaliov was strapped to a chair, blood trickling from a gash on his cheek. He sat under the spotlight with his eyes shut. Outside the light stood Shugar and Zubulin. Yazov opened fire. Zubulin bent forward, the green fabric of his uniform jacket stretched tightly over his back. Bullets ripped the cloth and the holes smoked with small puffs of green material and dust. Zubulin crashed over Kovaliov, overturning the chair.

A call just made to Shugar's wife had informed her that he was leaving Brzina Street in ten minutes. . . .

Four bullets exploded against the walls, kicking up large puffs of white dust. Another fragmented in an armchair behind Shugar, three others bowled him across the room. Kovaliov rolled with the chair from under the white light. He saw Yazov and imagined, mistakenly, he was to be freed. Yazov held the gun still.

'They know everything,' Kovaliov said, exhausted, waiting for Yazov to untie his bonds. Yazov killed Kovaliov with a single bullet that exploded through his neck, severing his spinal cord, and making him kick convulsively once.

Downstairs, Anatoli Kobolov had just put on a hat and a long, grey coat, and was on his way to collect Shugar and go home. He and Shugar shared their Fiats on alternate days because they lived in the same tree-lined street. He met Yazov on a corner landing.

Bullets exploded on the corridor floor and made big puffs of white where they ran up the wall behind Kobolov. He tried to reach his Tokarev 33 automatic pistol. A burst exploded in his chest, knocking him down. He lifted himself painfully and lurched against the pock-marked concrete wall and died on his feet.

Yazov ran down the stairs, stepped into the corridor, swung the gun sideways, looking down through the cream-coloured arches. There was an acrid smell of gunsmoke as Yazov slipped another magazine into the gun's hot barrel.

He found Tanya Posanska tearing a long telex message off a machine in the corner, near a window with its venetian blind drawn. A bullet hit a teleprinter and there was a spray of small, broken metal keys, black ink and rubber roller. The next hit Tanya Posanska, and she crashed against the window clawing at the venetian blind.

General Zerov sat at home in his pyjamas, in a large, comfortable armchair, worrying. He had slept badly. The Kovaliov investigation kept him awake. The more he thought about it, the clearer it seemed he was being hasty. Badly handled, the case would seriously damage morale.

After agonizing for hours, he finally decided to halt the investigation. He would himself tell Shugar. He was already overseeing Department Three, and it struck Zerov with some annoyance that he was now obliged personally to control a Department Four project as well.

He reached for the phone, dialled, listened to steady, even buzzing. There was a soft crackle, and he heard Galena Romanova.

'Good morning, Zerov here.' He gave the day's coded password.

'Good morning, General,' Galena Romanova said deferentially.

'Get me Department Four.'

'Very well, sir.'

General Zerov heard no more for a minute. Instead, he sat holding the plastic receiver. The longer he waited, the harder he froze.

'Sorry, General, there's no reply.'

'No reply?'

'No, sir.'

'What seems to be the trouble?'

'The phone keeps ringing. Shall I ask someone from Department Three to check and then ring back later?'

'Yes.'

'Very good, sir. I'll call you back in a few minutes.'

Zerov replaced the black plastic receiver. He sat slumped

in his pyjamas a short while, then got up to make coffee while he waited.

The big wooden doors to Department Three were carved with Bulgarian wild flowers. Yazov slowly pushed a door open, and positioned himself under a large gold-edged clock above the doors.

A phone buzzed near Barolski, who stood up in fatigue. He pushed the paper away from him, yawned widely. His cheeks rippled in Yazov's Zeiss lenses.

'Somebody answer the phone,' Vassilovich said from the Canada desk.

Barolski walked to the phone and his head bobbed up and down in Yazov's cross-wires. The assassin steadied them on the bridge of Barolski's nose.

As Barolski reached for the receiver metal fragments from Yazov's bullet sheared off the top of his head. Without pausing, Yazov fired at Vassilovich, who was reading Canadian trade reports and making notes about grain exports. A heavy-calibre bullet smashed through his neck, exploded against his lower right jaw and slammed him backwards over the chair

For a moment, Pavlov could not grasp that they were under fire. Then he dived under a desk, reached frantically for his pistol, and pulled the table down for cover.

Yazov aimed at the overturned desk and fired a long burst. Gunfire raked over the wood, the desk flew apart in large and small splinters. Some wood caught fire and briefly smoked. Pavlov pulled himself up from the floor groaning, blood running from splinters of fragmented wood and metal. He kneeled unsteadily on his right knee and there was a sharp crack as he fired a Tokarev 33 from twenty paces with a shaking hand. The pistol flashed and a bullet buzzed by Yazov. Two high-velocity bullets dropped Pavlov back to the floor for the last time.

The room was quiet and wisps of blue smoke and nitrous

gases which rose from the barrel's mouth smelt badly. It was 0414 hours when Yazov pulled the door closed and made for the stairs.

He ran into Galena Romanova, the laboratory assistant from Department Two and the lobby guard; they had heard the shooting. Galena Romanova was in front. The lobby guard had unshouldered his PPS sub-machine gun which he was swinging round at Yazov.

Yazov fired first. Four bullets exploded in the guard's stomach, chest and neck to blow him apart. Penkovsky, the laboratory assistant, had been developing microfilms. He rolled down the stairs with his skull shattered while bullets repeatedly bounced Galena Romanova against the wall.

Yazov looked at his watch. The glass was spotted red; the time was 0415 hours. He moved to the armoury for his explosives and, as he passed Galena Romanova's switchboard, he heard a buzzing. Somebody was trying to reach the Bulgarian Secret Service.

The operation, in its entirety had taken nine minutes and thirty-six seconds.

13

General Zerov stirred the large cup viciously and spilled coffee. The Bulgarian Secret Service was in trouble, that he knew. He was sure that it was heavily infiltrated by the CIA – and by the KGB. The Russians trusted nobody. They not only directed the Bulgarian Secret Service but spied on it from within. Morale was low, yet what was he to do? He had to please the KGB but he also had to press his investigations carefully. What morale remained in his service could easily be destroyed.

He rattled the coffee cup against the saucer impatiently. Surely Galena Romanova had called Department Four by now. Zerov reached for the phone and dialled Brzina Street. He sat in his armchair, drumming his fingertips against the table top while the phone buzzed.

Five minutes later, Zerov slammed down the receiver. He dialled again. This time he slowly fingered each number and released the punched, spring-loaded circle with great care. The phone buzzed on. Zerov was suddenly alert. His impulse was to phone Sofia State Police headquarters. Then he realized the Secret Service had enough problems without inviting outside gossip. He told himself there must be a fault in the line, and dialled the home number of the head of Department Four. The phone buzzed loudly in his ear and this time there was a click.

'Good morning, Colonel, Zerov here,' he said and spoke the code.

'Morning, General,' Mikozev replied sleepily.

'There's something not exactly right at headquarters.'

'Sir?'

'Earlier, I got through to Romanova and she could not put the call through to your department. They are busy with Kovaliov there aren't they?'

'Yes, General. They should be.'

'And now I can't even get through to Romanova. So I want you down there. I want you to leave right away.'

'I understand.'

'And by the way, the reason for my call to your department was to stop the investigations. I've thought about it again and I have to say that we must be careful not to antagonize the service. I think we may have to move much more carefully.'

'Yes, sir.' Zerov's nervousness came as no surprise to Mikozev. The rot in the MGB started with him. Mikozev was sure that, whatever else happened, Zerov would soon go.

'So when you get there, take Shugar off the interrogation.'

'Yes, sir.'

'And Mikozev, I want a very full report on what's happened this morning. I really am getting sick of it all. I think we're going to have to deal very hard with Romanova. I mean, this is absurd, totally absurd.'

'I agree, sir.'

General Zerov slammed the phone down. From the kitchen came the kettle's whistle. He decided to have another cup of strong coffee.

Yazov switched on the lights in the vast basement armoury. The area, which stretched out under most of the Secret Service building, smelled old and musty. In it was stored everything the service was ever likely to use. The assassin walked between thick concrete columns. Explosives of all kinds, carelessly stacked: crates of dynamite, boxes of plastic incendiaries and time bombs, grenades and old Russian TM-40 anti-tank mines. The latter, containing two-kilogram explosive charges, had lifting handles riveted to their sides; their fuses were pressure-operated.

Needing help, Yazov climbed the stairs to his office, unlocked the door and found Hofman seated at his desk. Colour had returned to his face, life to his eyes.

'I killed everybody in the building,' Yazov said simply.

Hofman blinked.

'We've got a little time. Now I want to blow the place up. That'll bring a big diversion and will help you to escape more easily.'

Hofman merely nodded.

'I'll want you to help carry explosives,' Yazov told him. 'We have plenty, so there's no problem. I'll lay them out. I want the top floor to go first, then the second floor, and the ground floor and basement last.'

Hofman continued nodding his head.

'Are you all right? Can you help?' Yazov asked.

'I think so.' They were the first words Hofman had spoken since Yazov had killed Novikov.

They moved quickly down the stairs. Hofman felt his knees weaken as he hurried past the victims of Yazov's carnage. The walls were spattered with blood, blood soaked the green carpeting, gunsmoke clung in the air.

Yazov put his gun down on Romanova's desk in the lobby. Her board still buzzed with an incoming call.

Once in the armoury, Yazov explained what he wanted, pointing to crates and explosives. He found a couple of green canvas duffle bags, which they filled with as much as they could carry, then went up the stairs.

'I'll lay them out,' Yazov said.

Now his role was that of saboteur. With all the flair of a demolitions expert, he set and placed the time bombs, taped plastic explosives to the walls, positioned the old TM–41 mines and incendiaries.

Within twenty minutes both men were sweating. They

worked hard and barely spoke. Hofman piled explosives in the corridor; Yazov took them from there. Hofman knew he might be earning his freedom and that thought kept him going.

By his sixth trip to the basement, he had ceased to be distressed by the carnage. He helped Yazov move four mines into the telex room where the machines clattered on and trailed long papers. He hardly noticed Tanya Posanska lying dead in the corner, under the venetian blind. And when he moved into Department Three all he thought of was that he was tired but there was not much more to do.

Before sunrise, Yazov had fastened sufficient explosives in the building and wired enough plastic charges to detonate everything. He worked quickly to pattern, laying more explosives in the lower floors because he and Hofman made more trips there. The hardest work was in the wiring of the basement. But when that was completed, twenty minutes remained before the first charges would detonate on the third floor, and Yazov made another two trips upstairs with Hofman. He would have made more but for Colonel Mikozev, who arrived as Yazov and Hofman had carried four TM mines to the second floor.

On his way down Yazov heard Mikozev's steps on the marble floor. He moved quickly to Galena Romanova's desk, but Mikozev got there first. He called out but there was no reply. He looked for the lobby guard, then saw Yazov walking towards him.

Yazov looked unkempt, his uniform was loose and Mikozev was pleased to see him button his tunic as he approached. The Head of Department Four leaned against Galena Romanova's desk and shrugged. He raised his eyebrows.

'What's going on?' Mikozev demanded. 'Where's Romanova? Where's Zaroubin? The whole damn service is falling apart. I think . . .'

Yazov hit Mikozev with a hammer first to the nape of the neck. As Mikozev went down, Yazov turned him around and with his knee broke Mikozev's pelvic girdle; once again, death was instantaneous.

Retrieving his gun from Galena Romanova's desk, Yazov called to Hofman and they left the building. Outside, the first streaks of a new day were in the sky.

The Fiat started with the first turn of Yazov's key and headed down Eleksandar Stambolisski Street to Sofia's railway station. Inside the car, Yazov passed Hofman a folder.

'Tickets, money and a passport. The photo isn't good but it's good enough,' he said. Hofman opened the folder checking its contents as well as he could in the grey light.

'You're booked on the Sofia–Belgrade train, and you'll find the train at platform four.' He shot Hofman a quick glance before moving his eyes back to the road. Hofman was recovering fast.

'There'll be a girl in the coupé marked eight. She's going to travel as your wife,' Yazov went on. 'There won't be any trouble. The train will be safe, just keep inside the coupé. There'll be a lot of confusion when the building goes up.' As he spoke, Yazov jerked his head backwards from where they had come, in the direction of Brzina Street.

'Seems pretty simple,' Hofman said, pocketing the folder.

'It is.'

'What about the border?'

'Your people will meet you after Dimitrovgrad, on the Yugoslav side.'

Then they were at the old station and Yazov braked the Fiat to a halt. He opened the door, the small interior light went on and, in the additional grey light of the dawn, Hofman saw Yazov's face fully. It had a quizzical expression that suggested things only Yazov knew.

'All right, good luck. Goodbye.' Yazov smiled.

'Sure.'

'And don't worry. You'll get out safely. I know you will.' The way Yazov smiled and spoke, Hofman felt quite sure he would.

The Fiat's exhaust rattled slightly as Yazov drove away. Hofman walked into the station. At platform four there was only one train. The coaches were dark green and marked 'SOFIA BEOGRAD VENEZIA MILANO LAUSANNE PARIS'. A variegated collection of passengers were boarding. They had attended an international yoghurt conference in Sofia and were returning all over Europe with crates of yoghurt.

Hofman walked down the platform, climbed aboard and found compartment eight down a red-carpeted corridor. He knocked lightly and when somebody said 'Come in,' he slid the door open, then closed it.

'Hi,' a girl said. She was brushing her hair.

'Hi,' said Hofman. 'I see you're expecting me.'

The girl nodded. And as she did, Hofman heard the first explosion. As the others followed, concussion rattled the train's windows.

The first blast had shattered the top floor, causing tiles to fly off the roof and break on the cobbled streets. The rest of the roof collapsed into the third floor as charges blew away or weakened supports and internal walls collapsed. With the bursting of the incendiaries, fires started. Dust rose and shone in a clean straight line where it crossed into sunlight above the roof; papers blew out of the windows and played in the breeze.

Even before the charges on the second floor detonated there were people in the streets. Some wore dressing gowns, others were in their pyjamas. They all stayed well clear. The second floor exploded. Because of the way Yazov timed the devices, those inside detonated first, then the explosives in the outer rooms.

The red tiled roof sagged, hung and crashed down through the third floor into the second. Showers of masonry forced the growing crowds to draw back. Fire gripped the building and burning papers and dust swirled on hot currents of air. The first floor went and the whole building shuddered under a mass of debris, as everything from the top floor down to the first cracked or broke. The explosions threw up more dust; all the lights in the building went out. Flames came out of holes in the rubble and through windows. Sirens started all across Sofia.

At last, the arsenal in the basement exploded. It went up with a tremendous blast and some of the crowd put their hands to their ears. The whole building seemed to lift up from the ground. A split second later it fell and settled itself with a great slap; dust and debris fanned high into the air; people took cover where they could.

The blasts showered glass and building fragments over several blocks and concussion shattered many windows in nearby buildings. Cracks radiated along the cobbled streets close to the site of the basement explosion, and each blast seemed to blow out the fires before the blaze came back more strongly than ever over the ruins.

With their lights flashing and sirens sounding, the first of the ambulances and fire engines drove into the square.

By the time Hofman's train clattered out of Sofia station, the Secret Service headquarters was unrecognizable. Nobody who did not know the building could have told what it looked like before the blasts, where the windows were, where the main doorway had been, how many floors there were.

Hofman saw black smoke rising in the east. By then the train wheels rattled hypnotically, woodwork creaked, and long, deserted corridors swayed. The engine's whistle blew as it passed a large hoarding which advertised yoghurt and the conference.

General Zerov met Major Branski of the KGB at 0600 hours in Zerov's black Volga – a Russian-made car given to high officials. Outside, 100 metres away, Sofia's fire department played silvery jets of water on the still burning, blackened building and the dead were being loaded into ambulances.

Branski knew Zerov was going to Moscow later that day. Already the KGB had pieced together enough information to know that Yazov had massacred Zerov's agents, blown up the building and escaped with Bernard Hofman.

Zerov shifted from behind the Volga's wheel, opened the door and walked round to the car's front. He slumped backwards over the bonnet and stared into the blaze with his hands deep in his large overcoat pockets. A little later he pushed himself off the Volga and got back into the front seat.

'Ivan Yazov did all this?' Zerov shook his head.

'That's what the Centre cabled.'

'But why? What for?'

'Money, blackmail. The other side bought him. We suspected him.'

Zerov turned to Branski with a strange smile. 'I'm going to have to go to jail,' he said sadly.

'You go to jail?' Branski tried to sound incredulous.

'Yes, Major, me. Jail, possibly worse. Obviously I'm finished. The Centre has sent for me today.' Zerov glanced at his watch. 'I'll have to go to the airport soon.'

'I don't know . . .' Branski tried to say something but Zerov cut him short with a sharp look.

'We don't have to go through all that, Major.'

Branski said nothing. He watched firemen struggle through the rubble. Two firemen were carrying a body out and they placed it in a pine casket. Others had already collected a pile of debris from the disaster and dumped it on cobblestones: a woman's shoe, a pair of spectacles, a lunch pail, a charred telephone directory. A bomb squad moved carefully through a jumble of overhanging, twisted pipes, electrical wires and loosely dangling slabs of insulation.

'What am I supposed to do when anybody with a map knows that Bulgaria will always be a Russian client state?' There was more of an edge to Zerov's voice now. 'And yet you are everywhere. Once, Major Branski, I was rash enough to complain to one of your generals about your massive penetrations here. I was crass enough to do that once. Do you know what he said?'

Branski looked up from the bombed headquarters.

'He said, "We will keep you honest if we can remind you that you can't move anywhere, report anything, without us knowing." That's what he said.'

Firemen still watered the smoking, broken spy centre, and there were cries from the bomb squad when a wall slowly collapsed in Brzina Street.

'Anyway, your masters in the Centre have told me to place you in charge of the search for Hofman and Yazov. I'm sure you knew that before I did.'

Branski nodded. For the first time he looked at General Zerov in a way that at last acknowledged their respective roles. Zerov gestured at the rubble. 'You've got all our resources at your disposal,' he said. 'And you've got my office too, Major. It's over there.' He pointed deep into the ruins.

They had already found Yazov's Fiat abandoned in Tolbunin Street near the monument to the Soviet Army. Yazov himself had disappeared. Men with dogs were already in the area but Branski guessed they would find nothing. He lit a cigarette, pulled on the door handle and let himself out of the Volga.

General Zerov watched him round a corner. Seconds later he turned the key in the starter and drove away. The Volga stopped three kilometres from Sofia airport after pulling off the tarmac. Wheat fields rolled from both sides of the road. Zerov watched the wind moving through the grain, and the way the yellow wheat rippled calmed him. He sat behind the wheel for a long while, past the time of his Aeroflot flight to Moscow.

The big Tupolev jet would wait. They would send a search party out along the road if he lingered too long. From the Volga's glove compartment he took a Nagant revolver, a double action model issued to officers. It was the standard Russian revolver of the Second World War.

Everything in Bulgaria, Zerov thought bitterly, was secondhand and Russian-made.

He pushed the Nagant's muzzle gently between his lips. For at least twenty seconds the spy chief rested the barrel on his yellowing bottom teeth. Then his eyes closed, he drew a sharp breath and blew off the top of his head.

Moscow's *Pravda* newspaper made no mention of General Zerov's suicide and reported the Brzina Street explosion in one paragraph.

Sofia. There was a large explosion here yesterday at 45 Brzina Street. It is believed that the old Sofia Supreme Court was used to store army surplus ammunition. There was an accidental blast in the stores area.

In Sofia, the Bulgarian press carried two paragraphs of firemen controlling the flames. The reports were a little longer than *Pravda*'s and praised the Sofia fire brigade. A brief, three sentence television news review covered the fire fighting.

A correspondent of *The Times* in London heard of sabotage and killings in the building. He tried to interview a news vendor who had a kiosk not far from 45 Brzina Street. The man's name was Grigori Kholkhov and all he could tell *The Times* was that he had been talking to a taxi driver when there was a dull-red flash, a tremendous explosion and he had seen red tiles fly off the roof. While he was speaking, a man in plain clothes interrupted to talk briefly to Kholkhov; the newsvendor would say no more to *The Times*.

14

The CIA's station chief gave the real facts to the United States Embassy. His report was encoded by the CIA's agent in the embassy and flashed at 100 words a minute to a phalanx of teletype machines housed in Langley's sophisticated seventh-floor operations centre. McLaren himself stood by the receiving machine as it decoded the message instantly, and he read the long report, word by word, even as the keys tapped on the advancing teleprinter carriage.

Then he tore off a long printout and walked to his office down the hall from the operations centre, through a room papered with huge maps. On his beechwood desk he had yellow, green, blue, red and grey phones, all equipped with scramblers. McLaren reached for the green phone and called Harper and Mallory. They hastened to his office and from behind the desk McLaren read the news to them. He read in a flat, satisfied monotone before passing the printout to Mallory. 'Yazov's a remarkable man. Zerov wasn't minding the store,' he said. 'And Hofman's on the train.'

Mallory passed the report to Harper; he would read it later. 'What happens when he gets out?' he asked.

'I don't know,' McLaren said thoughtfully. 'That's going to be tough. Mr Hofman has proved himself, shall we say, unpredictable. The question is what we do with him when he gets to Yugoslavia.'

He did not seem to be expecting an answer and the two men were silent. McLaren got up and walked to his stuffed trout. He asked Harper to remind him if he had ever been to his fishing cabin in Vermont. Mallory had been several times. Harper said he had not. 'You are going to get to see it,' McLaren promised.

He ran a finger over the trout's fin, then looked at Mallory. 'It seems to me that the moment Hofman escaped they killed themselves,' was all he said.

The two other agents exchanged alarmed glances which McLaren saw. He changed the subject and started talking about Project Fireplay. On *Pacific Klondike* Carson was preparing the first step in *Doneska*'s recovery. Mallory and Harper were to keep constant contact with *Pacific Klondike* and report hour-by-hour progress.

'If anything comes up, call me even in the middle of the night, okay?' McLaren got ready to leave.

'I will,' said Mallory.

McLaren reached for the door and smiled. 'I'm not trying to get any bouquets for this. There's just not going to be any blackmail. There are no good choices in a case like this.'

'No,' Harper said uncertainly.

'Just take the least bad one.'

McLaren, the others realized, was trying to make killing Yazov and Hofman more saleable to them.

Dawn broke at 0529 hours over the Pacific and like a sentinel the ship's high derrick loomed above the two-foot waves that washed against *Pacific Klondike*'s hull. Men were already out on the decks, sweeping the water that accumulated from the night's mists. A dry deck was needed if workers were not to slip and fall on the steelwork.

The forecasts were for a week's good weather and at 0600 hours, under open skies, a blast of the ship's klaxon began the complex operation to raise *Doneska*. As big engines started to throb and beat, they set in train long cycles of dirt, grease and foul language, with nowhere to go after a twelve-hour shift but the showers and a hot meal and just two beers. But the pay was good.

As men on the barge opened her sea cocks, sea water rushed into *Omega 1*'s vast ballast tanks. The barge sank slowly like a submarine into the Pacific to 150 feet. At that depth, men in water-tight compartments shut her sea cocks and *Omega 1* hung submerged in calm water.

Scuba divers peered through plexiglass windows into her floodlit chamber. Inside this huge bay – a vast, empty rectangular space that stretched across the barge from bow to stern – they could see stored the giant grabs to be lowered on to *Doneska*. Other divers swam above the barge, ready for the next operation. They carried underwater television cameras and kept a lookout for sharks.

Guided by these underwater cameras, Conrad manoeuvred *Pacific Klondike* directly above the submerged barge. The mother ship in place, men in blue hard hats worked around her 150-foot docking legs, carefully lowering massive, fifty-inch steel cylinders to lock into matching holes through *Omega 1*'s superstructure. Inside fifty minutes *Omega 1* was moored at all four corners 150 feet below *Pacific Klondike*. Barge and mother ship were safely connected and hands, faces, trousers and shirts were soaked with sweat, smeared with rust and grease.

Another blast of the klaxon. Men, their backs glistening, clustered around the ship's main, 200-foot derrick and eight powerful winches. Steel clanked on steel, there was a smell of diesel fumes, electric motors hummed, workers grunted. They pushed, pulled, dragged heavy equipment and worked with all kinds of tools.

Pacific Klondike slowly slid open the floor to her hull while, on the barge, the domed roof was cranked away. Derrick workers lowered through *Pacific Klondike*'s well the first sections of sixteen-inch diameter pipe. Through the well, too, winch drivers passed multiple three-inch steel ropes with huge steel hooks fastened to their ends. Scuba divers waited for the pipes, ropes and hooks to reach the deep interior of the barge's open chamber before guiding them on to the huge boom resting on the barge's steel floor. The boom was a web of steel sections, braces and cross-pieces, heavy bolts and strong welds, designed so as to swing at its centre of gravity around a massive stub axle. The axle's housing embodied a five-foot long, sixteen-inch diameter neck; inside the tubular neck were cut heavy, thick threads.

Into the neck three scuba divers screwed the first sections of pipe lowered from *Pacific Klondike*; two others hooked steel ropes into eighteen-inch holes in either end of the boom: by 1203 hours the grabs were securely connected to *Pacific Klondike* through boom, pipe and steel ropes.

The barge reverberated as powerful, water-sealed electric motors inched open its floors. At last, the grabs hung free in the water, suspended from *Pacific Klondike* through the barge 16000 feet above *Doneska*. Scuba divers swam around to make visual checks.

Carson ordered the testing of the electric motors attached to each grab, and below deck a technician pressed buttons on a console. On a bank of fluorescent screens huge metal claws opened and closed like pincers. Once again Carson blew *Pacific Klondike*'s klaxon. Before the sharp blast died on the water, workers on the derrick were lowering steel pipe, section after section, hour after hour.

Project Fireplay's engineers had utilized a complicated multiple-rope system. If a rope snapped, three others remained to take the strain.

The next day at 0713 hours, as the boom passed the half way mark to *Doneska*, Williams and Barroso went down again in *Explorer*. The bathyscaphe left the surface, her gentle rolling ceased, water gurgled softly, the depth gauge slowly deflected. Light through *Explorer*'s two thick plexiglass ports thinned and faded. Outside, water temperature dropped. Moisture in Barroso's breath condensed on the hull to form tiny beads of water, lights in the control board glowed like a Christmas tree. In the outside darkness, Barroso saw small forms of sea life: fish, like a series of tiny lights strung together, floated by.

Barroso sat relaxed. At 8000 feet, he heard Carson.

'*Explorer*, this is *Klondike*. Your present position is X23, 6Y 49, 2.'

'This is *Explorer*,' Barroso replied. 'We hear you clearly.'

Sonic transponders that Williams had dropped made *Explorer*'s navigation hyper-accurate. Emitting sound pulses every thirty seconds, so that her precise position could be plotted on a computer printout, the bathyscaphe slowly descended and reached the boom and grabs at 16000 feet. By then *Klondike* was trailing long strings of steel ropes, steel pipe and electric cables as well. The electric cables hung loose in the bathyscaphe's lights, because workers on *Pacific Klondike* had paid out slightly more electric cable than steel rope to avoid snapping the cables if the ropes suddenly broke. No danger of that had yet arisen; the strain would only come with lifting *Doneska*. If the steel pipes broke, nothing would be recovered and costly, sophisticated equipment would be lost on the sea floor.

Meanwhile, strong currents had dragged the long strings of metal slightly from the vertical. Barroso and Williams would have to manoeuvre the grapples carefully on to *Explorer*. The task was delicate. Williams had to steer *Explorer* and keep a check on her safety systems; Barroso would operate the grabs.

For Barroso's purpose, Fireplay's scientists had designed an ingenious electronic control system. His key piece of equipment was a small plastic computer, hardly bigger than a pocket electronic calculator, with a thin electric cable which ran to the surface from plastic-coated wire connected into a bank of mini-computers on board *Pacific Klondike*. On Barroso's small computer – and a spare replica – rested success or failure for Project Fireplay.

Five layers of buttons, similar to an electronic calculator, lined the computer's face. Through this row of black, plastic buttons, inlaid with white symbols, Barroso controlled the finest movements of *Pacific Klondike* from 16000 feet down: he could drive *Pacific Klondike* in any direction through a series of water jets and small propellers spaced at intervals along the mother ship's hull. Barroso had had months of drilling with his computer in a Los Angeles simulator; for hundreds of hours he had sat in a mock-up of *Explorer*'s cramped interior, working the buttons until his fingers hurt with cramp.

Along with his fingertip control of the ship and grabs, Barroso knew every inch and angle of *Doneska*'s disposition on the sea floor from a close study of thousands of *Mary Jane*'s photographs. For hours he had circled around the wreck in *Explorer*; for many hours, too, he had flipped through the latest photographs taken of *Doneska* by *Explorer*. He had studied particularly how *Doneska*'s conning tower lay ten degrees off vertical. The whole design of the boom and grabs was based on that: the conning tower's shallow slant enabled him to drop the grabs on to *Doneska*'s hull without causing boom and tower to collide.

Assisted by computers, Conrad's crew and the machines aboard the *Pacific Klondike* were able to position the boom and grabs within five hundred feet of *Doneska*, and only fifty feet above her conning tower. Barroso took over and depressed the black buttons. Reds and greens and numbers glowed on the computer's face. Within moments, silently, the boom and grabs steadily glided towards *Doneska*. With the boom thirty feet from *Doneska*, Barroso punched more buttons. Moments later, they hung stationary and Barroso steadied himself for the next series of crucial steps.

The boom had to be aligned in three different directions: he would swing it parallel to *Doneska*'s length along the sea bed, something involving two directions; thereafter the boom had to be moved directly over the sunken submarine.

At Barroso's nod, Williams raised *Explorer* a hundred feet above *Doneska*'s length, being careful not to entangle *Explorer* in the thick, spaghetti-like ropes strung out between *Pacific Klondike* and the boom. Below him, Barroso saw *Doneska* bathed in floodlights. Again he pressed black buttons on his computer and the boom moved silently, until it neatly superimposed itself on *Doneska* in a cross. Yet more buttons were pressed, causing the cross to dissolve into two roughly parallel lines. Finally, Barroso moved the boom delicately back and forth, until, so far as he could judge, it hung parallel to the length of *Doneska*'s hull.

Another nod and Williams reversed *Explorer* – free of ropes, cables and pipes – to drive the bathyscaphe directly over *Doneska*. In turn, Barroso used his computer to align the boom over its target. On *Pacific Klondike* Carson was jubilant as he watched the operation on the monitor. Now Williams moved *Explorer* out and to the side of *Doneska* and the boom. Barroso had only to complete two further, major operations. With *Explorer* safe – midway between the boom and the sunken submarine – he fingered more buttons to tilt the boom 10° to the sea floor. Now all that remained was to drop the grabs on to her hull; and with Barroso counting each foot of the way, Conrad signalled winch and derrick operators to lower the grabs inch by inch.

As the tips of the grabs dropped to within a couple of feet of *Doneska*'s hull, Barroso called a halt sharply. While Williams piloted *Explorer*, he realigned the boom and grabs to precisely where he wanted over *Doneska*. '*Explorer* to *Klondike*. I think that will do the trick,' he reported.

'*Klondike* to *Explorer*. Roger.' Conrad assented.

Metal dropped on metal with a dull clunk as Conrad dropped grabs on to *Doneska*'s hull. Carson happily blew *Pacific Klondike*'s klaxon. For a few moments, men above and below deck broke the long tension-filled hours with congratulatory smiles and talk.

In the deep waters Williams floated *Explorer* all the way around *Doneska*'s hull, while Barroso began another phase. He checked the positions of each of the eight, gaping claws that he was about to pinch around *Doneska*'s twenty-five-foot diameter hull.

Williams hovered *Explorer* close by the massive claw nearest the submarine's bow and Barroso delicately operated switches on a small console inside *Explorer*. He raised, lowered and twisted *Explorer*'s small pick-up claw to grasp part of the grab and push it carefully into place. A play of buttons on the hand-held computer closed slowly and inexorably the grab's claws around *Doneska*'s hull.

Barroso repeated the process three more times to finish with the sternmost claw.

Doneska was ready for raising. Williams sailed *Explorer* 150 feet from her and peered with Barroso through the plexiglass ports. On board *Pacific Klondike*, Conrad alerted winch and derrick operators for Project Fireplay's decisive phase.

Nobody could calculate accurately what force was needed to tug *Doneska* free of the bottom ooze. Fireplay's scientists had allowed big safety factors, but nobody could be certain how fast *Doneska* was stuck, or whether the winches and lifts were strong enough for the strains to come.

The sun streamed fiercely from blue skies. Crewmen, technicians and scientists worked tensely above and below decks. At 1603 hours, with the derrick on *Pacific Klondike* casting a long shadow, Carson signalled with three long klaxon blasts the final phase.

Powerful electric winches and the derrick's lift took up the strain. Synchronized by computer, the drums on the winches and the derrick's lift moved in time with one another. Thousands of feet of steel rope and pipe stretched with strain as the motors pulled harder. *Doneska* stayed stationary, stuck in the ooze; ropes stretched hundreds of feet without shifting the wrecked submarine.

The water-line lapping against *Pacific Klondike* rose slowly. The big ship shuddered as electric motors smoked and shrieked in falsetto pitches. Thousands of feet below the water-line, strain overcame a three-inch thick wire rope to the hook on the boom nearest *Doneska*'s stern. Slowly the rope unravelled, silently it snapped. Aboard the mother ship, the rope's winch drum spun out of control and tripped out. Three ropes to the sternmost hook jolted to take up the suddenly increased tensions. Red lights flickered on the console in Carson's control room to confirm the spinning winch drum. He stood undecided, valuable moments slipping by.

'Engines close to seizing,' came the laconic report from the winch controller.

'Rope tensions near snapping points,' came further word from the computer console.

Carson knew that within seconds either half-a-dozen new reds would blink brightly on the Christmas tree – or *Doneska* would break free.

'What do you think?' he called to Barroso.

In *Explorer*, Barroso stared at *Doneska*'s floodlit stern. Unmistakeably, he saw the first puffs of lightly-coloured finely ground muck rising off the sea floor. Was the submarine at last coming unstuck? As he watched, the sediment, soft as powdered talc, exploded into a vast, shining cloud. Soon the cloud billowed into a huge cumulus and totally hid the submarine.

Barroso's voice crackled through the underwater telephone. 'I think we've done it.'

On board *Pacific Klondike* Carson ordered a halt, he felt a little limp. The high pitch of the electric motors softened, the ship bounced slightly in the water and reverberations ceased.

An hour and twenty-three minutes later, when the clouds of powdered sediment had thinned enough for *Explorer* to make a closer inspection, Barroso found the wreck of the Russian ballistic missile submarine hanging free thirty feet above the sea floor.

'It's looking good,' he reported. 'But somewhere the rope snapped, I guess at the weakest point. Maybe X-rays didn't pick up the flaw clearly.' Barroso referred to rigorous checks that had tested the ropes after their manufacture in Los Angeles. 'I'll need to shift the loads and equalize the distribution along the grapple boom. Do I have a go-ahead on that?'

'You've got it.'

Barroso pressed the computer's black buttons and changed

the boom's angle to reduce strains on the sternmost hook. A little later, Carson restarted the winches and lift. Slowly, carefully – foot by foot – operators hauled the prize steadily to the surface.

Williams sailed *Explorer* clear of the submarine and the steel strings trailed by *Pacific Klondike*.

'*Klondike*, this is *Explorer*. We are running low on battery power. How does it look up there?' he asked.

'All clear. Come on up,' came Carson's voice.

A pull of a switch released ballast and *Explorer* rose slowly. Below the bathyscaphe *Doneska* faded away into darkness and distance. Soon, the only traces of the submarine were the muted pings of *Explorer*'s sonar. *Explorer* rose at an increased speed; but even when she broke surface she was only moving three-and-a-half miles an hour.

Two days later the weather changed. Although she was safely locked into *Omega 1*, *Pacific Klondike* bobbed in ten-foot waves that sent spray high over her decks. Men worked in the rain in thick, yellow oilskins and winds moaned through the ship's sensitive antennae.

At 1800 hours Williams relieved Barroso's watch of the Christmas tree. 'The weather is really lousing up,' Barroso said. Williams unzipped his waterproof jacket with an unhappy nod. They all knew that the three steel ropes which remained attached to the hook closest to *Doneska*'s stern had been overstrained in lifting her out of thick mud. Hours of raising the submarine had probably further fatigued the metals.

Doneska was still 2354 feet submerged when three red lights blinked successively on the control panel. Along with the fourth, they formed a neat row. The three ropes had snapped. Far below, the grapple boom swung immediately and violently about its stub axle. Williams stopped all engines, everything. He woke Carson.

The Fireplay executive rushed into the control room,

unshaven, but wide awake. In the harsh, underwater flood-lights, he saw on a television screen how *Doneska* hung precariously. The submarine's image rippled and she seemed to sway. Physicists were already calculating to see if the pipes and the four steel ropes nearest the bow would hold. Nobody knew how much the metal had fatigued.

Carson's eyes glazed. 'We are going to have one helluva time,' he said sadly. 'I wish it was Friday.' *Pacific Klondike*'s long-range Sikorsky Sea King had already flown to Midway to wait for McLaren. He was due on Friday.

15

Wild grass grew off the tracks between Sofia and Dimitrovgrad. The slipstream of the Sofia–Belgrade express flattened
the grass and stirred wheat in the fields just beyond. The
wagon-lit was hot. Outside, Hofman and the girl – code-
named 'K' -- heard snatches of conversation. It was so hot
that she slipped off her shirt and skirt and sat in bra and
panties. The tension was telling on her and she reached
into her case for a phial of white tablets.

'Nothing to do but wait. I'll sleep through it,' she told
Hofman. 'I'd like a glass of water.'

Hofman poured water out of a lukewarm carafe.

The girl swallowed two tablets and settled down to sleep
on top of the bed made up with checked blankets. She was
soon breathing rhythmically. The thief sat alone with his
thoughts. A little later he reached for K's tablets, and a
couple went down with the warmish water. Hofman checked
the compartment door's short, heavy chain which was
covered in leather against rattles. He lay next to K, grew
drowsy and dozed off.

Later, the train's whistle and the flapping of the window
blind woke him. He shook his companion gently. She lay
still sleeping, so he pushed her harder. All that did was stir
her slightly into saying something in her dream. Hofman
was suddenly aware of the girl's perfume. Her silken hair
smelled fresh and flowed over her shoulders; Hofman
stroked them casually. Then he pulled the elastic of her

panties and let it snap against her. K moved uneasily, but slept on.

The carriage rocked to and fro, making Hofman increasingly aware of his physical contact with her. She lay nearly naked, on her side. The man unzipped his pants, hooked his thumbs into the elastic of her panties and pulled them down to her knees . . .

Hofman and the girl walked safely through the Bulgarian frontier at Dimitrovgrad. The CIA had provided a fast white Mercedes Benz 350 SE with the registration number BE 26941. A CIA contact man, Bracic, drove Hofman and K from Dimitrovgrad to a rendezvous five kilometres outside Belgrade where he stopped alongside a big Citroën. Hofman and the girl transferred to the French car, which was driven by the CIA's station chief in Belgrade, a man called Heckler. K was taken to a safe house in the capital.

At this stage Hofman became demanding. He asked to be dropped along a bus route on the outskirts of Belgrade. Heckler refused and drove him instead to another CIA house in Banatska Street in the old area of Belgrade, not far from the Clock Tower. Hofman refused to go into the small apartment building, threatening to leave immediately. The station chief managed to calm him, then drove to the Hotel Argentina and booked Hofman into room 535. They arranged to meet next day.

A man was posted to watch the Hotel Argentina from across Cara Dusana Street. The receptionist in the Argentina, like Bracic, was also used sometimes by the CIA, and Heckler arranged for her to keep watch, too. Somewhat at a loss for what to do next, Heckler cabled McLaren a long message from the United States Embassy in Belgrade. 'Hofman is totally unreliable,' he concluded.

McLaren and Mallory were waiting for Harper in McLaren's small Vermont cabin. The Fireplay director was packing for his trip to Midway, from where he would helicopter on to *Pacific Klondike*. Now that he had heard from Carson, he was anxious to take control of the operations as soon as possible. Even at a depth of a mere 2000 feet, *Doneska* remained as inaccessible as ever. If there were a big storm, Carson had warned, they might lose her altogether. Otherwise, Fireplay's physicists believed the pipes and ropes would hold. But they could not haul her up without straightening the boom, and technicians were already busy with a method of levelling.

The weather was still bad.

Mallory thought McLaren had taken the news well. He calmly packed a couple of suitcases, careful not to crease a cool, clean white linen suit. He even packed his fishing hat and some fly-tying gear.

'How much time do I have?' The older man looked up from his packing.

'You've got forty-five minutes,' Mallory consulted his watch. To fill in time, he walked around the small, two-roomed cottage. It was neat and tidily stacked with rods, reels, fishing baskets, waders, nets, boxes of fishing line. Two walls of the cottage were covered by large bookcases which stretched from floor to ceiling, and Mallory idly read some titles. There was a big collection of hardcovers and paperbacks on everything about the Soviet Union: Russian novels, poetry books and a thick pile of old *Pravdas* and *Izvestias*. McLaren read and spoke Russian.

Another selection of books covered all major political and economic aspects of the United States. Also stacked in the wooden bookcases were most of the books ever published on the KGB, CIA and other major spy services. Mallory saw paperbacks on psychology, philosophy and religion. Oddly, there was a small section of sex manuals and Mallory pulled out a book entitled *Every Man Can*. He was surprised to see some passages underlined: he looked up at McLaren and wondered.

A knock on the cabin door caused him to replace the slim volume, and Harper came in. 'Hi, sorry I'm late,' he said.

'I've got my report.' To each of them he handed three closely typewritten pages.

McLaren sat down, adjusted his spectacles and read Harper's short and reasoned memorandum about Hofman and Yazov. His conclusion was that Fireplay was so valuable that the only safe course was to kill both men. If the CIA was to reap full benefit from Fireplay, the operation must remain secret for many years. Hofman's intentions, now he was free, were unpredictable: the Belgrade agent's report was a disquieting indication that he might be making fresh demands.

So far, the only person Hofman was likely to have told about Fireplay was Yazov, if Yazov had pressed him. To Hofman's demands must be added Yazov's $2 000 000, and even after they had paid these vast amounts the CIA would always be open to blackmail. The agency might eventually have no option but to dispose of the two men. Accordingly, shouldn't it be sooner rather than later? They could use Higby – and killings outside the United States were always simplest.

McLaren tapped his fingertips on Harper's memorandum. 'It makes sense,' he said. 'Bill deserves credit for clear thinking.'

'I see the problem differently now,' Harper recalled his initial reaction and defended his about-turn. 'I am looking at it more realistically, and there seems to be no choice.'

'That's two to me,' McLaren said, looking at Mallory.

'For a start, it's illegal, even for us,' Mallory said quietly.

'Okay, it's wrong,' said McLaren, 'but think what's at stake. Hofman and Yazov both are a danger – not only now but as long as they're around. Do you deny that?'

'I can't deny it.'

'We can't minimize them or ignore them – so we must liquidate them. That's all there is to it,' said McLaren decisively. 'Now who do we use? I think Bill's right. Higby's our man.'

With both his cases closed and strapped, McLaren took

off his spectacles and cleaned them. 'I'm not talking about morality, John, I'm talking about the agency's vulnerability,' he said gently.

'Yes, Mac.'

McLaren turned to Harper. 'I want them nailed. This week.'

'Can you get hold of Higby that soon?' Mallory asked Harper.

'Yeah,' said Harper. 'We'll send an airplane for him.'

'Fine. You work on it. I've got to go.' McLaren looked at his watch and collected his baggage. Outside it was warm and sunny. On the way to the airport, McLaren gave them both more details of Carson's message. Harper mentioned that Heckler had somehow persuaded Hofman to move into the safe house on Banatska Street, at least for the weekend, by assuring him of his personal protection.

'Heckler's been a great help,' said Harper.

At the CIA's private airport McLaren stepped out of the air-conditioned car into the September heat, waved goodbye, and picked up his bags. Then he disappeared into the airport buildings.

Mallory slipped into the front seat alongside Harper. He said, 'He's a ruthless son-of-a-bitch.'

'No kidding,' Harper replied.

16

Besides being a CIA-trained killer, Keith Higby was a fine golfer. At 1600 hours on the September afternoon, as McLaren's plane rolled down the long concrete runway and Mallory and Harper drove back to Langley, Higby was hitting out of a bunker to within three feet of the cup at the sixteenth hole of Westchester Country Club.

In Zürich, Ivan Yazov prepared to collect his $2 000 000 – the procedure agreed with the CIA's Sofia station chief when the massacre plan was accepted.

In Belgrade, Hofman had found a nice German-style restaurant, Café Kranzler, at 5 Kamenich Street, where the kassler rib and sauerkraut on which he dined were good enough to encourage him to return the following night.

On board *Pacific Klondike*, scientists were at the point of solving the problem of how to swing the boom and *Doneska* parallel to the surface of the ocean.

And in another part of the Pacific, in the cold, dull dawn of the following day, light grey fighting ships of the Russian navy sailed from Vladivostok into the Sea of Japan. Admiral Yashin, aboard *Kresta*, commanded a special task force on another secret mission ordered by Department A of the First Chief Directorate of the KGB through the office of the commander in chief of the Soviet Navy.

From *Kresta*'s bridge, Yashin felt invulnerable. Gun for gun, it was the most powerful flotilla the admiral had ever commanded and he exulted in the power given him by four cruisers, eight guided-missile armed destroyers and fifteen escorts. The ships sped across the Sea of Japan in tight formation, cutting creamy V-wakes in blue water.

Nearly 10000 sailors manned the fighting ships, men who justified the admiral's pride in the Russian navy. Not long ago, as late as the fifties, his navy had lagged far behind the army and air force. It was weak and defensive, based mainly on diesel-powered submarines. But the United States' deployment of Polaris-carrying nuclear submarines and the Cuban missile crisis had changed everything.

Now Russian warships outnumbered those of NATO in the north Atlantic and the United States' Sixth Fleet in the Mediterranean. Russian warships were faster and newer than in any other navy, sailed everywhere, anchored in friendly ports along the Mediterranean, African and Asian coastlines.

Yashin's flotilla provided ample evidence that the Soviet Navy was a potent fighting, political and diplomatic force, its mood offensive, not defensive. *Dmitri Lazarev* was a 16000-ton *Sverdlov*-class cruiser heavily armoured, with a speed of thirty-four knots. She carried fifty-six guns, twenty-one torpedo tubes and two guideline surface-to-air missile launchers.

Kashin- and *Krupny*-class destroyers carried, between them, four helicopters, forty-four torpedo launchers, sixty-four guns and Strela and Goa missiles. A combination of *Mirka- Petya- Kola-* and *Riga*-class escorts were armed with barrel rocket launchers, anti-aircraft guns, dual-purpose 100 mm. guns and torpedo tubes.

Kresta herself mounted two twin Goa missile launchers and two quadruple surface-to-surface missile launchers housed forward and aft. Her surface-to-surface Shaddocks were the largest Russian cruise missiles armed with nuclear warheads. Well aft, *Kresta* carried a twin helicopter pad upon which rested two KA-25 Hormone helicopters. The twin-turbine, general-purpose helicopters possessed inflatable pontoons around each landing wheel for emergency landings in water. Doors under the fuselages enclosed weapons bays for anti-submarine torpedoes, nuclear depth charges and other stores.

On *Kresta*'s aft deck, close by the helicopters, twenty-four Russian marines drilled. They were naked to the waist and had exercised without rest for an hour in four neat rows of six, sweating in the cold, whirling twenty-four AK-47 assault rifles. Not even Yashin knew their purpose yet. The Russian navy and KGB were running a joint, top secret venture. The mission's secrecy nagged Yashin, who worked best when he planned ahead. He was meticulous, and he hated surprises.

A day out of Vladivostok, new, coded orders made him none the wiser: he was to race the flotilla 3900 kilometres across the Pacific to an area south-west of Vladivostok. On a map in the chartroom he checked where the coded co-ordinates of 39°N and 165°W intercepted: nothing there but open sea. Idly, Yashin stretched a pair of dividers between that spot in the ocean and the United States naval base at Midway. They wanted him 1900 kilometres or about 1200 miles north-east of Midway: two days' sailing. The American bombers at the base, though, were only a couple of hours away. The trouble with the Russian navy was that it lacked air cover, as Yashin had often argued.

Meanwhile, Yashin busied himself plotting a new course to take the flotilla between the Kurile Islands of Matua and Shiyashkotan. It was a good route, he thought, for a secret mission.

When his helicopter landed on *Pacific Klondike*, McLaren was out before the rotors stopped spinning, hair blowing all over his face. Carson and Conrad had been awaiting him with some misgivings, but his warm greetings completely disarmed them. 'Dick, it's good to see you,' he exclaimed as he shook Carson's hand. Moments later he pumped Conrad's hand. 'No one's fired,' he said with an exaggerated smile. 'Not even him,' pointing at Carson. 'Have you had a busy day?'

Carson nodded. According to tests, he explained, metal fatigue was not a major problem in the remaining steel ropes and the pipes were holding well. *Doneska* could remain safely suspended indefinitely. The problem was how to raise her. The physicists maintained that to do so without re-distributing the load would impose too big an additional strain.

Fortunately, a method had been devised of fixing fresh steel ropes to the boom and levelling out. The idea was to reconnect ropes to the lowest part of the boom. Workers on *Pacific Klondike* had already rewound the winches up to 4000 feet of steel rope and had looped the ends of the steel ropes into huge nooses. Each rope was clamped at the ends and welded together over 100 feet. Whatever else went, the nooses were sure to stay.

The simple plan was to drop the steel ropes and nooses close to the boom. With a thermal lance attached to *Explorer*'s claw, Barroso had already successfully cut away the useless steel strands which had dangled from the boom's end. Now he would work the nooses on the boom with *Explorer*'s claw. Once the nooses were in place, the winch operators would gently pull on them to level the boom. After that, the raising could start afresh.

'The risk is minimal,' Carson said.

McLaren nodded. 'Fine. Let's do it.'

In the television room, a black and white screen mirrored what was going on 2000 feet below. McLaren clearly saw the huge boom at about 45° to the vertical, hanging sus-pended by four thin threads hooked to its upper arm. A thicker line on the screen was the length of sixteen-inch pipe which connected with the boom's centre.

On another screen in the console he saw a close-up of *Explorer*. Barroso had grasped in the bathyscaphe's claw a steel noose long enough to encircle the boom's bottom cross-section. He was having difficulty and somebody told

McLaren that he had been trying to lasso the bottom end of the boom for over three-quarters of an hour.

Barroso sweated and every few minutes he swore. He had struggled without success for what seemed like hours to fit a noose on the boom in the floodlit working area immediately forward of the plexiglass. He had a clear view of what he was doing, and had gripped the three-inch rope in a dozen different ways, inside and outside the noose. Every time he managed, after much effort, to slip the noose on the boom, it failed to hold.

Explorer's manipulator was designed to work like a giant human arm: the arm swivelled in every direction about a socket in its shoulder joint and the manipulator swivelled too in all directions from its elbow and wrist joints. From shoulder joint to mechanical claw, it measured ten feet. Barroso could move the flexible mechanical claw into countless positions by using nine buttons on *Explorer*'s console. After months of practice he was very skilful, but the long months of training had not included threading a giant makeshift noose to the boom, and he had to improvise and adapt as he worked. His eyes watered, his face was set, he was losing patience. Impatience only made it worse because the job needed delicate, deft handling. Frustrated, he stabbed yet again at the boom and the claw clanked dully off the steel.

'Try not to force it,' Carson warned him through the undersea telephone. 'A broken claw is the last thing we need.'

'All right,' Barroso restrained himself, realizing he had been rash. Twenty minutes later, he wanted to give up. 'It just can't be done,' he complained dejectedly.

For the first time, McLaren took a hand. 'Hi, how are you?' he said into the telephone. 'Trying to frighten us to death?'

Barroso managed a laugh. The knowledge that McLaren was there, watching, galvanized him into a fresh, sustained effort. Thirty minutes later the knack suddenly came to him.

At last the noose was grabbed at a magic point on its circumference and slipped over the boom. It held. Inside an hour, Barroso fixed the remaining nooses into place.

By then he was bone-weary, and Williams reversed the bathyscaphe thirty feet away from the boom. On board *Pacific Klondike*, at Carson's order, the winches slowly turned, and gradually the boom levelled. Carson stopped the winches a little before the boom had completely straightened, slightly tilting it to stop the ropes from slipping off.

The bathyscaphe surfaced in the slanting rays of the late afternoon sun and *Pacific Klondike*'s skiff churned over to the *Explorer*, where Barroso and Williams stood on deck.

Technicians reballasted and recharged *Explorer*'s batteries, checking out other vital equipment. Carson wanted *Explorer* down for the next phase, with her mechanical claw at the ready in case a rope started to slip out of place. He also needed step-by-step, eye-witness reports of the raising as *Doneska* was inched towards *Omega 1*'s gaping bay; television cameras were useful but not enough, since the screens did not throw three-dimensional images. The two-dimensional screen could lie and Carson needed Williams and Barroso on the spot. The two men lay face down on tables in *Pacific Klondike*'s sick bay, while the ship's doctor worked over their cramped muscles with firm, practised hands.

The weather was changing yet again and Carson wanted *Explorer* down by 2300 hours. Forecasts warned of rising winds over the next few days; inside forty-eight hours it would blow hard. By then *Doneska* should be safely in *Omega 1*'s belly.

17

In an antiseptic office in the Directorate of Operations, Harper paged through Higby's dossier.

Keith Peter Higby, born 7 November 1939, at Grand Forks, North Dakota. Columbia Law School. Recommended to CIA by a college professor. Standard training, near Williamsburg. Weapons ranges, jump towers and border crossings through a full-scale, communist-style frontier. Explosive bullets, silenced machine guns, explosives from simple, everyday materials. Countless parachute jumps and amphibious operations. Light artillery training. A heavy weapons course, post-graduate training at Fort Bragg in North Carolina. Jungle work at Fort Gullick in the Canal Zone.

Assigned to the Covert Action Staff of CIA's Directorate of Operations. Action in Laos. Nearly killed by claymore mine in South Vietnam. Assassinated CIA targets in Lima, Istanbul and Cairo, and twice in West Berlin.

There was a soft knock at the door. 'Come in,' Harper called. Still wearing his golfing kit, Higby entered.

'Hi, Keith,' Harper said, pushing away the dossier.

'Hi, General,' Higby said lightly.

'How was the golf?'

'Half good and half bad.'

The Fireplay executive told Higby bits and pieces about Hofman, Yazov and the blackmail that the CIA feared, omitting mention of Fireplay. To a professional killer all assignments were impersonal. 'You just want them hit?' Higby said.

'That's right. And that means keeping it off the agency. You have to keep it off Covert Action Staff, and off station chief, Belgrade, too. Right?'

'Okay,' Higby said. 'Have a nice evening.' He got up to leave.

'Good luck,' was all Harper said.

The flight to Belgrade was uneventful. Unarmed, and carrying only an overnight bag, passport and American Express cheques, Higby went through passport control without trouble to meet Heckler outside the airport buildings. They walked to a black Volkswagen. In the car, the station chief passed him a flat black leather zip bag.

'Hofman's eating cabbage and boiled pig's trotters in Café Kranzler. His hair is dyed black, cut short and he's got heavy, horn-rimmed glasses,' Heckler said. 'He is eating like a nervous cat.'

As the Volkswagen reversed, Higby swallowed an anti-poison pill of sodium thio-sulphate. He removed his light-weight jacket and unzipped the leather case. In the semi-dark of the Volkswagen's interior, he examined the weapon he had ordered, running his fingers lightly over the thin, metal tubes and checking with his fingertips that all the components of the weapon were there. The cyanide gas gun was assembled by Higby with hardly a downward glance in the semi-dark.

Three sections of light steel tubes were screwed together on their finely machined threads. The first section housed a spring-operated firing pin: once sprung, the pin fired a tiny percussion cap to push a metal lever in the weapon's mid-section against a glass ampoule in the muzzle: when the ampoule was crushed, the weapon sprayed a fatal dose of vaporized cyanide – a colourless, tasteless and odourless gas that left no traces. The CIA's Special Projects guaranteed instant death from gas fired into anybody's face at up to two feet.

Higby strapped the metal tube into a neat, mock-leather

harness under his right forearm. Into the firing pin section of the tube he screwed a hooked, highly flexible and thin spring steel wire which ran up his right arm, across his shoulders, down over his left arm and hand to terminate in a ring for sliding on to the middle finger. After he had carefully put on his jacket again, the weapon's muzzle extended a quarter of an inch past his sleeve into the palm of his right hand. A slight jerk of the flexible wire around his left-hand middle finger would fire the pin and detonate the percussion cap with a barely audible pop.

As they neared the Café Kranzler, Heckler slowed down. The streets were old and narrow here, and people were taking the air because it was still too hot for sleep. The windows to small flats were opened wide. In a doorway, a man sat with a small electric fan blowing his hair and people laughed.

Heckler drove about a hundred yards past the café to park in a small, clear side-street. The VW's engine died and its lights faded into darkness. Higby walked back slowly down the street towards the Kranzler. Outside the café's door grew a big oak tree, and from its cover Higby peered inside until he spotted Hofman from the CIA man's description. He sat in the furthest corner of the well-lit room, his back to the wall, and was still eating. Higby stood a short while, surveying the scene, then stepped through the doorway.

The café was about half full. Its owner was at the cash-desk drinking black coffee, waiting for closing time at midnight. The waiters were university students doing holiday work. A low buzz of café talk mingled with a smell of sauerkraut and pork dishes; three single-bladed fans whirred wearily up in the ceiling.

Higby made for an empty table next to where Hofman was eating. The blackmailer sat hunched over the table. Only his eyes strained over the tops of horn-rimmed glasses to watch the people in the Kranzler through the steam which condensed on the lenses. His face was damp and pink and he was shoving a small, round potato on the end of his fork into his mouth when Higby stooped down on his way to the next table to extend an empty right hand in a kind of greeting or gesture. When the victim saw the black hole of the muzzle extending slightly into the palm of Higby's hand it was already too late. Hofman's teeth stopped in the middle of a potato as Higby jerked the ring on his left mid-finger. A small plop followed as if somebody had dropped a sugar cube into a cup of coffee from six inches, and cyanide gas washed over Hofman's face from about one-and-a-half feet.

Higby reached the chair at the next table and sat down just as Hofman fell into the plate of pork and cabbage, mashing a portion of boiled potatoes. Horn-rimmed spectacles bounced off his nose and back again, coming to rest at a queer angle. Hofman's head smoked with the steam which rose off the plate.

Seconds passed before one of the students said, 'Now, what the hell . . .' By that time Higby had inhaled vapour from a capsule of amyl-nitrate, yet another cyanide antidote, and pretended to read the menu.

A minute later, one of the diners pointed at the pig's trotters and said, 'Is there anything wrong with that?' The owner came up. 'Nothing wrong with it,' he said aggressively. One of the waiters said that Hofman had overeaten.

Higby left before the ambulance arrived, moving carefully out of the café, through people trying to enter. In the Volkswagen, on the way back to the airport, he dismantled the weapon and threw its separate components into the Sava River while he and Heckler drove over a bridge near the central railway station: three easy throws as they slowed down a little. The station chief wondered when the Yugoslav authorities were likely to identify Hofman.

Higby jetted out of Belgrade airport two hours, twenty-three minutes after he had touched down. All the way to Zürich he longed for some pig's trotters and boiled potato with sauerkraut. The smell in the Café Kranzler had made him hungry and he hated airline food.

The weather remained kind to Project Fireplay. White gulls wheeled and soared in clear skies and blue water lapped gently against *Pacific Klondike*. With every hundred feet that *Doneska* rose, McLaren, Conrad and Carson felt rising confidence. McLaren had now taken control over the slow, delicate operation. There would be no second chance. If any two ropes slipped off the boom, the two which remained would snap under the sharply increased load. With that, the boom's arm would slam down in an arc and the fresh impact simply snap already overstrained ropes and the metal pipe. Together with the boom and grabs, *Doneska* would sink to the sea bottom.

From below, in *Explorer*, Barroso gave a minute-by-minute commentary. To keep the steel ropes from slipping, the boom was kept slightly out of kilter, something that demanded fingertip control over the winches and lifts. For that reason operators stood by, ever ready to halt motors any time the boom's fine balance shifted.

McLaren and Carson sat in *Pacific Klondike*'s television room where images picked up by underwater cameras rippled on six screens. Their eyes smarted with the fluorescent glow and uneven pictures on the screens. To relax his tense muscles, McLaren shrugged his shoulders and crooked his neck. Whenever he did so the chair creaked.

Along with ballistic missiles, torpedoes, ciphers and codes, Project Fireplay was expected to recover the bodies of the crew who had gone down with *Doneska*. CIA surgeons were on hand to conduct post mortems on some of the corpses – and thereafter the dead would be reburied at sea.

For the purpose of planning the ceremony, Carson had paged through Russian naval manuals and a copy of the Geneva Convention. He had already cleared the bizarre ritual with McLaren. *Pacific Klondike*'s loudspeakers would relay a recording of the Russian national anthem at the conclusion of a funeral service in Russian and English and each body, shrouded in canvas, would slide off a plank into the sea. CIA cameramen would film the burials in colour and sound.

'We are making history,' McLaren said. If Project Fireplay were ever publicized, years later, he did not want the CIA charged with desecrating the bodies of Russian seamen. Carson agreed that public sentiment in the United States, as well as Russia, would be antagonized.

When *Pacific Klondike* sailed out of Honolulu even her complement believed she was undertaking a deep-sea mining operation for Trans Acme Corporation. By the time Barroso had slipped the last cable on to the grapple boom, there was not a man aboard *Klondike* who did not know her true purpose. Now men gathered in knots about the winches and the powerful lift, and stood quietly in the hot sun to watch the slowly rotating winch drums. Layer after layer of three-inch steel rope clicked into place while workers on the 200-foot derrick lifted, through *Pacific Klondike's* well, section after section of sixteen-inch pipe. These normally boring operations had become spell-binding and made men talk softly and keep a wary eye on the weather. Hope was high.

With the secret so completely in the open, Conrad asked McLaren to allow small parties of crewmen into the television room. McLaren agreed and, in groups of four, party after party filed past the banks of screens like sightseers. They saw bubbles of air streaming off *Explorer*, dim lights shining through her plexiglass ports, and the vast, ghostly shape that was *Doneska*. Parts of the long hull were floodlit, other parts were dark, making for an eerie dappling effect. There was no mistaking her profile, the large fin and rounded missile hatches: even under the grabs *Doneska* looked sleek and lethal. Above the submarine, they saw the boom teeter, held precariously by huge nooses over her stern end.

As the sun died on the water, the forest of derricks and antennae on *Pacific Klondike* threw long, slim shadows over the decks and across the inky Pacific. It was 1855 hours when *Doneska* was finally cranked into *Omega 1*'s belly. Scuba divers swam in the underwater spotlights to fit long semi-circular steel ribs upon which *Doneska* would be laid and minutes after that task was completed an operator slid shut *Omega 1*'s gaping bottom doors.

The winch and lift drivers very gently lowered *Doneska*'s keel on to the specially shaped steel rips. Compressed air hissed into *Omega 1*'s ballast tanks to expel seawater and increase her buoyancy. For the first time in days, the winch ropes went slack and the length of sixteen-inch pipe buckled as *Omega 1* took up the strain of carrying the giant prize.

At last the strain for men and machinery was over; men cheered wildly, even before Conrad ordered six blasts of *Pacific Klondike*'s klaxon. McLaren was still in the television room when he heard the blasts followed by shouts, whistles and the stamping of feet.

Conrad now gave orders for the tasks that still remained. The submerged barge had to be made safe, the boom and grabs stowed, the docking legs removed. Crewmen had to lower the skiff to recover Barroso and Williams from *Explorer*. The bathyscaphe had to be winched aboard.

Instead of a time for carefree celebration, there was an air of urgency about the way in which the orders were given. Only a handful of men knew the reason. Fifty-seven minutes before the winches and lift had laid *Doneska* to rest in *Omega 1*'s belly had come the first fragmentary, sometimes contradictory, reports of a powerful Russian task force. These ships were sailing at full speed in *Pacific Klondike*'s direction and fifty-seven minutes later were still on course and hardly a day's sailing away.

Conrad began worrying about the range of Russian Shaddock missiles.

18

New, fast and well-armed ships of the Soviet Pacific Fleet cruised steadily south-eastwards at thirty knots, led by the missile cruiser *Sevastopol*. Aft of her, in giant V-formation, guided-missile armed destroyers and escorts churned through her wake; inside of them, in a smaller V, sailed the cruisers, *Gordyi*, *Lazarev* and *Revolutsia*. Yashin's flagship *Kresta* held its position at the point. They were to rendezvous with a group of six Russian submarines close enough to *Pacific Klondike* not to slow down the cruisers, destroyers and escorts.

The admiral stood with Sergei Rudnev on the bridge of the *Kresta* in the gathering dusk. He had read and re-read the orders from Moscow and had even asked for confirmation. The orders and confirmation nestled in his inside jacket pocket, as real as the forms upon which they were printed. And painfully clear.

'In brief, Sergei,' Yashin explained to Rudnev, 'we are to intercept *Pacific Klondike*, command her to heave to, radio her that if she does not halt we'll place a warning shot across her bow.'

'And if she sails on, sir?'

'We stop her as best we can and get a search party aboard. We'll get more details about that from Moscow. The KGB is behind all this. There's been too much secrecy all along.'

'Yes, sir.' A frown creased Rudnev's forehead.

'I hope they know what they're doing, that's all. I hope to God they understand the possible consequences of a direct, point-blank confrontation between us and the American ship.'

Rudnev nodded.

'I imagine she's some kind of spy ship,' Yashin went on thinking aloud. 'But this could end in confrontation between the Soviet Union and the United States. Unless we surprise and overwhelm *Pacific Klondike* in a single sudden stroke, all will be uncertain. And what do you estimate our chances of that kind of surprise are?'

'I doubt that it's possible, sir. The Americans will flash a warning hours before we're close enough to send in a boarding party.'

'Of course, that must be right, Sergei. And we're too damn close to Midway for my liking. We can't hope to match the fire power of their carrier fleet.'

Sailing somewhere not far off Midway, as the Russians well knew, was the nuclear-powered guided missile cruiser, *Stormy Beach*, a ship that displaced over 14000 tons and cruised easily at thirty-five knots. Her weaponry included forty Talos and two hundred and forty Terrier missiles, two five-inch dual-purpose guns, an eight-tube rocket launcher and two triple torpedo tubes. Russian intelligence reports stated she was equipped, too, with surface-to-surface Harpoon missiles. The missiles were comparable to Shaddocks but were newer, more advanced.

Other ships regularly called in at Midway: guided missile light cruisers, guided missile frigates, guided missile destroyers. Taken together, these ships had a host of missiles, six-inch, five-inch and three-inch guns and weapons systems which no doubt included torpedo tubes and rocket launchers.

Yashin and Rudnev both knew also that most of the United States Navy's modern ships carried anti-submarine helicopters and used ultra-sophisticated three-dimensional radar. 'Their carrier pilots probably include several Vietnam veterans,' Yashin said. 'They've already faced our missiles, they're skilled with their bombs and rockets. If they want to, Sergei, they can knock us out in minutes rather than hours.'

'There are land-based aircraft on Midway too,' Rudnev completed the gloomy assessment. '*Pacific Klondike* must be within easy reach.'

'There's no room for miscalculation. I hope Moscow realizes all the dangers as clearly as we do.'

Rudnev nodded and stared fixedly out to sea, glad that he was not commanding the entire operation.

'We must call for fresh intelligence on American ships in the area,' Yashin said. 'We'll rely on daily reconnaissance flights from the south and Vladivostok. And, of course, there's the Cosmos satellite system.'

As Yashin finished speaking a *Kresta* officer stepped smartly up to him, saluted and handed him a sealed, white envelope. Yashin opened it and read the orders from Moscow.

'They've found *Doneska*!' Yashin looked up in concern. '*Pacific Klondike* has found the submarine. We are ordered to challenge the American ship with removing our dead into a barge they are towing; that's what our search party is all about.'

Captain Rudnev felt even more relieved that his was not the final responsibility. Even so, his stomach fluttered, his mouth dried and he sweated in the stiff breeze.

'They are risking our naval prestige,' Yashin said bleakly. 'It could be the Cuban crisis all over again. Once more our ships are sailing to the brink.'

It was mid-September 1975. Mallory was fishing from a small boat in the Potomac when a CIA helicopter approached, hovered over him and dropped a plastic bottle attached to a large, red balloon into the water. He pulled out the message and read it while the helicopter hovered overhead. McLaren wanted him on *Pacific Klondike*.

Stowing his fishing tackle and fixing his life jacket,

Mallory swung into a harness and the co-pilot winched him aboard the helicopter. At the CIA's air base near Washington, Mallory was helped into a flight suit and then strapped into a pencil-slim SR-71B. Someone clapped an oxygen mask on his face.

Behind the small cabin, two Pratt and Whitney turbo-Ramjet engines were mounted in the wings and they whined and blew grit and small stones on the runway. Mallory was pressed hard into his seat as the J-58 engines rammed Blackbird down the long strip of concrete. Blackbird was a CIA-developed strategic reconnaissance aircraft that flew over 2000 miles an hour, higher than 80000 feet. The unarmed two-seater consumed 8000 gallons of fuel an hour – a costly way of getting to Midway, but the fastest way possible. Mallory knew there must be major trouble.

Twice the jet dropped from 80000 feet to 25000 feet and slowed to under 500 miles an hour for refuelling in mid-air from US Air Force jet tankers. Mallory flew the 6000 miles from Langley to Midway at an average speed of 2230 miles every hour. At Midway Harper was waiting for him on *Pacific Klondike*'s Sea King helicopter. Mallory was more concerned than ever as Harper told him the latest details. The all-weather helicopter flew more than 600 miles in under four hours to land on *Pacific Klondike*'s small, aft apron. When the Sea King landed, *Pacific Klondike* was towing *Omega 1* straight for Midway at twelve knots.

They walked immediately into the operations room. Once again the four Fireplay executives sat together round a table. McLaren reported that United States reconnaissance aircraft had now confirmed that the Russian task force was only six hours' sailing time away. *Pacific Klondike* would be caught on the open sea, hundreds of miles from Midway.

'Our cover's blown. Who knows how? Hofman? Maybe Yazov? It looks as if the whole operation to get Hofman out of Sofia was a disaster. And we've blown Yazov in the process,' Mallory said.

The CIA had got Hofman from the KGB and saved

nothing. Somehow the Russians knew about Fireplay and McLaren had guessed wrongly. Mallory smiled inwardly but without pleasure. This was not the moment to remind McLaren of the misgivings he had always felt about the Sofia operation, misgivings which were not allayed by Harper's report that Higby's mission to Belgrade had been successful. Hofman was dead, and Higby was now on his way to Zürich.

'So Yazov will be the next one,' Harper said. 'We got Hofman, and we'll get Yazov.'

McLaren listened quietly but Mallory was glad to see that even he showed faint traces of alarm.

'What's wrong with that?' Harper asked.

'Now the Russians know about Fireplay,' said Mallory, 'there's no need to kill Yazov.'

McLaren agreed and put a few questions to Harper about the Zürich operation. 'It's a little silly to hit Yazov now,' he said. 'There's no need. All it can do is provoke the Swiss.'

'You want me to call it off?' Harper said.

'I mean I don't want it done right now. It's not urgent. I don't care about Yazov any more. Let's just keep Higby away from him for the moment. Okay?'

'Sure, if that's what you want.' Harper reddened, got up quickly, and hurried to the radio shack. When he returned, he said there was still time for the message to stop Higby.

'Fine, that's all we can do,' McLaren said. 'Now let's try and save Fireplay.'

Lighting a fine Havana cigar, he held the flame at the tip for over ten seconds while he drew on it. His eyes moved from Mallory to Carson to Harper while he did so, then he blew thick smoke into the room across them all. It was McLaren's kind of crisis, full of high stakes and measured responses.

Within twenty minutes, they had canvassed most of the unacceptable alternatives. Nobody wanted to abort Project Fireplay by sliding open *Omega 1*'s underwater bays and dropping *Doneska* back on the Pacific sea floor. It had cost too much in terms of men and money.

Mallory wondered if they could hide *Omega 1* by submerging the barge below the sea's surface where she would float 100 or may 150 feet under water and perhaps evade detection – an option soon discarded, even by Mallory. When the Russians saw that *Omega 1* had disappeared they would surely guess what had happened and to find the barge at shallow depths with their sophisticated electronic gear was easy.

'That leaves the third plan,' Carson said. 'Run for it. Otherwise Fireplay will fail.'

'It is a terribly high risk,' Mallory said.

'All the same, that's what we have to do,' McLaren said simply. He had already made up his mind. 'We're all in it too far,' he said and looked at each of them as he weighed his words.

'You know,' he said, 'I've had a lot of dealings with the other side, one way or another. I want to tell you something that happened to me in Berlin.'

It was a crude give-away. Mallory knew that McLaren was about to try and soften up their resistance to a dramatic proposal. He was striking at their weaknesses: none of them had done much in the field and McLaren always held that advantage.

'When I was in Berlin I took a busload of troops through the start of the wall at Friedrichstrasse, just to prove that Berlin was still a free city. One of the East German police at the barrier, a Vopo, demanded to see our identity cards, but I said no very plainly. I told him that the rules were that we only showed ID cards to the Russians.

'I told the Vopo that the bus was going through in ten minutes. Ten minutes later I started the engine and he stepped back. I just wanted to tell you this because there's only one way to beat the Communists and that's to be tougher every time. And Fireplay is another of those times.'

It became clear to Mallory where this was leading.

'I'm against calling the president, the director, or anybody else who'll take this thing out of our hands,' McLaren went on. 'It's a reasonable gamble. The risks are big but so is Fireplay. And we're beautifully set up to bluff our way through.'

The others listened quietly, watching McLaren steadily. In turn, he spoke calmly, unemotionally, persuasively.

'Maybe we'll have to tell the president later; there's no need to bring him in now. Even if we told the director, he'd have to bring in the president. They could sacrifice Fireplay too soon. I'm not saying we won't have to do it in the end, I'm only saying let's not do it too soon. Let's not panic.'

Mallory, Harper and Carson all respected McLaren's experience of tough tense situations. Now he reminded them of the *Pueblo* incident in January 1968, when North Korean torpedo boats seized the 906-ton spy ship in the Sea of Japan. The Koreans had given the ship to the Russians who had won a valuable prize even as the United States Navy suffered a severe loss of prestige. Throughout the long, embarrassing enquiry that followed, the question that had dogged the navy was: why no air cover?

'We'll radio for help from the nearest carrier, tell them we're being harassed by Russian ships and make it look like there could be another *Pueblo*,' McLaren said.

'The response to harassment is to call in a flight of jets. Jets over *Pacific Klondike* will raise the stakes for the Russians and maybe drive off the flotilla. If not, that'll be the time to call the director or the president.'

All they could lose was a little time, McLaren ended, adding as an afterthought, 'And our jobs.'

Carson, Mallory and Harper had listened intently. McLaren's arguments rang soundly. He was staking thirty-two years in the CIA and OSS on Fireplay. But if it was impossible to rebut his conclusions, it was equally impossible to support him.

Both Mallory and Harper said that McLaren would never

convince them that the president or director ought not to be told of the new situation.

'You're glossing it, Mac,' Carson explored. He talked eloquently about the risk of war, and suddenly McLaren conceded defeat.

'Okay,' he said, 'I'll call the president, but later, not now before we know what the navy can do to help us.' He got up to go to the radio shack, and the men with him realized that they had failed to persuade him to contact his own superiors. None of them had the courage to go over McLaren's head.

Experts calculated that the Russian task force would overhaul *Pacific Klondike* shortly after dawn, and McLaren contacted the attack aircraft carrier *Galveston* at 2203 hours. On *Galveston*, an orderly carefully shook awake Rear Admiral Scott M. Smith. McLaren told him that *Pacific Klondike* was on a routine CIA spy ship mission. Since Russian fighting ships were in the area, he wanted *Galveston* to run hourly flights over *Pacific Klondike* commencing at 0600 hours.

'I don't expect trouble but I don't want to risk another *Pueblo*,' he said.

'That's right,' Smith promptly agreed.

'Give them an hors d'oeuvre and maybe they won't come back for the main course,' McLaren said. 'Your jets will stop anything before it even starts.'

'Sure. By the way, you know you're on an open line?'

'Maybe it won't do any harm.'

'You want to let them know that we're coming?'

'Yes.'

'Well, it's not such a crazy way to think,' Smith conceded.

'Good luck,' McLaren said. 'And have a good night's sleep.'

Smith certainly did not want another *Pueblo*. The navy had well-rehearsed contingency plans to dispatch planes or ships to surveillance vessels in any kinds of peril. It no longer depended on the safety provided by the time-honoured freedom of the seas.

Before retiring, Smith gave orders. He passed routine messages to Pearl Harbor and Midway and altered the course of *Galveston* and her four destroyer escorts to intercept *Pacific Klondike* some time the next day.

McLaren returned to the officers' mess where Carson, Harper and Mallory were talking animatedly. When the door opened they fell silent. McLaren looked at each in turn before he solemnly reassured them of the air support on its way. Then he returned to his quarters via the ship's doctor, from whom he gratefully accepted a sleeping pill. He sank into his bunk exhausted.

19

The big Swissair 707 landed at Zürich airport, taxied down runway twelve and stopped close to the airport terminal buildings. Keith Higby boarded a bus and drove to the terminal in thin, drizzling rain to meet the Zürich chief of station, who drove him away in a bright red Passat. Higby sat in the back, alongside a small, nervous man who managed the Bank of Swiss International and Overseas Services, a CIA proprietary in Zürich. He now repeated to Higby a conversation he had had that afternoon with Yazov.

'He said, "I'd like to see you alone. Tomorrow." I said "Fine". He asked whether there was any problem about the money and I told him he could get a million dollars right away.'

'Do you think he was in any way suspicious?'

The banker thought a little. 'No, I don't think so. He asked if I would be available all day, and I said I would be.'

'Thanks,' Higby said.

The Passat stopped outside the Hotel Dolder Grand on Kurhaus Street. Higby dined well, slept soundly and woke at 0630 hours central European time. After a shower and a shave, he studied himself closely in the mirror for a few minutes. Outside there were storm clouds.

Zürich's station chief had handed over a cyanide gun which Higby strapped into place. If equipment was all that mattered, the CIA generally had the better of the KGB.

Higby pulled a cream mackintosh over his light grey suit and into a pocket of the crumpled coat went a slim Colt .45.

He glanced around the room, making sure he had left nothing behind. Outside the Hotel Dolder Grand a taxi waited to take him the short distance between the hotel and Pelikan Platz. Had Higby known Zürich well enough, he might have walked.

He met the chief of station in Pelikan Platz, near the botanical gardens. The big Platz was surrounded by old, stone buildings with large windows and colourful, candy-striped awnings. Brass plates, inlaid in black, disclosed that most were banks. It was early morning, the drizzle was thinning, and the sun began to break through. Bright patches of light came and went in the Platz. News and coffee vendors were busy and people held steaming coffee cups.

Higby sat on a bench opposite the Bank of Swiss International and Overseas Services, a depository for CIA money from the black markets. Yazov was that day going to walk up the six steps to the main door of the bank, try to collect the money, and walk out. Presumably, he would come in disguise and Higby was ready for it. The CIA's man in the bank had a walkie-talkie, so did the chief of station: it was a cigarette lighter device from the Technical Services Division of the Directorate of Operations.

Their quarry had been careful, made no precise appointment, specified only the day. Even then, he might not come; maybe the next day, or the day after. Higby would wait to meet him in fine rain or drizzle or patchy sunshine. In daylight, in busy Pelikan Platz, with people hurrying about their affairs, Higby would push his right hand out, stretch his fingers and say 'Hi'. A plop and Yazov would pitch forward.

The CIA had reservations on flights out of Zürich to New York on Pan American, Swissair, Alitalia, Lufthansa and Air France. Within the shortest possible time of killing Yazov, Higby would be out of Zürich.

Now he and the station chief sat in the Platz on a bench from which they fed pigeons. Sometimes they stood up and walked. A man in a dark grey suit took photographs of his little girl who stood with pigeons sitting all over her outstretched arms and shoulders and on her head. She looked scared. A little boy pushed a dead butterfly across a small pool of the night's rain.

To make conversation Higby asked how his companion kept fit. 'I always run upstairs,' the station chief replied. 'And I stopped smoking about six years ago.'

'I never started.'

A man running into Pelikan Platz, pushing through the people, interrupted their conversation. The station chief stood up. 'That's Burns, my assistant,' he said.

Burns ran up. 'Well,' he panted, 'I think Yazov wins.'

'Why? What's happened?' the station chief asked, surprised.

Pulling out a decoded cable, Burns read the new instructions quietly to them. Higby was unconcerned that the mission was scrapped. Gently easing the ring off his finger, he stood and stretched his stiff spine.

'Somehow I'm glad,' the chief of station said.

Higby merely smiled.

At 0300 hours Ivan Yazov was in his room at Obersalzburg Gasthaus in Flora Strasse, close by the lake of Zürich, when the first scrappy report came from a trusted Belgrade contact. It had cost a lot, the brief message, but Yazov reckoned it was money well spent. Hofman had been taken ill – food poisoning. At 0323 hours he knew that Hofman was dead and Higby was on his way to Zürich. The assassin considered his position and how the news affected his plan to collect the fee for his services from International and Overseas. It was a huge sum, even for the CIA to pay. He thought they would probably try to take him outside in Pelikan Platz.

The porter woke him at 0600 hours. Yazov breakfasted on chilled tomato juice, corn flakes, grilled bacon and poached eggs. He ate thin toast, wiped the crumbs off his mouth, drank three cups of black coffee and packed into a small canvas bag a blue overall, a raincoat, his gun and three clips of explosive bullets. Into a worker's box he placed a packet of thinly sliced Zugarelli's Parma ham, Planter's peanuts, some bread and cheese, and a bottle of Ruffino Chianti. The box also contained binoculars, a rope, a silenced Lüger pistol and two hand grenades.

He left the small gasthaus dressed in plimsolls, blue jeans and a pale polo-necked sweater and drove to a small wood outside the city. There he resighted his gun by firing into pine cones at a hundred metres. He exploded eleven pine cones before he was satisfied.

Yazov got back into his rented Volkswagen and parked it about 600 metres from Pelikan Platz. He went into a public lavatory and came out wearing a thick blue overall. A short walk took him to a side entrance of one of the banks – the Bank of International Swiss Finance and Development. He looked like a repairman.

Yazov asked the bank's security guard to help him to the roof because he had to work on a flaking sign which read BANK OF INTERNATIONAL SWISS FINANCE AND DEVELOPMENT. When the security guard looked uncertain, Yazov put down the worker's box, reached into a pocket of his blue overall, pulled out the silenced Lüger pistol and pushed it into the guard's ribs. He pointed to the worker's box, the guard lifted it and together they climbed up four narrow, winding flights of steps. At the top the guard fumbled with his keys at the door leading to the flat roof, pushed it open and walked into fine rain. When the door closed behind them, Yazov bashed the guard's head in with such force that part of the skull was torn away. He hid the body in an old red-and-white striped piece of canvas awning and locked the door.

Close by the big sign Yazov pulled on his mackintosh and removed from the box the pair of Zeiss binoculars. He peered into Pelikan Platz, a large paved rectangle, where scores of people moved below him. Directly opposite, about a hundred metres away, was the Bank of International and Overseas Services. He removed his gun from the canvas bag and, for the second time that day, snapped and screwed the thin, small and finely-machined mechanisms into place – the tubular stock framed like an A, and the high-powered telescopic sight with cross-hairs. Much of the morning he spent scanning Pelikan Platz through the binoculars, confident of his ability, after twenty years with the CIA and MGB, to recognize the man or men he sought. There were hundreds under his gaze – window shoppers and bench sitters, people feeding pigeons, people on business, casual strollers. Two men, sitting on a bench, both in mackintoshes, had caught his eye. They had been there a long time. From time to time they stood up and strolled.

Yazov rubbed his eyes, put down the binoculars and opened the packet of ham. He ate a slice with a piece of bread, and washed it down with a tilt of the bottle of Chianti.

He had a piece of Camembert cheese in his mouth and the wine bottle in his hand when Burns ran into the Platz. Yazov put down the bottle and took up his binoculars to watch Burns greet the two men on the bench.

The binoculars went down, the gun came up. The man who ran into Pelikan Platz had a piece of paper and read the contents to the others. One of the men stood and stretched like a cat. The Bulgarian steadied the gun, and squinted down the tube and the cross-hairs bounced on Burns's back. The bullet hit Burns a little to the right of the seventh spinal disc and blew out an irregular hole about a foot wide. The dead man bounced a pace under the impact and fell into Pelikan Platz. For a moment, passers-by stood gazing. Then they suddenly ran for cover, as more bullets smacked the pavement around their feet.

'What the hell is this?' the station chief screamed. He ran hard after Higby who was already halfway across Pelikan Platz, zig-zagging through people who were running in every direction. He had to jump over others who had been hit by fragments of metal and now lay on the street.

A bullet struck the ground two metres ahead of Higby as he ran full tilt, showering his lower legs with fragmenting shrapnel. He hit the stones with a splintered fracture of the left tibia, and lay still. From the bank's roof he seemed dead.

The shooting stopped. Some seconds later, people picked themselves up and came out from under cover. Crowds gathered in the platz and stood in excited knots about the wounded who were dragged into the shops or lifted on to nearby benches.

The station chief ran back into the Platz and found Higby lying on his back, blood leaking from sharp, tibial splinters that stuck through his trouser cloth.

The injured agent's face registered a mixture of pain and rage as the chief of station bent to speak to him and give him some comfort. He lifted Higby's head off the pavement and looked around for something to use as a pillow. Beside himself with pain and fury, Higby screamed, 'You god-damned idiot.'

Up on the roof, behind the bank's sign, Yazov saw the movement. He held the back of Higby's head in the cross-hair at the end of his telescopic sight. As a police van swung into the Platz, siren blowing, Higby's head shattered in the hands of the Zürich station chief.

Seconds later, Yazov had stripped off his mackintosh and overall, stowed the metal box, and hurried from the roof down the worn stairs. A Swiss gendarme was climbing up stoically while Yazov took the steps two at a time. Yazov shot him three times and the gendarme's body bounced between the walls of the narrow stairs.

Much later, up in his room, Yazov watched a television announcer point out white streaks on the street where bullets had exploded. The camera also filmed his position behind the bank's sign, taking in the crumpled overalls, the mack-intosh, the box, some cheese and bullet casings. A bottle of

Chianti lay on its side, and the wine had spilt into a small puddle.

Then there was a brief shot of the station chief as, white-faced and remonstrating, he was bundled into a police wagon. Yazov guessed they had found the cyanide gun.

20

The United States Pacific Fleet is the most powerful striking force afloat and one of the largest and most powerful ships of that fleet is the aircraft carrier *Galveston*. It is 1020 feet long, carrying 4493 men aboard and displacing 80 800 tons of salt water. As she sailed towards *Pacific Klondike*, *Galveston* met the fuel tanker *Patricia* and the two ships sailed 140 feet apart while the carrier took on engine and jet fuel from two thick umbilical lines that hung suspended between them. Next *Galveston*'s four destroyer escorts took their turn before sailing back into formation.

Among the scores of jets tethered on the carrier's canted flight decks were A-7E Corsairs that had first entered combat service in May 1970 off Vietnam. However, these subsonic, single-seater tactical fighters were too slow for Rear Admiral Smith's requirements. Instead, men in bright red, green, yellow and blue overalls were working on batwinged F-4N Phantom II's. The men wore radio headsets and bubble-like sound muffs; antennae for walkie-talkie sets stuck out of their helmets. Their job was to check the twin engines of each of the all-weather fighters as well as their load of 1000-pound bombs, Bullpup air-to-surface missiles and packets of surface-to-surface rockets. Small, yellow diesel trucks towed the planes into a launching pattern. The quickening activity on the flight deck was a sign that soon there would be orders to warm the engines.

Lieutenant Commander Bob Wooler was thirty-three

years old and a little disgruntled when they called him at 0450 hours to attend the briefing in a low-ceilinged room below the flight deck. After the briefing, which Smith had left to a junior officer, Wooler enjoyed a breakfast of a mound of crisp bacon, scrambled eggs and coffee.

Over 2300 hours of flying were charted in his log book, which was liberally sprinkled with green entries representing more than 400 combat missions over Vietnam. Now, he zipped his flight suit over a t-shirt, and around his body he wrapped a g-suit, survival gear and parachute harness.

A lift deposited Wooler and Joseph Pugulisi, his back-seat man, on *Galveston*'s flight deck. Their Phantom stood refuelled, chocks ready for removal, and Pugulisi started his own pre-flight checking of the systems and armament. The plane was three years old and needed forty hours of maintenance for every one hour in the air.

Noise and tumult rose to a crescendo as a yellow diesel truck towed Wooler's Phantom to a catapult hidden below the flight deck. A green-shirted handler dived under the Phantom to hook it to a catapult shuttle on a steel track. Then a plane director signalled with his hands, saluted and pointed to the bleakly short bow ahead. Behind the plane a water-cooled blast shield swung up from the flight deck. The Phantom's twin jets flamed as the pilot stoked the after-burners.

In a cloud of steam, the catapult – a giant piston – whisked the Phantom from standstill to 140 miles an hour in two-and-a-half seconds, pinning Wooler and Pugulisi to their backrests. The flight deck jerked from under the jet's wheels, and by the time Wooler pulled his head free of the rest, he and Pugulisi floated in smooth, calm flight. The Phantom banked steeply into the dawn, climbed to 20000 feet and waited to be joined by three more aircraft. Then as they sped towards *Pacific Klondike* at 1200 miles an hour, Wooler's voice crackled over the radio,

'Missoula Montana, Soap Box, Head Band: are you happy?'
They all waggled their wings.

Shortly after first light, as the hot sun dried the mist off the sea, the horizon filled with specks that became smudges, smudges that turned into ships. *Pacific Klondike* was firmly held in Yashin's net.

Soon the light-grey fighting ships were showing their lines. There were the big *Sverdlov*-class cruisers, with their twin stacks, twin radar booms and heavy guns mounted fore and aft. *Kashin*-class guided missile-armed destroyers carried four separate towers of complicated electronic gear, radar dishes whirring slowly about the high towers. Sleek *Krupny*-class destroyers and smaller *Kola*-class escorts claimed attendance on *Kresta*, whose menacing silhouette sailed into view. The cruiser presented an outline of four radar towers, missile launchers, two Hormone twin-jet helicopters. A long, white wake frothed behind her as she bore down rapidly on her quarry.

The encirclement of *Pacific Klondike* in a contracting steel ring had not surprised McLaren. For over an hour, drinking cups of strong, black coffee to dispel the after-effects of his sleeping pill, he had sat with Conrad studying the Russian build-up on radar screens. They admired the task force's clockwork precision. Once the Russian ships had completed their encircling formation, with *Pacific Klondike* netted near the centre, they slowed down and the vast circle shrank as ship after ship slotted home.

On the underwater radar screens, blips indicated the presence of submarines. Overwhelming forces were disposed against her. No hope existed against ships almost three times her speed. Moreover, she had *Omega 1* clumsily in tow.

They depended utterly on the sudden appearance of the naval jets, McLaren grimly told Conrad, before he went off to broadcast a short, simple message over the ship's loudspeaker.

'I have to tell you, there's going to be trouble,' he said. 'We've already got through to the navy and help is on its way. All we can do is wait.'

There was no audible reaction from the men who stood in small knots, but the tension could be felt.

'We've contacted the proper authorities,' McLaren went on. 'I don't have to detail all the obvious dangers, but let's keep calm. Just stay alert and follow your orders quickly and quietly. And good luck.'

When the Russian ships got in close, Conrad gave crisp orders. *Pacific Klondike*'s complement donned life jackets and sealed off the ship's compartments as tightly as possible. They took what cover was available, moving from positions exposed to gunfire. Two CIA agents, one in the bow, the other in the stern, stood armed with Belgian FN rifles. Teams stood ready with fire-fighting equipment, other squads prepared to lower life boats.

Kresta sailed within fifty yards of *Pacific Klondike*. A Russian officer put his mouth to a loud hailer. He spoke English and his voice boomed over the water.

'*Pacific Klondike*: you must heave to, stop engines and prepare to receive a boarding party. You have aboard Russian dead from a Soviet submarine, *Doneska*, missing in these waters after sailing from Vladivostok. We claim our dead and our submarine under international law.'

'Your message is not understood,' McLaren boomed back from *Pacific Klondike*'s bridge. 'We know nothing of your submarine or dead. Our ship is in international waters. We are unarmed and engaged in lawful deep-sea mining pursuits. We shall resist any attempt to board us.'

'To resist is useless. If there is no Soviet submarine aboard your sister barge, you will be permitted to sail on after a brief inspection. Do not resist. Heave to or we will open fire.'

'We are in international waters and claim our right to freedom of the seas.'

'We are preparing to board your ship. Do not resist.'

The twin props of two Hormone helicopters coughed into life aboard *Kresta*. Russian marines in battle dress and armed with Kalashnikov AK-47 rifles could be seen preparing to climb aboard.

'To stop this ship or to attempt to board her is an act of war against the United States of America.' McLaren's voice boomed over the water again. 'Such an attack by Russian fighting ships upon our unarmed, deep-sea mining vessel is an attack by the Soviet Union on the United States itself.'

'Do not resist! Do not resist!'

'We are in contact with our government,' McLaren retorted. 'Units of the United States Navy have been alerted. We cannot yield to your demands.'

'Do not resist!'

'I demand to speak to your commander. I earnestly hope that these serious provocations will not be endorsed by your commander.'

The two-fold answer came in actions rather than words. First the Hormones lifted from *Kresta*'s launching pad. Armed men sat in the open cabin doors, their legs dangling. Two other helicopters rose off *Krupny*-class destroyers. All the helicopters trailed long ladders.

Second, a small *Kola*-class escort broke formation and sped towards *Pacific Klondike* from the south-west. Men stood at the rails with rifles ready. To cushion the impact, the small ships had rigged to their sides rubber tubes and rope mats. Another *Kola*-class escort raced in from the south-east.

Pacific Klondike faced armed boarding parties from sea and air. The CIA agents with FN rifles waited for orders, hoping they would not come, knowing any resistance was hopeless.

'Do not resist! Do not resist!' the Russian said over and over, through his loud hailer. 'Everybody get out on deck and raise your hands . . .'

McLaren could do nothing but wait. For some minutes, *Pacific Klondike*'s air-surveillance radar had been picking up signals of an incoming flight of jets moving faster than sound. They could only be from *Galveston*. Every ship of the Russian flotilla had picked them up too. 'Comrades, attention!' *Kresta*'s loudspeaker blared in Russian. 'Aircraft approaching! Aircraft approaching!' Russian sailors were running about the decks to their action stations. Hooters blared warnings, and the neat Russian ring of ships broke up into defensive disarray. As their wakes criss-crossed with split-second timing, it seemed miraculous that they avoided collisions.

The cheers and applause rising from *Pacific Klondike*'s complement were premature, and Conrad ordered his men back under cover.

A flight of four F-4N Phantom jets came in from the south, very low. The fighter-bombers streamed over the Russian flotilla only ten feet above *Kresta*'s tallest radar, scattering helicopters. Zipping off the water thousands of feet into the sky, they burst out of formation and circled back.

McLaren clearly saw surface-to-air missile launchers rotating into attack positions on the Russian ships. Needle-like Guideline and Goa missiles rolled smoothly in their launchers, tracking the Phantoms as if by magic.

And then, unable to believe their eyes, the watchers saw smoke trickle from the back of a Goa surface-to-air missile on *Kresta*'s forward launcher. A split second later, a huge cloud of white smoke billowed upward. McLaren saw the slim missile slowly rise off its launcher, hang there for a split-second, and then shoot into the sky. His mouth ran dry, his shoulders and arms tensed. . . .

From his F-4N fighter-bomber Wooler too watched in amazement as the missile burst lazily out of the cloud of white smoke. Less than half an hour had elapsed since he had been hurled into the inky blue sky off *Galveston*. It was a type of mission to which he was not wholly unaccustomed. Since Russia had joined the United States as a naval super-power, both navies had become inclined to jostle each other for space, asserting their right of way with reasonable good humour, though the Russians were known to cut dangerously across the bows of American ships, even of attack carriers.

When they indulged in this kind of mischief, it became almost routine for American carrier jets to buzz the Russian vessels in retaliation, and Wooler himself had taken part in four or five such operations. Thus he was not too worried as he led the four Phantoms in simple diamond formation down the invisible track computed by Pugilisi's dead-reckoner. He hoped *Pacific Klondike* was still on the course given at the briefing and was almost relieved when Pugilisi detected traces of Russian radar bounding off the Phantom. Soon jamming devices sealed the F-4N in its own protective bubble of electronic screens.

Then, dead ahead, Wooler saw the Russian flotilla moving slowly forward in perfect formation. According to the briefing only five to ten Russian ships were expected. Somebody must have miscalculated. Wooler had never buzzed a flotilla of that size before.

'Twenty to thirty fighting ships bearing 315 degrees, distance twenty miles, course 120 degrees, speed ten knots,' he radioed *Galveston*.

The orders were to give the Russians a light buzzing and Wooler led the flight into a steep dive, flattening over the Russian warships which broke up in disarray. As he whooshed over *Kresta*, making the helicopters veer crazily, he wondered about the wisdom of his orders.

The F-4N climbed high into the sky and circled back, and the Russian missile, as it slowly rose into the sky, looked like a flying telephone pole. Its aim was harmlessly wide, but Wooler shouted into the radio: 'I believe they may be targetting on us!'

21

Rear Admiral Smith was breakfasting alone in his quarters. For a man who worried as intensely as he did, he had a deceptively mild appearance. When Wooler's report was handed to him by a naval orderly, Smith's features twisted in alarm. The only reliable information in his possession had come from the CIA's McLaren, who assessed the Russian force at between five and ten ships. News of the Russian flotilla's size shocked Smith. He hurried out of his quarters down a telescoping vista of the carrier's bulkheads, and into the communications room.

Now the shock contorted his mild appearance out of recognition. White faced, he agonized over the other flights he had almost casually ordered off *Galveston*. The briefing had been left to a junior officer. Now his jets had moved the United States into a major confrontation with Russia.

The implications were so numbing that a great weakness tingled behind his knees. He was grateful only that the missile had gone wide. Now he had to make a quick, instinctive decision. By nature he favoured weaker rather than stronger responses: he called off the buzzing runs, ordering the remaining Phantom flights to circle clear of the flotilla and to spy from a distance.

That done, and anxious to shift some of the responsibility, he radioed a full report to United States Navy headquarters in Hawaii. 'I think we've run into the middle of a CIA covert operation,' the message ended.

The carrier's multiple early-warning radar systems placed

on full alert should be more than capable of shielding *Galveston* from disaster, but Smith hoped fervently they would not be tested.

Wooler's flight was running low on fuel and his voice crackled over the open intercom to say that he was flying back.

'I think it may have been a mistake,' he spoke more calmly now, revising his initial reaction. 'Maybe some guy with his finger on the button got nervous and slipped. The missile was aimed right the other way.'

'What happened to it?' Smith asked.

'It blew a long way from any of us. I don't think anybody down there wants war after all.'

'What's happening around *Klondike*? Anything new?'

'Pretty static, sir. A waiting game.'

Fresh alarm flushed through Smith. Perhaps he had called back the other flights too soon. If the Russians realized that he had pulled back his jets, they might be tempted to try again. He wished the orders from Hawaii would come.

'Keep the rest of the jets on stand-by,' he ordered *Galveston*'s air controller.

For a long time, Smith tried to break a lifetime habit of biting his nails in a crisis, but now the nails of his right index and middle fingers were already broken and he started on the third finger. He felt that somehow he had been duped. Would there be a navy Court of Inquiry? In that stark auditorium at the Naval Amphibious Base, California? Just like *Pueblo*?

On the bridge of *Kresta*, Rear Admiral Yashin too watched in amazement as white smoke rolled in huge clouds in front of him from one of his own Goa missiles. His immediate reaction was that some over-anxious missile operator must have clumsily depressed a firing button. Yashin's stomach muscles contracted rapidly and painfully as the needle-pointed missile streaked off into the air. He watched it streaming smoke, weaving erratically.

The planes burst untidily out of formation, swooped and swerved crazily over the sky. Fortunately, the Goa missile flew on harmlessly to blow up in a bright red and orange fireball.

Outwardly Yashin showed no emotion. With black fragments of the Goa missile still falling out of the sky, he turned to the white-faced Rudnev who stood beside him with a telephone receiver to his ear.

'Stop all boarding operations, Captain,' Yashin ordered. He spoke with icy calm. Even as Rudnev transmitted the order into the telephone, the Hormone helicopters veered sharply off *Pacific Klondike* and the escorts, with their boarding parties at the ready, sailed clear.

'Order all missile operators to stand clear of their firing buttons,' Yashin went on. 'Order all ships to break into more scattered defences against air attack.' Rudnev spoke once more into the telephone, before receiving his final instruction.

'And, Captain, arrest that missile gunner, immediately.'

Yashin left the bridge to prepare another urgent message for Moscow. On the way to the radio room he called in at the operations room and watched as a radar operator, his scope scanning the sky for miles, relayed information to an air-control officer. The latter stood before a transparent plotting board operated by a man, whose face glowed in the red and green lights. Yashin watched him chalk in more 'bandits' – bandits too near for comfort.

A realist, content to follow orders, Yashin had never seen the sense in disposing of so vast a task force. Surprise had been essential to the success of his mission and the key to that had been speed and secrecy. Left to himself, Yashin would have dispatched a couple of the Pacific Fleet's fastest destroyers which might have sailed unobserved and could have stopped *Pacific Klondike* dead with a couple of shots across her bows or else swiftly landed marines from a helicopter. The action would have been over before any confrontation started. In short, a quick, cunning *Pueblo*-style hi-jacking should have been used.

Instead, the Russian ships were strung out on the Pacific, far from home without air cover, close by Midway, with attack carriers in the area. If the United States Navy wanted, it could sink every ship of the task force. American air superiority, from ship and land, would be decisive. This was because Russian strategists had for years scorned attack carriers as floating coffins, confidently predicting that the United States' entire carrier force would go down within the first hour of any nuclear war. Yashin agreed, but he also recognized that the sinking of an attack carrier was unthinkable in anything short of all-out nuclear war. Carriers with their powerful air arms were still invaluable in limited actions.

Convinced that the game was up, Yashin went in to the radio room and signalled to Moscow his latest assessment in a long, secret message. He had temporarily called off the boarding parties when the jets had flown into view, he reported. If naval headquarters and the KGB were relying on bluff, it may have failed. The United States Navy had raised the stakes, and the confrontation with *Pacific Klondike* was slipping into perilous uncertainty.

Risking demotion, or worse, Yashin also reported the careless firing of the Goa missile, adding that the operator was under close arrest. The missile had strayed far off the mark and, after initial uncertainty, the carrier pilots had themselves probably realized that it was fired in error. He asked for permission to call off the boarding parties altogether.

Having sent the message, the careworn admiral relaxed and returned to the bridge. Rudnev greeted him with the information that the Americans had not flown another run.

'That's good, Sergei.' Yashin was relieved.

'Also our surveillance radars have picked up several four-plane flights that have turned back. The others are circling safely out of effective range of our missiles.'

'Good. Clearly the Americans want to avoid provocation. I only hope our superiors in Moscow will do the same.'

Yashin turned his binoculars on to the barge being towed by *Pacific Klondike*, staring at the thick, impenetrable walls. 'It seems deserted,' he said. 'A mysterious craft.'

'Hard to believe that *Doneska*'s resting there, sir. And strange to have found her so far from where we looked all those months ago.'

'The whole business is a mystery, Sergei. Why send us so far across the Pacific on a mission that was bound to end up in some kind of confrontation? There was never a chance of surprise. Something's been cooked up. They've had me on a leash throughout this *Doneska* business, right from the start.'

'You thought there was something funny when we started the search in that sweep down past Chile,' Rudnev recalled.

'That's right. Once the KGB was involved, it didn't smell right, and now it smells even worse. I wish to God they wouldn't always treat us like children.'

Yashin swept the binoculars along *Pacific Klondike*'s decks, across a maze of machinery over the superstructure and a thicket of sophisticated electronic gadgets. Occasionally, he saw crewmen pop their heads from under cover.

'If they've got *Doneska* inside there, it's been a good effort, Sergei,' Yashin grudgingly gave *Pacific Klondike* her due. He rubbed his eyes and the binoculars hung against his chest. An officer stepped up smartly with a fresh message from Moscow and Yashin read the script quickly.

'Damned curious, Sergei,' he said, halfway through the long signal. 'The KGB has ordered the release of our careless gunner. What do you make of that?'

'What are we to do about *Doneska*, sir?' Sergei Rudnev was more interested in their immediate prospects.

'We're pulling out.'

Yashin finished reading the latest orders from the office of the commander in chief of the Soviet Navy and Department A of the First Chief Directorate of the KGB. As usual, they were long and detailed; as usual, they left him no room to exercise any discretion. Yashin felt more like a puppet than admiral of the fleet.

'You know, Sergei,' he said thoughtfully, 'maybe our careless missile gunner wasn't so careless after all. You'll probably find he works for the KGB.'

The first indication of the Russian reaction came when *Kresta*, from her position within a hundred metres of *Pacific Klondike*, veered suddenly to the north-east. From the bridge, McLaren and Conrad watched the Russian flotilla regroup. The ships sailed without fuss into a new formation of cruisers screened by the smaller destroyers and escorts.

The manoeuvre was completed with well-drilled precision, and as the Russian task force moved steadily away from *Pacific Klondike*, McLaren guessed correctly that it was on course for Vladivostok.

High overhead a new flight of Phantoms flew in large circles. The crisis was over. His staff realized that. McLaren had won. He had gambled on deceiving Smith, he had upped the stakes for the Russians, he had defied his own committee of Harper, Mallory and Carson. Everybody had been deceived. To compound it all, the Fireplay director offered everybody his congratulations.

First he broadcast over the loudspeaker a short message of praise for *Pacific Klondike*'s crew. Later it was the turn of Carson, Mallory and Harper, in the blue carpeted boardroom to an accompaniment of popping champagne corks. Fireplay would make up for Sofia, and the possible repercussions from Belgrade, McLaren said.

'You're the three most valuable members on the General Advisory Committee. We don't have to go into it. It's not just bull, it's the truth.'

The three others shifted a little uncomfortably with embarrassment at McLaren's extravagant praise. 'I always respected your opinions,' he said, 'even when I went against them. But I'm the guy with the ultimate responsibility, and if I have to, I'll carry the can for all of this in Langley.'

'Well, it's worked out all right in the end,' Carson said, a trifle uncertainly.

'Sure. My view has always been: get to the edge first. *They* got to the edge first in Berlin and Hungary and won. *We* got to the edge first in Cuba and today – and *we* won. That's what I've learned in thirty-two years in the business.'

Only Mallory seemed uncertain. He swivelled the thin-stemmed glass in his hand, spilling champagne. The plain truth was that, whatever the ultimate success, McLaren had risked nuclear confrontation. And, as Mallory said quietly to Carson, McLaren had no business running that kind of risk.

'The truth always comes out in the end,' Mallory said. 'The director will want this investigated.' Mallory was sure there was going to be trouble. He looked across the room at McLaren who stood straight as a ramrod, champagne glass in his right hand, a grin on his face, beguiling a small group of scientists.

'I don't think anybody is going to leave this room with views that aren't essentially Mac's,' Mallory said thoughtfully.

Wooler put the F-4N into a power glide, aiming for *Galveston*'s swaying, canted flight deck. The plane thumped on the deck at over 150 mph with the throttle open until its tail-hook snagged on to an arresting cable. The hook caught, Wooler was hurled forward in his shoulder harness and the F-4N quivered, signalling the end of the mission.

He walked towards the shower but someone told him to report to Rear Admiral Smith at once.

He walked to the operations room, knocked, walked in,

saluted. Smith was seated behind a small, portable Sony tape recorder. 'You've got to tell me everything that happened,' he said. 'This is the CIA's problem, but there'll be an inquiry. Let's get it down while it's still fresh.'

He put the microphone in front of Wooler who spoke in a flat monotone for ten minutes without pause. The evidence was available if anybody asked for it.

22

It became known as 'the day McLaren defeated the Russians'. Not until the task force had disappeared from sight did the Fireplay directors have a chance to inspect their prize. Harper was eager to go aboard, supported by Mallory and Carson. McLaren confessed that he was exhausted by the crisis. He was not as young as he had been, and said he would take another sleeping tablet and spend the rest of the day in his bunk.

The three younger men climbed aboard *Klondike*'s Sikorski helicopter, fluttered across the short distance to *Omega 1*, and then clambered down to the barge's dome-like roof. They used another ladder to step down the thick sides of *Omega 1*'s hangar-like walls and trooped through a water-tight door into a vast echoing chamber.

Ahead, under a string of makeshift floodlights, the Russian submarine glistened wetly. Out of the water, settled on steel supports on *Omega 1*'s floor, she seemed vast. The conning tower loomed over her relatively slim, cigar-shaped bulk and ran ninety feet over the centre of the hull, almost one-third of her length. Three vertically-mounted tubes were sited immediately aft of the tower's stubby mast. The whole of the fin was neatly streamlined and rounded off with a series of small, square, air vents cut into the tower slightly above the hull line. The hull itself was badly discoloured with large reddish brown patches where rust had stained the light grey paint.

They climbed down yet another ladder into the huge bay in which the submarine nestled. The whole area smelled of salt water, and everywhere moisture dripped off the sides of walls. A small work detail was busy around the conning tower and another at the stern. Close to the submarine, dozens of canvas bags were neatly spread. Alongside each bag was placed a large, red calico flag, marked with hammer and sickle, to serve as shrouds for the dead.

Sparks flew from the conning tower like a small fireworks display as men with blow torches burned access into the submarine. Bursts of light from the burning torches threw weird shadows against *Omega 1*'s interior walls and roof.

Clanks and thuds came from the stern area as Mallory walked over to it with Carson and Harper. It must have been a massive explosion. Bright, portable spotlights lit up enormous masses of torn, twisted steel where workers tried to enter *Doneska* through massive tears in the hull. Silently they watched men with large hammers and crowbars attacking the bent and twisted shapes which barred access. Mallory realized that entry would be difficult even when the torn steelwork was straightened.

A cheer came from the conning tower and the small party moved across to find that blow torches were cutting through the last thicknesses of steel hatch. Already the first section of the conning tower had been breached and work was finishing on the second hatch. There was the hiss of hot gases and the smell of acrid fumes. At last the bright light of the torches died out as the final obstacles to access into *Doneska* from the tower were removed.

A strong, portable light was handed to Mallory who placed a green surgical mask over his face. After months of suspense and waiting, the moment planned so long ago in McLaren's office was at hand. No western spy had ever examined the intimate, interior details of a Russian submarine. It was a major intelligence coup.

As McLaren's deputy, senior to Carson and Harper, Mallory would be first down the hatch. Unable to contain his excitement and wait for the hot steel to cool completely, he gingerly eased himself feet first down into the submarine.

He waited in the control room, under the conning tower – and even here *Doneska* smelled dank and salty. Sea water had got in everywhere. Mallory swung his lamp over the submarine's Christmas tree and the vast board glistened moistly and dully. A swing of the periscope made it creak in its mounting. Harper and Carson joined him and the three men walked in single file through narrow spaces to *Doneska*'s stern, the bright light of their powerful lamps washing over the submarine's interior and wreckage. They lingered in the missile bays, standing over a battery stowage area, and then picked their way into the engine room to see three huge diesel and three electric motors that were tangles of twisted metal. A control panel spilled brightly-coloured wires like spaghetti.

As they neared *Doneska*'s stern, rear torpedo stowage and aft trimming tanks, the clanking sounds of hammers and crowbars grew louder. Little lights glowed through ribbons of twisted metal and the indistinct sounds of men's voices could be heard.

Mallory was careful not to tear his clothing on sharp pieces of fractured metal as he carefully examined the torpedo stowage. Twisted metal barred access to the submarine's stern torpedo tubes, otherwise he would have checked that area, too. They moved silently back to *Doneska*'s missile bays, lingered another five minutes, then passed through the control room once more into the captain's quarters, wardroom and chief petty officer's mess. This part of the submarine was not very damaged but it was still wet and paint peeled off the surfaces to expose rust.

Under the crew's quarters – a series of bunks in a confined space – was built another torpedo stowage. And forward of that, Mallory found *Doneska*'s bow torpedo tubes. They spent fifty-six minutes in the examination of *Doneska*, compartment by compartment. On two occasions they had trouble with rusting doors and, while Mallory held the lamp, Harper and Carson grunted and got them open. As the truth dawned on them, Mallory thought of the hundreds of millions of dollars spent on raising *Doneska*. In the process, though nobody could control Yazov, the CIA had destroyed a large building in Sofia, killing a dozen people. McLaren had risked nuclear war. All for nothing.

For by now Mallory was satisfied that aboard Doneska *there were no missiles, no torpedoes, no code books or ciphers. No sea burials would be necessary, since there were no dead.*

In the yawning, empty missile bays Mallory stood in shocked silence in the place where they had expected to find Serb ballistic missiles. He recalled that Geiger readings were registered by *Explorer*: the only explanation was that the Russians must have used radioactive paint in the empty missile bays and in the gaping torpedo stowages and tubes.

Mallory felt giddy as he climbed back with difficulty up *Doneska*'s conning tower. He mounted a guard and gave orders that nobody was to enter the Russian submarine. Work stopped on the stern and workers moved out of the vast bay. McLaren would have to be told.

From a catwalk secured to *Omega 1*'s massive walls, he turned to observe *Doneska* once more, his eyes running thoughtfully over the submarine's periscopes, sleek conning tower, radio aerials and gun platform. Feeling empty and hollow, he climbed the remaining stairs. The going was hard because his knee joints prickled with weakness.

Nobody spoke until they reached *Omega 1*'s curved roof to wait for the Sikorsky Sea King. Then Harper said with bitter understatement, 'Not quite what we expected.'

'What do you think, John?' Carson demanded.

'A disaster,' Mallory said. 'The whole thing's a disaster.'

Across the water the Sikorsky's turbo shafts coughed as the rotor spun. Slowly the stubby helicopter lifted off *Pacific Klondike*, its shadow rippling briefly over the deck.

'Yeah, sure,' Carson said. 'But what do you make of it?'

'God knows. The KGB must have dreamed the whole thing up. Maybe their Department A. *Doneska* was some kind of Trojan Horse.'

'How'd they get the submarine there?'

'That's the easiest part. A skeleton crew could have sailed her, probably took off by helicopter. If you check the navy's IBMs, you'll probably find a *Kashin*-class destroyer was near by, a couple of hundred miles off where *Doneska* was scuttled.'

'And the search?'

'Just more bait, Dick. Make-believe – like the confrontation. They baited some kind of trap.'

'Yes, but –'

'The missile, too. Another put up job, it was so far off target. Probably trying to impress *Klondike*'s crew.'

'It sure as hell impressed me,' Carson said.

'Nobody would have sent a flotilla that big halfway across the Pacific and thought it wouldn't be spotted,' said Mallory. 'Whatever the reason was, they faked that confrontation.'

'You mean they knew we'd call in help?'

'I think so. Jets or ships. Or even the president. Maybe they wanted to embarrass the president, try him out. But it was a hell of a way for the Russians to do it. Maybe I'm guessing wrong.'

'Someone will have to tell Mac,' Carson said.

'I'm now inclined to think even Sedlacek was a plant.' Mallory referred to the defector who had given them the codes.

'I'd hate to be McLaren right now,' said Harper.

'Yeah,' said Carson. 'He's living in a dream world.'

Mallory knew *he* would have to tell McLaren. He had never in his life wanted to do anything less. 'It's hard to know how to do it,' he said. 'Tomorrow's time enough. Let him have a good night's sleep. Even tomorrow a seance with McLaren's going to be hard.'

Carson thought 'seance' was the right word. Fireplay was dead.

McLaren was well rested. He had bathed and shaved by the time Mallory walked into his cabin, and wore crisp, white flannels. He was massaging after-shave lotion on to his face when Mallory broke the news.

McLaren sat down and minutes passed in agonized silence. At last he spoke. 'So we get nothing out of the whole damned thing?'

'I don't think we get a thing, sir.'

'A dry hole.'

'That's right. Junk. Trash. The sub will just about furnish a junk store.'

McLaren sat on the edge of his bunk. Then he said suddenly, 'Who was the asshole? Was it Shilling? Was it Morrows? The navy must have been nuts!'

Getting up from the bunk, he walked to a shelf upon which rested a bottle of Old Spice, and a few more dabs of after shave went on to his pink, clean face. 'If it gets out, it will crucify us.' McLaren ran thin fingers through his white hair. 'It will make the CIA look bad, and it's going to make McLaren, Mallory, Harper and Carson look bad. It's likely to blow the whole Sofia thing, which will be very unfortunate – both for the CIA and for American foreign policy.'

McLaren took off his white shirt. Mallory was annoyed to see him get back into the bunk, and prepare to go back to sleep in broad daylight. 'Okay, kid,' he said. 'See you this evening. Make it 1830 hours and bring Carson and Harper. I want time to think.'

'Right, sir,' Mallory said and started to say how sorry he was.

McLaren interrupted him. 'Get the hell out of here, kid,' he said softly. 'Whatever you have to say, say it to somebody else. Just don't bother me.' He shut his eyes and settled in the bunk.

The door closed quietly behind Mallory. For hours he and Carson and Harper went over the situation, consuming tepid Cokes, while McLaren remained in his cabin brooding in isolation. The first sign that he had stirred from his quarters was the sound of the Sikorsky helicopter lifting off its pad. It hovered over *Omega 1*'s arched dome and then McLaren, thin and looking frail, scrambled on to the roof and disappeared down one of the ladders. An hour later, he re-emerged.

Mallory saw him on the roof, outlined against the sky, standing with his legs apart, hands stuck in his pockets. 'Probably working on how to shift the blame,' Mallory said.

'That's going to be pretty hard work,' Carson retorted.

When they met at 1830 hours round the wardroom table, McLaren's white suit was rumpled, his face perspired, and his eyes were red-rimmed. He looked down at the table and, after a short, awkward silence, cleared his throat softly. 'Let's examine everything. Let's first go through all the facts, and see where that leads.'

For forty minutes, McLaren delivered a monologue about Project Fireplay, its planning, its execution, its importance. He left nothing out. It was a masterly exposition but it contributed nothing to a solution of their difficulties. The others remained silent, and McLaren neither sought their advice nor paused for comment.

Carson, Harper and Mallory all knew that Fireplay was finished. Somehow they would have to persuade McLaren that they must all accept responsibility.

When McLaren at last finished, Harper asked him what he thought the KGB wanted to get through Fireplay.

'Who knows what they want?' McLaren said. He breathed on his glasses and wiped them clean. The monologue continued. But what he was now proposing was a cover-up of Project Fireplay. A total cover-up. Fireplay's failure was to be hidden from everybody, even from the CIA hierarchy.

McLaren wanted to slide open the barge's sea doors,

drop *Doneska* back into the Pacific – and so erase the whole Project. They would report a total failure to recover the submarine.

Mallory shook his head. 'That's not going to work.' Apart from the ethics which he avoided discussing, too many people on *Pacific Klondike*, in and out of the CIA, knew *Doneska* had been raised successfully. It was impossible that the truth would not ultimately reach the director.

The next proposal McLaren put forward was that the aft two-thirds of *Doneska* should be hacked away with blow torches leaving a third forward of the conning tower. The aft two-thirds, including the conning tower, the missiles and code room stowage areas, could be sunk. He would write a memorandum explaining how *Doneska*'s hull, already damaged by the explosion and weakened by severe pressures, had cracked into two pieces and how the aft two-thirds had dropped back to the sea bed. The mission would only have recovered the useless forward third.

Harper hardly bothered to hide his contempt for this plan. Blow torches would leave molten edges on the submarine's hull, tell-tale signs of the deception. 'Besides,' Harper added, 'I don't want the CIA's trusted people to keep information from it. Also, everybody knows the whole sub was recovered and John's point still stands.'

'That's right,' Carson said.

'We have to give much more attention to what the KGB is planning,' Mallory interjected. 'We simply can't hide it from our side.'

'For one thing,' Harper said, 'they got us to waste a lot of money and effort. My guess is that they will leak the failure story, sling mud through their Disinformation Department, embarrass us at home and abroad.'

'Well, nobody's going to believe anything coming from them.'

'Don't be too sure. It will be confirmed by *Klondike*'s crew. A big story about how the CIA was made a sucker by the KGB.'

'Except nobody knows that, not yet,' Mallory said quietly.

'Just so, John. That's the danger. The failure has to be kept from personnel *outside* the CIA. We have to make it look like a big success.'

It was now evident that McLaren had, in some way, been excluded from the discussions. No one paid any more attention to what he had said. Fireplay had been his brainchild; now it lay in ruins. His decline escaped no one; if he had somehow succeeded in foiling the complex Russian plot, it had been through blind luck combined with his obstinacy in not reporting the course of events leading up to the confrontation.

Harper stressed that it was up to them to prevent a loss of prestige to the CIA, and that meant keeping knowledge of Fireplay's failure from the public. If they were to develop a cover-up, the essential thing was to plan for the immediate future.

Mallory turned to McLaren. 'Harper came up with a proposal yesterday. Carson was in favour and I . . .' McLaren's reaction checked Mallory. His face clearly showed that he resented their meeting without him.

'So why doesn't Harper give us the benefit of his ingenuity?' he demanded.

Harper needed no further encouragement. 'We act like Fireplay is a big success,' he said. 'If it had succeeded, there would have been Russian dead. So we stage a burial for the benefit of *Pacific Klondike*'s crew and everybody else on board.'

'All we need are a few trusted men to stuff the shrouds with some kind of filling. Maybe we should even do it ourselves,' Carson put in.

'No problem,' Harper said. 'All it has to look is realistic. When these guys leave *Klondike* they have to be convinced of Fireplay's success. That'll corroborate any version we publish outside the CIA, if it ever comes to it.'

McLaren sat impassively in another awkward silence, and again Harper tried to press his point home.

'Don't you agree, Mac?' he said. 'We must get the burial done. Let's do that anyway.'

For answer McLaren smiled bleakly at Mallory and pointed at Harper. 'He can make the decisions from here on,' he said. He got up stiffly and said he was going to his quarters. 'Let me know when I'm back on the team,' he said as he stalked out.

Harper shrugged.

'Bill, you're going to have to be very careful,' Mallory said quietly.

'Thanks, pal, I know.' The wardroom door shut behind Harper and Mallory turned to Carson. 'I think Mac will want to fix Harper.'

'Bill was too blunt,' Carson agreed. 'But we just don't have time for mollycoddling Mac's finer feelings.'

Mallory left Carson paging through a copy of the *Geneva Convention for the Amelioration of the Condition of Wounded, Sick and Shipwrecked members of Armed Forces at Sea*. It was dated 12 August 1949.

23

The weather was appropriate for a funeral: there was a heavy grey sky and a rising wind. The Fireplay cover-up began in the morning in light drizzle, with most of *Klondike*'s complement gathered in the stern of the ship, around the helipad. The men wore bright orange waterproofs and went bareheaded. Fine rain wet their hair as they quietly crowded the rails.

Mallory, McLaren and Carson watched from the back of the bridge. In his right hand Carson carried a well-thumbed copy of the Geneva Convention. Article 20 of the Convention regulated Burials of the Dead at Sea and Carson had arranged an appropriate ceremony.

From where he stood, through binoculars, he saw on the barge a row of bulky canvas bags shrouded in Russian flags. There were nineteen of them, and they neatly lined the barge's aft deck. To prevent any danger of a burial bag foul ing against *Omega 1* the burials were to proceed along the barge's port rail, close by the stern but clear of the propellers. Harper and Barroso, who both wore raincoats, had rigged a smooth pine plank to the barge's railing, specially designed to slide across the line of bogus corpses.

At exactly 0900 hours the first of the red shrouded containers was raised from the deck with exaggerated difficulty. Carson waited for them to place it on the smooth, light plank before he signalled again with his hands by waving the Convention. He read a short service in English and slow, stilted Russian. Powerful, scratchy notes of the Russian national anthem played over *Pacific Klondike*'s loudspeakers while CIA men filmed the scene. A cameraman on board *Pacific Klondike* filmed the sombre faces of men who stood silently on her stern deck.

Harper tipped the first burial container. The bag slid off the plank, well clear of *Omega 1*, and splashed, making dark water spout up amid tiny ripples where the rain fell. Solemnly, Barroso slid the plank along the barge rail opposite the next shroud.

So the burials continued with *Pacific Klondike* doing five knots. The only sounds were the churning of her propellers, the regular splash of bulky containers in the sea and taped music over *Pacific Klondike*'s public address system. Carson alternated the Russian anthem with the *Internationale*. When McLaren broke into the *Internationale*, Carson and Mallory sang along solemnly and *Klondike*'s complement heard them over the loudspeakers. Some men, curious, turned and briefly stared up at the back of the bridge.

Heavy rain held off until the last flag-shrouded bundle had dropped into the water. The *Internationale* died away and men broke quickly away from *Pacific Klondike*'s stern. They moved off in small knots, quiet and serious, talking softly about the bizarre but unforgettable scene. Moments later, the skies opened to hurry stragglers under cover, and above the rain's clamour, they heard McLaren's voice boom over the speakers with the volume up.

'I don't have to remind any of you of how much we want the things that happened here over the last few days kept quiet. If you want to talk about it at all, do so now, among yourselves. But once we get back to port, I want you to maintain silence. Always. For anybody here not impressed by what I've said, I remind you that you have sworn and signed oaths of secrecy. I'm making no threats, but this entire operation has been too delicate not to stress your pledges.

'Thank you once again for your help and courage. We've written a new page in the history books together. The fact that nobody's going to know about it back home for a long time is a pity – but that's the price of success. I'm sure you understand it all. God bless you and God bless America.'

There were no cheers. Rain washed in torrents against the glass panes of the bridge and, to Mallory, the Fireplay Director appeared to be back under control.

Mallory and Carson nodded politely to him and were already clear of the bridge when McLaren received a message from the radio room. Marked *Urgentest*, it brought the first news of the events in Zürich; Yazov had killed Burns and Higby. McLaren folded the paper neatly and placed it in his pocket.

Already he was composing the first line of Harper's resignation and, by the time he was off the bridge, a small secret smile was on his face.

Standard practice was what McLaren called it. He held xeroxed resignation forms from everybody who worked under him, signed in advance.

When Harper entered McLaren's office at 0700 hours next morning, in answer to a summons, his xeroxed resignation form lay on the table along with the Zürich report and two unsigned letters of resignation which McLaren had typed.

'Sit down.' McLaren had on his head a canvas fishing hat, neatly barbed with dozens of small, colourful trout hooks. An open box on the table had small compartments filled with assorted hooks, tracers, gut, fishing line, feathers, strips of cloth and silvery lures. McLaren was painting small red spots on an aluminium lure, and he hardly raised his eyes to Harper. A cigar smoked in a tray.

'You remember that we have talked about resignations, that I always require to have them in hand,' McLaren said.

'Yes,' Harper said.

With the back of a slim, fine paint brush, McLaren

pushed the Zürich report towards Harper. The younger man read it in silence, and understood at once how he was being made to pay for undermining McLaren's authority.

A minute passed while McLaren waited for Harper to absorb it. 'What do you think?' he finally asked softly.

'I think it ought to be Harper, Carson and Mallory,' Harper answered coolly.

'Well,' McLaren said slowly, 'I have them too. But I thought Harper may be enough at this moment.' McLaren pushed the two typescripts in front of Harper. 'I've prepared these two letters. One requests an immediate leave of absence. The other, of course, is just a straight resignation.'

'Yes.'

'I suggest that you sign both. Then I can decide which, if any, to use.'

Harper made no move to pick up the pen McLaren had rolled to him on the table. Instead, he re-read the scripts. 'What I would like to do is to draft an alternative letter putting in both options.'

'All right.' McLaren sounded disappointed. 'If you can give me something better, fine.'

'I would like to try.'

'Good. Why don't you use these as a draft?'

'All right.'

'Understand I don't want to aggravate your position at all,' McLaren said. 'But you have taken a helluva load, particularly the Zürich business.'

Harper knew he was finished. Forty-eight hours before, he could have sworn that McLaren had cracked. Now he was re-asserting all his old iron and claiming his scapegoat.

Harper said, 'You will have something within a couple of hours.'

McLaren reached up and gingerly lifted the canvas hat off his head. Slowly and patiently, he inserted a new hook and dropped the hat back on his head where it sat askew.

'Maybe in the end nobody will have any problems,' he

said. 'It's possible. But the whole Hofman and Yazov operation was your disaster. There'll be an inquiry within the agency at some point, a report to the Forty Committee. Somebody'll have to be thrown to the wolves and that person will have to be the one that causes the least harm. For the sake of the agency that person is you rather than me. But if it has to be me, too, I'll have to stand ready.'

'Like you say, Mr McLaren, I've got more to offer than anybody else.' Harper got up and left, knowing that when the ship docked he would be walking out of the CIA. There was a sour taste in his mouth. He moved to *Klondike*'s starboard rail and spat into the sea, then he went off to find Carson and Mallory.

After he left them, Carson and Mallory sat discussing Harper's story. McLaren joined them and he seemed agitated – certainly not cool and in control as Harper had described. His pale face was flushed and Mallory smelt whisky.

'I just wonder if the son-of-a-bitch had a recorder on him,' McLaren said. 'I didn't notice but I wasn't looking.'

'It's almost inconceivable Bill would try that . . .' Mallory said without thinking. But McLaren persisted.

'Is there any way that Harper might have walked in there with a recorder on him?' He stood so close that Mallory edged away. There was definitely whisky on his breath.

'No, that's too remote.'

'If he did, could it make trouble for me?'

Mallory was puzzled. 'I suppose so – if you said anything you shouldn't have.'

'I want to be certain that you are going to identify Bill Harper as the one who directed the Sofia and Zürich operations,' McLaren said. 'I think we could all get by on that without further casualties.'

Almost two-and-a-half years after *Doneska* sailed out of Vladivostok, she arrived ignominiously at a mooring off the Midway atoll in the belly of *Omega 1*. The barge's sea cocks were reopened and she took on enough water to sink to the sea's bottom 275 feet down. Inside her, she retained *Doneska.*

Barge and submarine lay safe on the sand with no practical way of reaching either, and until the CIA had cleared everything with the highest authorities, *Doneska* would remain off limits to all save CIA personnel. That time, it soon became clear to the navy, was distant.

McLaren, Mallory and Carson tried to allay the navy's curiosity with a series of secret but misleading reports and memoranda to the effect that the CIA had succeeded in raising the submarine – a remarkable technical feat, by any standards – but that much of the most valuable material had been lost. The huge gash in *Doneska,* and other damage, even the explosion itself, had seriously reduced the spoils. Either the Russian vessel had not carried a full complement of missiles and torpedoes, or else much of the armament had been blown clear by the vast explosion that had sunk her. What remained, severely damaged, had been retrieved by the CIA, and if it provided any useful information this would be passed on to the navy as soon as possible. As for the code books, they had been soaked into useless pulp by water which had flooded into the officers' quarters and radio room. These reports were interspersed with sly hints that the CIA might possibly attempt to renew the search for undamaged missiles, if any, buried deep in the Pacific sand. If they were found, a different recovery procedure would need to be devised – an ingenious explanation of why it had not been possible to tackle the problem at the time of the salvage.

It was a flimsy enough story that did little to smooth the prickly relations that already existed between the CIA and the navy, but its very simplicity made it easy to defend. Attempts by the navy to probe for details met with a stonewalling technique which, while it eventually reduced naval investigators to frustrated silence, was not entirely unexpected.

Having safely dumped *Omega 1* and the Russian submarine, *Pacific Klondike* weighed anchor and set sail for the Hawaiian Islands. She was seen off the island of Maui, where Conrad pretended to prospect for minerals on the sea bed. Her mysterious manoeuvrings over two weeks prompted an investigation by state officials into the ownership of mineral rights in offshore Hawaiian waters.

Late one night, in calm waters off Honolulu, Conrad executed a crew change with near military precision, hiring a private boatman who used his seventy-foot launch to carry 136 men off the ship and into the port. There they piled quietly into three waiting buses which moved off to Honolulu airport, where they boarded a Boeing 707 transport waiting for them on the runway.

An alert customs official tipped off a reporter from the *Honolulu Advertiser* and was paid $15 for his trouble. The reporter got to Honolulu airport in time to question crewmen hurriedly as they flung their baggage off the buses. Most of them were tight-lipped, but one seaman, who did not give his name, mentioned that *Pacific Klondike* had been mining for minerals in the waters off Hawaii during a long Pacific cruise.

Meantime, a private shuttle service ran supplies in a thirty-foot power boat called *Cindy* from Honolulu harbour to *Pacific Klondike*. The contractor who ran the service for $260 a day and fuel, told *Honolulu Advertiser* reporters that he rarely saw any men about on *Pacific Klondike*'s deck. 'You'd expect them to come out and get some sun once in a while,' he said. 'But it is like the ship ate them up.'

Pacific Klondike weighed anchor again and reached San Diego, California, on 23 October, eleven weeks after sailing out on Project Fireplay.

In San Diego a shore-based worker assigned to the ship told an NBC-TV reporter that he had seen *Pacific Klondike*'s crew fill twenty-five large trucks with heavy equipment and electronic gear. The trucks drove to Redwood City. By the

time he made this statement, most of the original complement had left to catch planes, trains and buses to all parts
of the United States. In fact, within two weeks of docking,
only six men remained on board and most of the time they
played stud poker. This inactivity and the delays in resum-
ing mining operations added to *Pacific Klondike*'s mystery.
Shipping experts were surprised that the costly ship was not
immediately refitted and put to work, and nobody knew
what had happened to the vast, ungainly barge she had
towed out into the Pacific.

The *Los Angeles Examiner* directed enquiries to Trans
Acme Corporation. Letters went unanswered, phone calls
were not returned. A reporter who tried to interview
officials of Omega Corporation was referred to Trans Acme's
public relations office who failed to reply.

24

As the weeks went by, more and more United States news-papers and news agencies began probing Project Fireplay with a post-Watergate fervour. The *Philadelphia Enquirer*, already alerted by a tip in late 1973 when building started in the dockyards, picked up an Associated Press telex which noted *Pacific Klondike*'s return for refitting in San Diego. The *Enquirer* moved in reporters who began to hear talk connect-ing *Pacific Klondike*, Trans Acme and a CIA mission. Follow-ing up an FBI leak on papers stolen from Felix Townsend's Manhattan penthouse, the newspaper was first with a page one report of a mission to recover a sunken Russian sub-marine in the South China Seas. In the second edition, the story was severely trimmed and printed on an inside page.

McLaren had continued the playing-down with a persuas-ive call to the editor. He confirmed the CIA had recovered a submarine, but from the Pacific; unfortunately, only the submarine's forward third was found to be intact, the rest having become so water-logged as to be valueless, its arma-ments and other secrets having been washed away. There-fore it was against the interests of the United States Govern-ment to publicize the CIA's partial success.

'You might put it on a national security grounds basis,' McLaren ended his call. 'It absolutely is. National security.'

It was already too late. A shipping reporter on the *Los Angeles Times*, who had for weeks sought *Omega 1*, drove his battered Ford on to a secondhand lot on the edge of Los Angeles to meet a sailor on shore leave from Midway. The *Times* printed a tentative story about the sinking off Midway under the headline: OMEGA I HOLDING RUSSIAN SUB?

McLaren was unable to stop this report from appearing in the *Times*'s following edition. From then on, it was a losing battle.

Harper had by now officially resigned from the CIA, but McLaren brought Mallory and Carson up to date. 'I had a call from Davis of the *Washington Post*, who is a reasonably close acquaintance. A reporter of character, if there are any. He said they had a report out of Midway that – let me use his words – "there's a Russian submarine sunk there by the CIA". He asked if there was anything to it.'

'What did you say?' Mallory asked.

'I said there wasn't a damn thing I *could* say, one way or the other.'

'So they will probably write a story on that. It's beginning to get out of hand.'

Together, they shared the press enquiries which steadily streamed in, always pleading that the story should be embargoed until a full assessment of the project had been completed and officially presented to the appropriate authorities.

'The timing is terribly important,' McLaren emphasized to these callers and quoted the names of news media that had agreed to withhold publication altogether. 'Don't write anything,' he pleaded. 'To write anything at all can only be damaging at this stage.'

Privately, journalists speculated on McLaren's apparent deviousness. The recovery seemed a kind of coup, good news for the CIA. Project Fireplay was highly imaginative. Was McLaren playing for maximum publicity?

It was clearly only a matter of time before the media became aware that it was the failure of the project that made Fireplay such a sensitive area, and the break came when a mid-western TV station interviewed a former, high-ranking naval man. The navy, it seemed, was unimpressed with the raising of a largely obsolete Russian submarine that carried little real military or naval significance. The direct question was put: Would publicizing Project Fireplay jeopardize national security? 'I think not,' the former officer replied.

Mallory was with McLaren as he watched the videotape play-back of the interview. 'Well,' Mallory asked, 'when do we make the announcement?'

'Why don't we do it tonight?' McLaren said. He had just seen Fiedler, the agency's assistant press officer, and added: 'Fiedler feels we have no more than twelve hours. He's got a tip-off from the *Times* and says that unless we take the initiative by nine o'clock tonight, it will be too late.'

Later there was a knock on the door, and Fiedler walked in to see McLaren sitting behind a large pile of typescripts bound in blue paper. Each typescript consisted of eighteen pages which he, Carson and Mallory had compiled to state their version of the Fireplay operation. Fiedler looked at them inquisitively.

'It's all in these books,' McLaren said. 'Get them out right away.'

By any reckoning it was the most intriguing item released in Washington for months. A press run of 3000 copies sold almost immediately and people started to line up for the next run at two o'clock in the morning in front of the CIA Printing Office.

Already, the slim blue-covered books had the feel of history. They furnished the basis of the long reports on Fireplay which every major newspaper in the United States carried in the next twenty-four hours.

The *New York Times* not only had headlines covering the successful raising of the submarine, the failure to retrieve missiles, and the burial of nineteen Russians at sea: it also carried photographs of *Pacific Klondike*, of *Omega 1*, and of a diesel-powered *Golf*-class Russian submarine.

Within the week, national news magazines had researched the story in greater depth. *Time* magazine devoted five pages to Fireplay which they headlined: THE GREAT SUBMARINE SNATCH. *Newsweek* called it: CIA'S MISSION IMPOSSIBLE. But the pictures and sketches that appeared in different magazines and newspapers made it clear that a good deal had been omitted from McLaren's blue books. Grapnels were shown extending from a series of long cables, or from a single thick pipe that passed upwards through *Klondike*'s bottom into her derrick. No one had thought of a bathyscaphe.

On the whole, both the stories and the editorials praised the CIA for their initiative. The *Los Angeles Times* editorial was fairly typical.

'Good intelligence,' it said, 'is essential to national security in a world of nuclear weapons and intercontinental missiles. The CIA is congratulated for this extraordinary effort, which unfortunately fell short of full success.'

A sour note began to intrude however. Reporting the probability of investigations into Fireplay, the *Washington Post* said:

The White House, the Pentagon and the CIA refused yesterday to talk about the CIA's reported attempt to salvage a sunken Soviet submarine this year. But congressional committee chairmen said they would investigate the project.

The disclosure of the attempt suggests that the intelligence community may be in need of a cost-benefit ratio. 'If we are prepared to pay Felix Townsend $350000000 for an obsolete Russian submarine, it's little wonder we are broke,' said Senator Dan Proudfoot.

Once the story was out, McLaren would say nothing, claiming he was not free to talk. All press enquiries were gently turned aside and, within two weeks, Project Fireplay came off the front pages and the television screens. The newsmen had still not heard about the confrontation between *Pacific Klondike* and the Russian navy, nor that the naval funeral had been make-believe.

Ten days after Fireplay died in the news, McLaren invited Mallory and Carson to a private celebration in his office. A crisp, white tablecloth over his beechwood desk was covered with trays of drinks and snacks: caviar, large green olives, Greek cheese, smoked trout and salmon. McLaren mixed martinis and poured them into fine crystal glasses. He was full of his old confidence, his eyes twinkled again, his step seemed lighter.

He had written for the Forty Committee a report which covered most of the facts. While admitting that Fireplay was unfortunate, a grand scheme that had misfired, he reminded the Committee that the whole Project had passed through several CIA channels, including a final review by the members themselves in full session.

The biggest mistake had been trying to kidnap Hofman from Sofia, and the Yazov affair had gone very sour. But Harper had been directly responsible for all of that, and since he had resigned, no further action seemed necessary. The only official complaint made by the Russians was a diplomatic note protesting the disturbing of their sailors' bodies. This could safely be ignored, McLaren wrote, since, in fact, there had been no Russian dead, though that had not been made public. He added that it seemed the Russians themselves were going along with the CIA's version of events, and this was all to the good. Nothing had been made of the buzzing by United States Navy jets.

Whatever losses the CIA had sustained in the operation, it had gained a new technology. Far from Fireplay proving wholly abortive, the CIA had for once enjoyed favourable press coverage.

In spite of McLaren's reassuring report, he was now being questioned on certain sensitive details. Why had the Fireplay director not notified Langley once the Russians came out in force? Would he please supply fuller reasons why he had taken it upon himself to call in the jets? What was his explanation for not leaving a ranking Fireplay executive at Langley during the crisis?

Nor was that all. He was required also to deal with certain criticisms of the CIA by the navy, which was planning its own secret inquiry into the events of the confrontation. In particular why had McLaren not informed Rear Admiral Smith of the true gravity of the crisis?

Knowing very well that his replies to these queries would themselves come under further and closer scrutiny, McLaren had contrived to drag his feet, using old, well-learned skills to stall the matter. Perhaps his days were numbered, but McLaren was too close to retirement for that to matter much. All he wanted was to nurse his part in Project Fireplay through its final stages.

Small wonder, then, that McLaren's spirits were high when he entertained Carson and Mallory in his office. But Mallory, still worried about Dan Proudfoot's threats to hold Senate hearings, remained unconvinced.

McLaren sipped his martini, chewed an olive, put the stone on a plate, and dismissed Proudfoot. 'There are no votes in it, John,' he said, placing his arm round Mallory's shoulder. 'You really can't worry about it all the time. Apart from Yazov, I don't see any major problems ahead.'

This, it appeared, was the real reason why he had asked them over to his office. Yazov was unpaid and free. So far, the press had not linked Fireplay to the killings in Sofia, Belgrade and Zürich; obviously, any such connection could provoke more front-page publicity – and a general outcry.

McLaren had expected Yazov to contact the CIA by then but the Bulgarian had not done so; they would have to go after him. His suggestion was that Mallory and Carson fly to Zürich and start looking around, for Yazov had somehow to be dealt with. The first task was to locate him – and convince him that he had not been abandoned by the CIA.

The next day, Mallory and Carson boarded a flight via New York for Zürich, the last known whereabouts of Ivan Yazov. After Zürich the next best places would be Paris and Rome, where it was known that he had contacts.

McLaren let it be thought he had given his two deputies a few days' leave after their labours. Meanwhile, the CIA's Forty Committee pursued its slow internal investigation of Fireplay.

25

Whether it went by the name of Cheka, GPU, OGPU, NKGB or NGB, the political police force of the Soviet Union has remained very much the same. Since 1954 it has been called the Committee for State Security, or KGB. Its Moscow headquarters are at 2 Dzershinsky Street, named after the founder of the Cheka, and there, some days before Fireplay came off the front pages of American newspapers, a committee of Department A of the First Chief Directorate met around an oval table, covered in green baize.

Department A's main purpose was to weaken, disrupt and if possible destroy the forces of law and order in the West and make easier the ultimate takeover by a Communist Government. For that reason the KGB and CIA opposed each other all over the world. The committee was meeting on this occasion to decide where to plant the true facts of the CIA's Fireplay operation.

To publish the story in *Pravda* or *Izvestia* would have been easy but obviously wrong. TASS and other communist agencies in the West were also inappropriate since the CIA would too easily discredit them. A more devious, necessarily convoluted route, not in any way traceable to the KGB, was required.

Thus, after considering advice from the press attaché and other officials in their Washington embassy, the Committee decided to plant the Fireplay story in a small, carefully selected town in Arizona. Skull Valley had a population of less than 10000 people and was served by the *Skull Valley*

Courier, which came out twice a week and had a circulation of 2330.

Numbered among Skull Valley's citizens was a young man named Peter Howick. He had been aboard *Pacific Klondike* when Yashin attacked, and KGB psychologists – basing themselves on their embassy men's reports – had compiled his personality profile. He was among the top men of the crew (so far as the members had been tracked down) rated by the KGB experts as bad risks for keeping secrets. His father had been a diesel fitter and his mother had died in Skull Valley. When Pete Howick was paid off in Los Angeles he returned to his home town as a motor repairer in Howard Moore's 4S Service Station. 'I guess I'm not really a very reliable guy,' he told Howard Moore after being late for work three days in a row.

A TASS correspondent and KGB operative, Boris Zhenov, gave Department A's plan its first push by anonymously phoning Bill Evans, editor-reporter-printer of the *Skull Valley Courier*. Did he know, Zhenov asked Evans, that Pete Howick had been a rigger on *Pacific Klondike*? No, he did not, replied a surprised Evans.

'He is not talking because he thinks he mustn't,' Zhenov said over the phone.

Bill Evans replaced the receiver and sat thoughtfully. So Bob and Carol Howick's boy had been aboard when they raised the Russian sub. It was a good, human interest story but before he had even thanked his informer the man had rung off.

The *Courier*'s editor was fifty-six years old. He wrote the paper on Saturday, Sunday and Monday and took photographs, too. On Tuesday, it was he personally who printed the *Courier*'s four pages. He became a reporter again on Wednesday and Thursday and printed on Friday. If there was not much local copy, Evans subbed material from the Associated Press news service, whose ticker constantly chattered in the room where he did the printing.

It was Wednesday – and Evans sat in front of an old

Remington typewriter with a green eye-shade over his glasses. More and more, he had taken to using AP's copy, a practice that was bad for a small-town paper because people wanted local stuff. The anonymous tip-off offered the first important local news story in a long while. Evans went into the printing shop, put a new roll in the AP ticker, pulled on an overcoat and banged the office door shut behind him. The December cold caught in his throat, and he looked forward with pleasure to a stiff whisky.

Howick and Evans sat in Bim's Bar, opposite the 4S. A woman played a piano, the soft lights twinkled off plastic table tops, and outside, a neon sign flashed on and off.

Pete Howick was in shirt sleeves, an anchor tattooed on his forearm. He downed the beers bought by Evans while the latter made notes in a spiral notebook. Not that there was, at first, a great deal to note. 'Those guys did a terrific job,' Howick said at one point. And later on, 'I was just one among them – nobody special to make a fuss about.'

Evans sensed Howick was holding back and unashamedly continued to buy him beer. So it came about that, as he downed his ninth beer, Howick became the first member of the discharged crew to speak to a newspaper man of the confrontation between *Pacific Klondike* and the Russian task force.

The jets, he said, came in very low, and as he demonstrated with his hand a beer can went flying to the floor of Bim's Bar. Then he stiffened an index finger and moved it through the air like a missile.

'I wish it was Friday,' said the editor of the *Courier* as he closed his notebook.

When Friday did come, the *Skull Valley Courier* carried the headline: HOW PACIFIC KLONDIKE BEAT OFF RUSSIAN WARSHIPS. There was a photograph of a smiling Howick, some old photographs of Serb missiles and G-class submarines copied out of *Jane's Fighting Ships*, and Howick's description of the Russian task force, the helicopters, the Phantoms – and the Russian missile. Evans gave the story the whole of the *Courier*'s front page. It was in due course to win him the Pulitzer prize. With his Friday edition out, Evans notified Associated Press. It was seldom anything of consequence came out of Skull Valley, but when it did, he passed it on to AP.

Perhaps because it was thirty-five years since Skull Valley had given Associated Press a worthwhile story, the regional news editor assigned a junior reporter to cover it. Charles Ungerer was a twenty-nine-year-old college dropout who normally covered local politics or reported on unsanitary restaurants and petty police graft.

He motored the hundred odd miles north-west of Phoenix in a broken-down Ford Pinto to interview Howick. Worried that he had broken his pledge of secrecy, the rigger was reticent at first but, confronted by Evans, he finally told his story again. Then he took Ungerer home to his second-floor flat, where another *Pacific Klondike* crewman had come to stay for a few days. Ungerer sat down and took notes from him, too.

Back in Phoenix, Ungerer handed his story to AP's regional chief. The chief acted speedily. A hand-picked team of reporters, from AP bureaux all over the United States, quietly began a massive probe. They went after *Klondike* crewmen in their homes and over the phone. The facts were checked and cross-checked. AP corroborated, to its own satisfaction, fact by fact, the drama of McLaren's brinkmanship on the high seas.

The news service had worked efficiently and quickly, and put out its full report to all the major United States newspapers and magazines, TV and radio stations. The story that its telexes clattered to all its customers began:

The CIA's efforts to raise a Soviet submarine earlier this year from the Pacific ocean near Midway came close to provoking nuclear war. It was followed by sustained attempts to suppress public knowledge of brinkmanship undertaken without presidential authority during which Phantom fighter bombers of the United States Navy were fired upon by a Russian navy task force. . . .

Once again Fireplay occupied the headlines, television screens and radio news spots, and the criticism of the CIA was all the fiercer because of the praise it had won earlier.

'Fears have grown that the US intelligence apparatus is no longer under control,' wrote the Washington man of the *Cleveland Post Dispatch*, and he ended his story: 'As far as is known, the White House was not informed of the risks taken to defend the CIA's submarine-lifting operation in which none of the vessel's nuclear armaments were recovered.'

WHO DECIDES WHAT? asked *Newsweek* in a headline to a four-page story. From further afield, and typical of overseas reactions, *The Times* of London complained that the CIA might have involved Britain in 'annihilation without representation'.

It was the CIA itself which officially named McLaren as the man who had controlled Project Fireplay. He went before a battery of TV cameras wearing a neat grey suit. His white, crew-cut hair was spiky and shone in the Klieg lights, and he blinked his eyes in the glare.

Reading from a prepared statement he accepted full responsibility for the project and then swiftly moved into the attack.

'I deeply resent the slanderous and false statements about me and the CIA,' he said with feeling, 'and I am sure certain elements are trying to stretch this into something more than it is. Nothing like the bizarre incident described by crewman Howick ever occurred. Most of what he has to say is grossly overblown and exaggerated.

'I was appalled at this senseless, illegal action by Howick and others and I was shocked to learn that employees of the CIA were apparently among those guilty of breaking their contracts, indeed oaths, to keep secret their work with so sensitive a government agency.

'We need secrecy. We have people whose lives and reputations depend on our secrecy. We have technical systems whose effectiveness can be annulled if details of particular activities are published. It is not in the interests of national security that all the facts pertaining to Project Fireplay be disclosed. Surely this must be obvious. An agency such as the CIA cannot operate under the glare of public scrutiny.

'It is also essential that we should not be so distracted by attacks of this nature as to cause the CIA to neglect the vital work before it, before this nation, before America, at a time of critical importance to America and the world.

'In the final analysis, the integrity of the CIA – public faith in the integrity of the CIA – will have to take priority over all personal considerations. I have to say that I have since learned that Peter Howick is an unstable, practising homosexual who has consulted at least three psychiatrists. He has changed jobs seven times in three years. He tried to commit suicide two years ago by slitting his wrists after an argument with a close male friend. I have nothing personal against homosexuals, or people who frequently move from job to job. I do not say these things make them liars. But such facts ought to be known.'

When the statement was over, someone in the studio asked, 'How come you employed Howick?' but the Fireplay director was already walking out through a side exit.

Extract from a twelve-page KGB memorandum outlining a new project named Operation Blue Stallion:

The American Press will become obsessed with *Doneska*. Under the guise of the press's right to explore the truth, there will be a massive volume of *Doneska* coverage by news organizations, thus enabling Blue Stallion to develop naturally and giving the opportunity for information to be planted almost at will. *Doneska* coverage will distort TV network news programmes, the front pages of newspapers and the opening sections of news magazines. The American public, it will be claimed, will want to know every scrap of detail about an organization wild enough to provoke possible nuclear way over an obsolete submarine.

CBS News interviewed Rear Admiral Smith. He sat in full uniform on a brown, chunky swivel-chair, in front of a map of the Pacific with big blow-ups of *Galveston*, *Kresta* and *Pacific Klondike* towing her barge. There was also a big, blurred, black and white photo of a Goa missile being launched.

Smith's face was drawn and he carefully hid from view the fingertips of both hands, for all the nails were bitten down. A typescript of his original notes made on the day of the crisis rested on a small table next to the swivel chair.

Why did he not report directly to the president? Was sending the Phantoms not a presidential-level decision?

'I regret all that deeply,' Smith said. 'Some of my judgments were wrong, but ever since *Pueblo* we had contingency plans that did not call for bothering the president every time a Russian ship sailed too close to one of ours. McLaren even mentioned *Pueblo*.'

What did he think of Howick?

'Well, Howick broke but it had to happen. Others who know will be under great pressure to talk as well.'

Could the CIA successfully cover up the full details of their involvement?

'I think not. The press is going to drag it out drop by drop, and it wouldn't take a sharp congressional investigator very long to do it because everything's there in the CIA files that they'd have to turn over.'

Why did McLaren do it?

'Everyone wants to win his place in a hall of fame.' Smith laughed. 'I understand McLaren was already something of a legend – OSS, Hungary and Berlin. Maybe he wanted more.'

What of the confrontation?

Smith shifted in his seat. 'Nobody ever told me that the Russians were after their dead. You don't wake up the president or secretary of defence just because some Russian boats are in the area.' He half reached for a glass of water, then pulled his hand back. 'Besides, I didn't want to undercut the CIA,' he went on. 'They just showed incredibly bad judgment, right?'

So he blamed McLaren?

'Well, he's not Mr Cool, you know. He is not as cool a type as they could have found,' Smith replied ironically. 'But you must realize that I am prejudiced against him.'

'You feel that McLaren started it?' persisted the interviewer.

'Yes. He did not give us the real facts and we acted in good faith.'

What of the CIA's future?

'I'm glad I don't work for the CIA,' Smith said grimly.

What of his future?

'I have never been a quitter but I shall leave the navy with regret at not completing my term.'

The interviewer said he was sorry, both men smiled, the TV picture faded. When it returned, Smith was gone and, in his place, Senator Dan Proudfoot sat and swivelled in the chunky, brown chair. Proudfoot's jowls jiggled, his eyebrows rolled up and down but his lips stretched in a gentle smile.

He announced that he would seek to establish a select committee of four Democrats and three Republicans to conduct a full-scale investigation of Project Fireplay and any cover-up.

McLaren clicked off his set. He had watched the programme from a deep armchair, drinking large whiskies.

His spectacles were perched halfway down his nose and fresh cigarette stubs littered a large ashtray. Some were only half smoked and the tobacco crushed through broken paper seams.

He put through phone calls to Paris, where Mallory was trying to track Yazov, and to Rome, where Carson was on a similar errand. McLaren told both men that he wanted them back in Washington. Senator Proudfoot would have no difficulty in getting his resolution through the Senate establishing the select committee and McLaren wanted to discuss strategy before the investigation started.

26

Mallory paid two francs for the *International Herald Tribune* at a news stand in the busy concourse and boarded a flight at Charles de Gaulle Airport, Paris, reading the front page all the way down the escalators and on to a waiting Boeing 747. He finished the latest long story on the CIA's crisis just as the Boeing rolled down runway five to lift sharply into clear skies over Paris.

The CIA agent turned the air nozzle on hard, directing a powerful jet of air on to his face. Under the impact, his brownish hair strayed slightly over his forehead.

CIA BELIEVED TO HAVE BLOWN UP BULGARIAN SECRET POLICE HEADQUARTERS, ran one headline, and another connected the assassinations in Belgrade and Zürich with Fireplay. Mallory had not found Yazov, but he had managed to establish that the mass killer had gone via Madrid to Canada. Only a little more time was needed to locate him.

The *Herald Tribune* had published Sovphotos of the smashed building on Brzina Street. Firemen played long strings of water on to smoking rubble. Mallory also saw a UPI picture of the Café Kranzler in Belgrade.

Under the headline, THE STORIES NEVER END, the *Herald Tribune* editorial said:

'Each day it becomes clearer that Senator Proudfoot's select committee's enquiry into the CIA needs to be bigger and bolder than was initially thought.

'The CIA stands uncovered as a reckless "rogue elephant", out of control, and the facts are not all in yet. Much information obviously remains undisclosed.

'There is some evidence that secrecy has been imposed to conceal questionable CIA actions rather than matters of legitimate national security. The result may be a head-on collision with the CIA over the issue of privilege. The revelations of dubious practices have led Senator Proudfoot to talk of holding public hearings whenever possible.' And they quoted a comment by the senator: 'In the absence of war, no government agency can be given licence to murder. The CIA is not a glorified Godfather.'

Mallory felt sick. What he needed to settle his stomach was a stiff cognac. The airline hostess obliged.

From New York, Mallory flew on to Washington and, tired out, reached McLaren in Langley in the evening. Carson was already there.

McLaren greeted him warmly.

'How's our latest coverage?' Mallory asked.

'The press is still playing it hard and mean,' McLaren said, 'but we'll have a chance to get back one day.'

Carson got up from a plastic chair to pour three full cups of black coffee. 'I've got notes on the people who are being unfriendly,' he said as he stirred in sugar. 'This will end someday and we won't forget them.'

'I like to think that.' McLaren's eyes glinted.

With a thumb hooked into his braces, McLaren paced up and down the olive green carpet of his large office. He smoked a chain of cigarettes, and the air in the office was a little stale.

'Let's talk about what kind of line to take,' McLaren began. 'We're back in the problem area. Proudfoot's investigation will use special prosecutors who'll want to make a name for themselves.'

'He already has a zealot in Clifford Blanzer – a fire-eater,' said Carson.

'They'll squeeze hard,' McLaren said. 'But how bad is

television for us? I am not sure it won't even help. CIA agents looking honest and sincere, talking about fighting the Russians with the gloves off.'

'Right,' Carson said. 'And putting their own lives at risk.'

'You know, even Proudfoot only wants to have a circus for a week because he thinks interest will fall off,' McLaren went on. 'He brings all the big shots up right away. He hauls in McLaren. He would like of course, to get Mallory and Carson . . .'

'. . . and Harper,' Mallory said softly.

'That is correct.' McLaren's eyes went steely.

'Who is going to be the first witness?' Carson asked.

'Harper,' said McLaren.

'If Harper does go in, that might ruin the whole week for us,' Mallory said. 'I'm sure he's ready to hurt the CIA.'

'You know, it hurt *me* to fire him,' McLaren said.

'If Harper testifies it's going to unscramble the whole omelet: the faked burial, the Yazov connection,' Mallory said in a soft, flat voice. 'We'll all look foolish and dangerous. Which is what Proudfoot wants.'

'Harper got sloppy, and he was fired. He has a lot to answer for,' McLaren said. 'He is a man with suspect motives, and he's going to do anything to save his ass. He's not credible. Nobody's going to believe him.'

McLaren took off his glasses, polished them, and put them on again – a sure sign he was coming up with a solution. 'The main thing is to handle it right,' he said. 'It may not be ideal but if Proudfoot gets a big fish to start with, that will take a lot of the fire out of the inquiry.'

'Yes?' Mallory was hesitant, not quite sure what McLaren meant.

It was at this point that McLaren explained that *he* would take the stand first, setting the tone of Proudfoot's investigation and using himself as a stalking horse. 'I think it could draw Proudfoot's fire and defuse the hearings. It'll be a rough and tumble, but I'm ready for it.'

'If I were you I would be reluctant to do it,' Mallory said. 'These men are going to be merciless.'

'I know that,' McLaren nodded, 'but I'm ready to risk it. I'll take all the heat and kill it that way.' He walked over to his prize trout and studied it awhile. 'There'll be a horrible two weeks, a big scandal. But that'll be it. I'll put on a show, just like I'm selling cornflakes.'

Carson and Mallory laughed, and McLaren joined in. His refusal to be beaten, his gallows humour, seemed to make the problem manageable.

Having established his right to be the first to testify as the man primarily responsible, McLaren wanted Carson and Mallory out of the country. Nobody from the CIA was going to appear at the hearings voluntarily. If Proudfoot tried to subpoena them, McLaren would explain that they had both been sent on a mission connected with the CIA's internal Fireplay inquiry.

He suggested they continue their search for Yazov – when it was all over, they would need him anyway. Mallory briefly brought them up to date, saying that the assassin was probably in Canada.

'That's fine, John,' McLaren exclaimed. 'Canada's the next stop for both of you.'

They went on to discuss the probable committee questions and procedures, the best legal men to employ as counsel, and the nature of their press releases prior to the hearing.

It was four in the morning when the session finally closed. They were all yawning, the coffee cups were cold. Mallory was still doubtful that McLaren would succeed in taking the stand first, when the committee had specifically asked for Harper, but he was too tired to press the point further.

Carson rang his wife to tell her he would be going away again. Neither he nor Mallory could return to their homes for fear of being served with subpoenas. McLaren drove them directly to the airport, and they wished him luck as they waved goodbye.

27

Dan Proudfoot wanted to be president of the United States. He had once run for presidential nomination and now he was ready again, an aggressive, ambitious, disciplined and dedicated politician who had worked hard and well in the Senate. Yet despite twenty-nine years in Congress, he was a public figure only in his home state of Louisiana; most other Americans hardly knew who he was, let alone what he wanted. With the purpose of remedying that, Proudfoot had gathered together, over the years, a team of skilled, professional campaign aides.

Fireplay could change Proudfoot's colourless, wooden image, and he was well placed to profit from the CIA's misfortunes. He was a dedicated conservative, mistrusted the Soviet Union, was unhappy with détente, and was against giving away presidential power.

'So the commander in chief isn't the commander in chief at all,' he told CBS News on the even of the hearings. 'He's just a problem; nobody wanted to inform him because he might have said "no".'

The senator was for the CIA but against waste and inefficiency. His campaign statistician had worked out that at $350000000 the Russian submarine had cost $153 192 a ton to raise. In the television studio Proudfoot pretended to do sums and scratched in pencil on a pad before finally tearing off the page and holding it high. 'Bring me a taxpayer who wants to buy junk at $153 000 a ton,' he said with a fine show of indignation.

The Senate resolution ordered the committee to investigate and report

the extent, if any, to which illegal, improper or wrongful abuses of power were engaged in by any persons, employed directly or indirectly by the Central Intelligence Agency, acting either individually or in combination with others, in the agency's so-called Project Fireplay and to determine whether in its judgement any occurrences which may be revealed by the investigation indicate the necessity or desirability of the enactment of new congressional legislation to safeguard against abuses of its power or potentials by the Central Intelligence Agency.

The resolution had been proposed by Senator Daniel Lewis Proudfoot, Louisiana Democrat, and in accord with Senate customs he became chairman of the select committee on the Central Intelligence Agency's Project Fireplay. The press immediately dubbed it the Proudfoot Committee.

It employed eight lawyers, four investigators and eighteen secretaries, typists and messengers in a large workroom on the ground floor of the Dirksen office building. Tacked to the oak door was a small, rectangular piece of white paper upon which someone had unsteadily inked: *Committee on Project Fireplay, please knock.*

Staff worked long hours, interviewing witnesses, correlating evidence, investigating leads, preparing questions for the committee's senators. Most of the workers were hired by, and responsible to, Clifford Blanzer, the committee's chief counsel. A former criminal law professor from Harvard, Blanzer was an independent, incisive cross-examiner and methodical organizer. He smoked pipes between supervising the interrogation of the major friendly witnesses. These included Smith, Wooler, Pugulisi, Harper, Conrad, Howick and five other crewmen from *Pacific Klondike*.

The committee's employees worked confidentially and, by Blanzer's order, scrap paper was shredded, typewriter ribbons were cut up, tapes locked away. As a further precaution, a guard was posted at the oak door with authority to search all staff members. It was Blanzer himself who worded a finely-printed *sub poena duces tecum* to be served upon McLaren, ordering the Fireplay director to produce for perusal by the Proudfoot Committee all the CIA's written record of Project Fireplay. His messengers also sought Mallory and Carson but without success.

McLaren had finally persuaded the Proudfoot Committee to take his testimony first. Dan Proudfoot was forced to concede the point. The man who was responsible for Fireplay was volunteering a full disclosure and was subject to cross-examination. To preserve his impartiality, Proudfoot gave way.

Harper was a late-nighter who liked a pre-bedtime snack. McLaren expected to find him still up when he called at his house. It was close to midnight. The hearings were due to start the next day.

McLaren walked round the house to the back and watched through the kitchen window as the ex-CIA agent fried a snack of Italian sausages and spinach. From where he stood, McLaren heard the meat sizzle, smelled its tangy aroma.

Dressed in shirtsleeves, a small apron tied around his middle, Harper bent over the cooker, moving the meat and spinach around the pan with a fork. A small can of beer, a clean plate and a slice of bread rested on the table beside him. He was dusting his sizzling snack with salt and pepper when a rap on the window pane made him start. Through the window, in the light burning outside the door, he saw McLaren's face. It came as no surprise – for some time he had expected McLaren to call.

Harper pushed the saucepan off the burner, cleaned his hands on the apron and walked across the kitchen to free the chain and open the door.

Outside in the yellow light, his face very serious, stood McLaren. Harper extended his right hand, but·let it fall when the Fireplay director pulled from his pocket a .22

Beretta pistol which had a thick sausage of a silencer wound round the barrel.

McLaren shot Harper seven times in the face, neck and chest in five seconds. His white shirt staining rapidly with red, Harper coughed, staggered and fell, bumping heavily against the door.

McLaren pushed the pistol deep into his overcoat, then walked back into the quiet, suburban street and down the kerb, keeping to the large black pools cast by big poplars. He passed nobody on the way to the rented car parked 300 yards down from Harper's home. All he left behind were seven .22 calibre shell casings.

Blanzer told Proudfoot of Harper's murder in a pre-dawn telephone call. The senator lay with his elbow propped on a pillow. The news of Harper's death jolted him alert.

'What do you make of it?' Blanzer broke the silence.

'McLaren's as sharp and tough as nails,' Proudfoot said, 'but with this we can break him. All we have to do is time it right. Meantime, keep the news off the streets.'

'Don't worry about that, Senator. Nothing will leak out.'

Proudfoot replaced the receiver and rolled his legs free of the bedcovers. His wife slept in the next room. There were faint streaks of dawn in a blue-grey sky as the Louisiana Senator thought about Harper's death, and wondered about the best psychological moment to use his information. Draping himself in a bathrobe, he walked to the shower. Warm water sprayed over his head and he was still thinking as he soaped himself. After a few minutes he turned on the cold tap, grimacing while icy water burst over his head for five seconds.

Four days after he got to Montreal, Mallory confirmed his tip-off that Ivan Yazov had flown in from Madrid. Once again, however, he had vanished from the scene, and the hunt settled down to a repetitive routine. Mallory and Carson sifted through passenger lists, conferred with the Canadian Secret Service, made telephone calls.

On the sixth day, at the Sentinel Hotel in lower Montreal, a clerk seemed to recognize a picture of Yazov. Wearing an armoured vest, Mallory knocked on the door of a room. He found a man dressed in his underwear, his wife and two-year-old son. Meantime, Carson had traced a hired car in a false name to Toronto, where he was making enquiries.

Unbroken, torrential rains made Montreal very dark on the tenth day. Later in the afternoon, Mallory checked a musty flat on East 13th Street. Nobody was home and when Mallory forced his way in all he found was a swarm of cockroaches. Three days later he hired a detective agency to assist with routine and wished he had done so earlier.

Newspapers and magazines were delivered daily to his hotel room. The news was mostly bad, but on the morning of the hearings, he read the first anti-Proudfoot editorial – a piece in the *New York Daily News*:

The whole thing smacks too heavily of politics. Not only is Proudfoot seeking the presidential nomination but Chief Counsel Blanzer is now rumored to have accepted the post as Proudfoot's campaign manager – if the campaign ever gets going.

The Fireplay affair is starting to smell like a publicity stunt and when Proudfoot says that he sees nothing political in it, we wince in embarassment for him.

Mallory phoned Carson in Toronto to see if he had read the editorial. Carson had seen it and was pleased at the development, but he too admitted that he was nowhere near finding Yazov. A small compensation was the fact that the Canadians were televising live the start of the Fireplay hearing, so Carson planned to stay in his hotel room for the rest of the day in front of the TV with a few cans of beer, a deep armchair and sandwiches.

28

McLaren took the oath at ten o'clock in Senate Caucus room C18 of the Russell office buildings. Giving a final reassuring pat to his breast pocket handkerchief, he raised his right hand high, his head slightly tilted, and took the oath.

'State your profession.'

'I am an intelligence officer – a spy – for the government of the United States.' McLaren was unrepentant.

'Where is your place of work?'

'Central Intelligence Agency, Langley, Virginia.'

'Now, before we start, was a subpoena served upon you personally to bring with you all files and documents relating to a project code-named Fireplay?'

'It was.'

'Have you complied with that subpoena?'

'No.'

Two microphones were placed on the witness table in front of McLaren. Cubes of ice floated in a clear glass pitcher. To his right sat counsel for the CIA, a bespectacled, white-haired man wearing a buttoned-down shirt and striped tie. The Senate Caucus room was lit by ornate chandeliers and Klieg lights were strung from a boom above McLaren's head. The room, with its ornate columns and marble panels, was filled with press and public. Cameramen operated a battery of television and movie cameras from places between the marble columns to McLaren's left.

Nine Fireplay Committee senators faced him from behind

a large green table, on which microphones and ashtrays, name plates and water glasses were neatly laid out. Behind the senators sat Fireplay's staff. At Proudfoot's right elbow lay a shiny, carved wooden gavel which he had used to rap the Caucus room into silence, the hearing into session.

McLaren, leaning towards the microphone, gave a slightly crooked grin and spoke in a monotone into millions of American living rooms.

'Why did you tell the messenger there are no complete records in existence?'

'Well, Mr Blanzer, the records were removed from my files and destroyed.'

The Caucus room stirred. Blanzer was momentarily non-plussed. 'Why were they destroyed?' he asked.

'They were destroyed because there was no special requirement to keep them.'

'Where they destroyed before or after the press revelations?'

'They were destroyed after the press revelations – and, Mr Chairman, there is no connection between the two.' McLaren gazed unblinkingly at Proudfoot.

The committee's chief counsel was deeply incredulous. 'Do you swear that these records would have been destroyed even if there had been no press exposure about Fireplay?'

McLaren replied evenly. 'I dispute any connection between the destruction of these documents and publicity about Fireplay.'

'Don't you think it is rather suspicious?'

'No, I don't think so, Mr Blanzer. It was entirely a routine action.'

There were titters in the Caucus room, and McLaren shifted in his chair.

'What a liar,' a senator muttered to himself, but his mutter was picked up by a live microphone, making the public laugh. Press bulbs flashed. Proudfoot used his gavel again.

Later, the questioning moved to the confrontation itself, and the Fireplay director was asked why he had, without authority, moved the United States to the brink of war. The chairman intervened. 'Would you tell me, Mr McLaren, what is your perception of the institution of the presidency?'

'The president cannot deal with all of the mundane problems that go on from day to day,' McLaren replied. 'He has to deal with greater problems.'

'Is the firing of a Russian missile a mundane, day-to-day happening?'

'It was a misfire,' McLaren retorted. 'It missed by a mile. Everybody in the United States knows that by now. But not in the Soviet Union – you can be sure of that, Senator.'

'And the armed helicopters, the frigates sweeping in, what about . . .'

'The CIA beat them, that's what, Mr Chairman.'

'Who gave the CIA authority to make war? What law is it that delegated authority to you to confront the Soviet Union?'

McLaren sat silent. Seconds ticked by before he replied. 'I have not found anything in the constitution, Senator.'

'Why did you not immediately advise the president of the Russian ships?'

'I was not prepared to countenance anything that would stand in the way of Fireplay.' McLaren maintained his defiance.

'The salvage of an obsolete submarine?'

'Anything atomic is important. We need to know everything that can help keep the balance of power, and through that, the peace.'

'By going to war?' Proudfoot demanded triumphantly.

In the silence that followed, the Fireplay director turned to his CIA counsel and spoke fiercely and audibly. 'It's a great trial being conducted up here, isn't it?'

There were fresh murmurs. McLaren seemed a little out

of control, and while the room buzzed, his counsel placed a warning hand upon his sleeve. Proudfoot shuffled his papers before gavelling the proceedings back to order. He nodded at Blanzer to continue, and the committee's chief counsel knew it would not be difficult to get under the guard of a witness who was so confident and combative, uncontrite, and arrogant.

'Would you lie at the present time to protect the CIA?' he fished.

In the hush that followed, McLaren gave another crooked smile. 'I would walk over my own grandmother for the CIA.'

There was an audible gasp in the courtroom, cameras flashed and press photographers scrambled to focus on McLaren's face. The witness himself seemed unaware of the disturbance, folded his hands neatly across his chest and waited unconcerned as the first few raps of Proudfoot's gavel went unheard in the hubbub, forcing marshals to restore order.

'Let us go back to the beginning,' Blanzer said. 'How did Fireplay start?'

'It started in the summer of 1973 with a file from naval intelligence to see if we could set up a perfectly legitimate intelligence operation. I sent for Harper and we agreed that naval intelligence was not the agency for the job. In retrospect, that was a bad decision, because naval intelligence is incredibly cautious and they would never have got us in the present jam.'

Some laughter broke out in the Caucus room. McLaren had scored a point and grew in confidence as he tried to spin a web of blame around the Fireplay executive.

'Harper was told to put together a plan, how we would run it.' McLaren sipped iced water.

'Did you go along?'

'Not at all. After Harper got it to us I said it was too full of holes. Carson and Mallory agreed. Harper was told to come up with something more realistic.'

Blanzer nodded as McLaren continued. 'As it now appears, we were badly misled by Harper for reasons which are still not completely clear.'

Changing tack, Blanzer asked, 'How did the Forty Committee take to the plan?'

'They expressed approval.'

'Mr McLaren, in spite of your disapproval of Mr Harper's plan, isn't it a fair statement to say that your report to the Forty Committee was wholly biased in favour of a pet project?'

'Your conclusion is quite unjustified.'

'But you had considerable power with men on the Forty Committee, did you not?'

'I don't think power is the right word.'

'According to a statement made by Mr Harper, the committee respected your opinions and listened to you. There was hardly any meeting you ever attended when you didn't manage to carry the majority. Is that a fair summary of your influence?'

'Judge for yourself. It doesn't look as if I'm carrying the Fireplay Committee,' the witness replied sharply, to win another round of laughter.

'Mr Harper has told us, Mr McLaren, that it was all your doing – that he had nothing to do with the major planning of Project Fireplay,' Blanzer said softly.

'A palpable, damnable lie.'

'What about blowing MGB headquarters in Sofia? Whose idea was that?'

'I claim privilege on grounds of national security,' McLaren said stonily. 'The law forbids an answer though I'm sure Harper's told you everything he wants you to believe.'

'What about plans to assassinate former CIA double agents in Belgrade and Zürich?' the chief counsel persisted.

'I'm not your best witness on that. This was not my beat. Ask Harper.'

'He has told us he got the orders from you. He said he

can remember it very vividly, and he asked you whether it was a proper assignment.'

'Another damnable lie,' McLaren snapped. He wiped his forehead, drank iced water and then talked more calmly. 'My involvement in what happened in Zürich was entirely through Mr Harper. We were badly misled by him.'

'Is that your only explanation, that it was all Mr Harper's fault?'

'Maybe I should have fired him sooner,' McLaren replied coldly.

With that, Dan Proudfoot took his cue, stirring from behind the silver microphone, shuffling his papers together. The chairman's eyebrows waggled, his jowls quivered and an air of expectancy spread through the Caucus room.

'Mr Harper was shot this morning, Mr McLaren,' Proudfoot said. 'He was shot seven times with a small calibre pistol and he is dead.'

Jumping to his feet, McLaren pounded the witness table. Ice and water spilt from glass tumblers as they overturned. 'Nobody told me Harper was dead,' he shouted. 'The agency knew nothing about it. We had nothing to do with it.'

The hearing broke up in confusion, with people on their feet amid a noisy babble. Flash after flash lit up the room as news photographers doubled their activities. The proceedings were past control, and Proudfoot hurriedly gavelled an adjournment before senators and their staff filed out in disarray.

The Fireplay director stood by the table, grasping the green baize covering. To the newsmen who surrounded him he said repeatedly, 'It isn't a fair trial, is it?' He shook himself free of his counsel's restraining hand, and when a reporter place a microphone before him and wanted to know whether he contemplated resigning, he seemed surprised. 'That's one for the CIA to figure out.'

A reporter suggested that such a request was likely. 'Maybe the director will call for my resignation,' McLaren said, 'because I hired Harper.' He seemed to regret the impulsive words as soon as he had spoken them and said more quietly: 'I'm not suggesting I'd like to resign. I would not like to. But if I'm required to resign and I can do so without creating any sticky problem for the CIA. . . .' He paused. 'Yes, I might even do that for the agency.'

29

In a darkened Montreal hotel room Mallory watched a large TV screen. The small, comfortable room had a red carpet, green mock-leather chairs, and the kind of hard bed that was good for his back. There was even a small cocktail bar and ice chest.

The CIA agent sat in shirt sleeves; and light from the TV screen made patterns on his face and white shirt. He had finished two double whiskies on ice and was on his third at the moment he saw the CIA's counsel half-dragging McLaren away from the witness table. Reporters in suits, sweaters and sport coats crowded the star witness with a small thicket of microphones that barely succeeded in keeping pace with him as he left the room.

Feeling sick, Mallory drank the small, neat whisky. The CIA would want McLaren's resignation. His own and Carson's as well. Everybody Fireplay touched would have to resign.

He phoned Carson in Toronto but got no answer from his room. Mallory stretched his legs and tried to relax deep in the armchair. The thought that was uppermost in his mind was that Yazov would have to be found. He would have to find him soon. Deep inside, a feeling began to grow that finding Yazov was the last service he could do for the CIA.

He called Toronto again without success.

Half dreaming, Mallory tried to penetrate the mists in his mind. The Russians had baited their trap brilliantly, he thought. The loss of a submarine close to the navy's sonar device, the search by the task force, Sedlacek's defection with the code that led them to Sofia, the ingeniously contrived 'confrontation'. It had all been a brilliant gamble. It was destroying the CIA. Throughout the night Mallory sat slumped in the armchair, getting up only for another attempt to contact Carson in Toronto.

By the time morning came he knew what he had to do. There was heavy stubble on his face. He ordered a breakfast of fresh orange juice, two poached eggs on toast and coffee, and had all the newspapers available delivered to his room. After his third cup of black coffee he once more tried Carson, again without success.

Mid-morning he turned on the television and was in time to catch a live CIA press announcement direct from Langley. Fiedler, the CIA's press officer, read from a prepared statement without pause – he even managed to smile faintly twice. Fiedler said:

'Ladies and Gentlemen: I have two announcements to make.

'The first relates to the appearance of Central Intelligence Agency officials before the Senate Fireplay Committee, better known as the Proudfoot Committee.

'All members of the CIA staff who participated in the project will appear voluntarily when requested to do so by the committee. They will testify under oath and they will answer fully all proper questions.

'My second announcement concerns the Fireplay case directly. As a result of serious charges which came to the CIA's attention, some of which were publicly reported at the time, the CIA began intensive enquiries of its own into the whole matter. Reports are being urgently compiled by responsible CIA personnel. I can report today that there have been major developments in the case concerning which it would be improper to be more specific now, except to say that real progress has been made in finding the truth.

'Today, in one of the CIA's most difficult decisions, the

agency has accepted the resignation of a key man in the directorate of operations, James Joseph McLaren. John Mallory and Richard Carson, associates of McLaren, will also be asked to resign.

'The CIA wants to stress that in accepting Mr McLaren's resignation, it means to leave no implications whatever of personal wrongdoing on his part or on the part of others who have been named. But in matters as sensitive as guarding the integrity of our democratic process, it is essential not only that rigorous legal and ethical standards be observed, but also that the public have total confidence that they are being observed and enforced by those in authority – and particularly by the CIA itself.

'The CIA wants to make it abundantly clear that it has nothing to hide in this matter. During the past weeks, the wildest accusations have been made; rumour, gossip, innuendo, accounts from unknown sources have filled the newspapers and television newscasts.

'As the Proudfoot Committee conducts its enquiry, the CIA considers it essential that its counsel should be present to cross-examine witnesses and introduce evidence in an effort to establish the truth. The CIA has agreed to make highly confidential records available to the committee. These documents will provide all the additional evidence required to put an end to the Fireplay controversy, so that the agency is left unimpaired for work that still must be done in dealing with the problems which affect the nation's security.

'Finally, I am authorized to state categorically that the Central Intelligence Agency bears no responsibility whatsoever for the death of its former agent, Robert William Harper which, in all the circumstances, the agency regards as a tragedy.'

After Fiedler read his announcement, copies were handed out by aides to the pressmen. His only unrehearsed action was to thank the press and explain that he could not possibly answer the questions they might wish to ask.

'We've been through many difficult times together and many historical ones,' he smiled faintly. 'I hope you remember the good ones too.'

Mallory pressed a button and the screen faded. He dialled Toronto again. There was no Carson. By now Mallory knew he was dead. He knew Yazov would find him too. . . .

He left his hotel room and when he returned twenty minutes later, he brought with him two thick, lined examination pads, a ball point pen, and two refills. He started writing in his neat, looping hand. By nightfall his hand hurt too much to continue. Throughout the afternoon he had forced his fingers into place, flicked his tired wrist and massaged the ball of his fist. He locked and bolted the door and ran a very hot bath.

During the next two days, Mallory completed his report. It ran to 273 pages. From time to time he had stopped writing and read the newspaper reports and comments. What he read filled him with dismay. The stories that were now appearing ranged far beyond the Fireplay revelations, and covered a whole catalogue of accusations that went back over the years, some of them based on evidence, some that could only have been the product of a lively imagination.

Time magazine quoted 'credible sources' who insisted that the CIA had been involved in assassination plots against at least three figures. They listed the assassination of the Dominican Republic's dictator, Rafael Trujillo; an attempt on the life of Fidel Castro with 'expert hired-gun help of US Mafia figures'; and an attempted bombing from the air of the palace of the late Haitian dictator, François Duvalier.

Other reports tied the CIA to the killing of South Vietnam's President Ngo Dinh Diem and the Congo's Patrice Lumumba, to attempts to kill Egypt's President Nasser and even France's President de Gaulle.

There were stories of CIA inefficiency. The agency had

misread the outbreak of the 1973 Arab–Israeli war, it was alleged. They had not known of the 1974 Cyprus coup; they had misjudged Turkish motives after the invasion of Cyprus; they had been surprised by the Viet Cong's Tet offensives in South Vietnam. Senator Dan Proudfoot was quoted as saying: 'If an attack were to be launched on America in the very near future, it is my belief that America would not know that the attack was about to be launched.'

A CIA official was said to have defied an order from the president to destroy cobra venom developed for a tele-scopic-sighted dart gun. There were references to a CIA project to discredit President Sukarno of Indonesia. The *New York Times* published a round-up of the CIA's illegal and secret surveillance of United States citizens.

To exercise his bad back, Mallory walked around the room. He only went out once, and that was to rent a xerox machine which he had delivered to the hotel. Apart from that, he stayed in his room because he did not want to miss the call from Yazov that he was sure would come. Indeed, he became increasingly impatient as he waited for it. He had made five copies of his report, and it was all that work that had made his back ache.

His meals consisted of sandwiches and beer, and he passed the time watching television. When Senator Proudfoot appeared yet again, this time being interviewed by Nicholas Wicker, Mallory had scarcely more than an academic interest in what he said.

The senator announced he was discontinuing the Fireplay hearings. He now wanted something much bigger – nothing less than a Senate investigation into the entire working of the CIA, and perhaps of the whole intelligence establish-ment. He read extracts from the National Security Act of 1947 and even from the constitution respecting the rights of the individual.

'We must have tighter oversight, a smaller, more effective

intelligence operation,' he said. 'I think one of the problems is the CIA's too big.'

The phone buzzed in Mallory's room.

Wicker asked Proudfoot if he was not trying to destroy the CIA.

Mallory put out his hand for the telephone.

'Who needs them the way they are?' Proudfoot retorted.

It was Yazov.

'Mr Carson asked me to contact you,' Yazov said. 'He had to go back to Washington.'

'Sure, I'd like you to come to Montreal. We need to talk.'

'I'd like to do that.'

'Fine. I'm staying at the Convention Inn.'

'We'll meet somewhere I'll decide,' Yazov laughed. 'You'll have to trust me rather than me trust you.'

'Sure,' Mallory said. 'I understand.'

30

Mallory flew the ninety-six miles from Montreal to Norton, Vermont, in a single-engined Piper Cherokee Cruiser which took off from a private air strip outside the city, across the St Lawrence. The small two-seater crossed the United States border at 9000 feet near Stanstead.

Below Mallory stretched green hills, freeways, small settlements, rivers and small lakes. Smoke rose from the stacks of fishing cabins; it was good fishing country.

Strapped into a reclinable seat, with copies of the *New York Times* and *Time* magazine on his lap, Mallory had given up trying to read the small print in the buffeting aircraft. He had taken some pills in Montreal, but he still felt sick and his back was hurting. The CIA's potential was damaged for months, even years, possibly permanently. Dan Proudfoot and other powerful men even wanted it dismantled. Fireplay had shattered the CIA as surely as a series of bomb blasts. If Russian agents had somehow slipped into Langley with satchels of high explosive, all they could have done was raze the buildings; Fireplay had destroyed the agency's credibility, its confidence, its secrecy.

While writing his report, Mallory had been reminded of the doctoral thesis he had written years ago when he had graduated from Harvard. Its title was *Risk, Decision, Prediction* and it had been his interest in the subject that had led him into a career in the CIA. In his thesis, he had analysed in detail what he thought was the greatest intelligence coup ever: the risks, decisions, and predictions of the Trojan Horse in 1194 B.C.

After the Greeks had withdrawn their fleet, pretending to lift the siege, the Trojans had dragged the wooden horse into Troy. And so Troy was taken, sacked and razed.

The KGB had done something comparable. The risks were there in both cases but the planning and timing were superlative. The grandeur of the KGB's scheme – its similarities with the Trojan horse – overwhelmed Mallory.

Doneska had been the Trojan Horse. But, of course, somebody had to be hidden in the horse – to open the gates. *That somebody had been McLaren.* All the KGB had needed was Jim McLaren. Without him, the Russian operation was too risky. With him, success was almost assured.

A Russian ballistic missile submarine was attractive bait. All the KGB wanted was a man to make sure the agency took it, a KGB man to push when Fireplay stuck, a man to 'confront' Yashin's task force with a flight of jets. They had to have an agent there for the brink-of-war hoax. The Goa missile was a hoax – a KGB agent probably got a medal for missing, Mallory thought.

Once the press broke Fireplay's secret – how could they ever have thought that nobody among hundreds of men would ever tell? – McLaren was inside the walls, ready to destroy the CIA's image. His performance at the hearings had been brilliant. The man with the frayed nerves, getting rattled by the questions, bumbling about resigning. Jim McLaren was not like that at all. That was what had given Mallory the first big clue. McLaren was icy cool. He knew him too well, there had been too many years together.

Mallory thought back past Fireplay, to a day years ago and to a leafy glade where he had lain beside a green-eyed girl while pages of *Risk, Decision and Prediction* marched through his mind.

'*What are you doing?*' she had asked him.

'*I'm working.*'

'*What kind of work are you doing?*'

'*I'm thinking.*'

'*What are you thinking about?*'

'*The Trojan Wars and how in God's name did Ulysses calculate the risk?*'

She had gone away and married somebody else. And now when Mallory recalled that day and the way he had chosen instead to take his vows with the agency, how it had all been, what he was going to do, how it was all ending, he just smiled.

The only time things had gone solidly against McLaren on *Klondike* was when he, Harper and Carson together drew the line. Mallory wondered whether McLaren had killed Harper. He was certain Yazov had killed Carson.

Nobody would believe him. It would be his word against McLaren's. There was no way of conveying all the nuances, moods and manipulations. It was impossible to present concretely the atmosphere and evil genius of McLaren's machinations over the months, the way McLaren smiled sometimes, spoke softly, the enigmatic expression of his face. How McLaren wiped his glasses that night he tricked them into flying out of Washington to leave him alone with the Proudfoot hearings. The nod he gave Harper to kill Hofman in Belgrade. McLaren had wanted Higby recalled from Zürich. Mallory wondered whether he had already calculated it was too late – or was Higby's death a bonus? There were some things he had not worked out.

He half believed that the KGB had allowed Yazov to destroy the badly penetrated Bulgarian Secret Service. How convenient for them to have General Z kill himself.

All the Russians had sacrificed was a submarine that was probably being phased out of service anyway. For them, it was a reasonable gamble, *provided they had McLaren*. Where had the KGB recruited him, he wondered. How long ago, how did they do it? Had they blackmailed him or was he dedicated? Did he really believe in Karl Marx? Had they caught him in Hungary, in the building, after that famous telex printer had gone dead? Or had it happened in Berlin?

McLaren had sprinted across to the American sector ahead of Russian tanks, or so the story went. Or had they got at him through some kind of sex aberration, a favourite KGB blackmail ploy? Mallory wondered, thinking of the one book in McLaren's library which had seemed out of place.

The Piper Cherokee came in to land on a rough strip in trout country. The CIA agent saw the shadow of the plane ripple in the longer grass to the side of the runway and felt the wheels bounce under him. It rolled to a halt in under 200 yards and the prop spun out. Mallory climbed out and said good-bye to the pilot.

He walked over the grass and soon he was out of the clearing. Thin smoke led him to McLaren's fishing cabin. The door was open and Mallory walked inside. He had been there before and found nothing new: a fireplace, a Franklin stove, a table, a bed; an assortment of trout fishing rods and colourful flies. There were a couple of fishing baskets. Mallory tried on a pair of rubber waders.

On the table was a plate with the remains of a freshly cooked trout, with tiny pieces of white flesh still sticking to the fish's skeleton. Mallory gave the head a perfunctory glance. The eyes were missing. McLaren always ate the eyes, prising them out with a fork, eating them last.

Carrying the waders with him out of McLaren's cabin, Mallory walked slowly down a narrow, sandy track and suddenly, on the crest of a small hill below him, the green country opened up. The stream was down a steep slope. There were trees around the stream, and he could not see McLaren.

Mallory heard water rushing and paused to take in the quiet beauty of the scene and the smell of grass warming in the sun. Smoke drifted from another fishing cabin that was hidden in a small belt of trees. He thought of what lay in store, and his spine froze, his mouth went dry.

Leaning back a little as bracken crunched and gave underfoot, he slipped carefully down the slope. To balance himself, he took a wader in each hand. Ahead of him the noise of the stream got louder, birds sang in the trees. Then he found himself on a flattish rock, and in the stream he saw McLaren.

The double agent had his back to him. He was up to his thighs in a quiet stretch of water, wearing a hat covered in trout flies and a red and black checked shirt. McLaren was casting with easy grace. The younger man watched him trail the fly, pull the line in and send the hook out again and, gently with a practised hand, guide the loop of the line. The trout rod bent and as the line hit the water there were tiny circles.

Pulling on the waders, Mallory inched into the water. He was a little unsure of his footing so he moved gingerly and took tiny steps. He got a third of the way across to McLaren and halted in the water.

'Hi, comrade,' he called out.

McLaren turned slowly to smile very peacefully, an enchanting smile.

'Hi, comrade,' he said, casting his fly in a relaxed easy fashion.

Mallory had given much thought to how to set about it. He would move obliquely, go sideways until he was ready to move head on.

'How are you feeling?' Mallory asked.

'Fine, a little tired.'

Opening his creel, McLaren showed him three scarlet-spotted trout glistening wetly against fresh green ferns that lined his basket. Then he pulled on the fishing line.

'I think you have a problem' Mallory said.

'Yes? What sort of problem?'

'Carson' said Mallory. 'Carson has some wild ideas.'

McLaren stopped pulling in the line and turned slightly to face Mallory with a quizzical look. He smiled, looking slightly puzzled, then he pulled in more line. Mallory waited for a fresh cast before he went on.

'Carson has a bizarre theory. Really absurd.' Mallory spoke haltingly. 'He figures that you've destroyed the CIA.

He says that the agency has become such a dirty word that maybe we ought to just give headquarters to the Defence Department for an annex and go up to Pittsburgh, rent an apartment and start all over again.'

'Carson's crazy of course,' McLaren said without turning. 'We all decided everything together. Do you mean Carson figures I was working for the other side?' McLaren laughed. 'That has to be crazy. Do you go along with any of it?'

'I know, Mac, it sounds crazy.' Mallory hedged. 'I'm just telling you what you have to know. There'll be some kind of investigation after Carson tells the director. Maybe I shouldn't be talking.'

'Thanks, kid. I'll survive any investigation, with or without you.'

'I'm sure you will.'

'The trouble with Carson is that he has motives, just like Harper.'

'Carson figures you killed Harper.'

'It gets crazier and crazier.'

'I know. It shocked me too.'

'I want you to know, I'm not shocked, kid. Sorry it had to happen to you.' The old sarcasm was back.

'One of the problems Carson has is that he's not sure what *is* true at this point.'

'Well, John, out with it all, and I'll tell you what to say to Carson.'

Given this opening, Mallory listed all the accusations against McLaren he had just put in his report, but he still attributed the whole thing to Carson. All the while, McLaren lazily launched cast after cast on to the clear, gently running stream. Once a two-pound trout took the fly. During a brief, skilful struggle, McLaren played it. Reeling in, he netted the trout, carefully removed the hook and pushed the dying fish through a small hole in the basket.

At last Mallory finished. McLaren nodded. 'It's not such a wild theory, the way you've put it across, John. It hangs together in a crazy kind of way.'

'Carson says this whole operation was done by Department A of the First Chief Directorate, and there must be a helluva party going on there right now. He says you were in on it from the start, right from where *Doneska* was scuttled. And you've got your monument to yourself all right, even if it has to be in Moscow.'

Mallory waited as McLaren dropped a fly within two inches of a trout's nose. He could see the spotted back of the fish through the clear water, the way the trout flicked its tail and moved upstream.

'I asked him what he was going to do with all this speculation. He said he means to give it to the director. I said that it was all hearsay and guesswork. He just shrugged and said he'd still have to do it.'

'That's interesting. Whatever his theory is, let me add a footnote. It won't help him a bit, not a damn bit.'

'Sure, Dick's in trouble unless he can somehow effectively peddle to the director a theory that the K G B were running Fireplay through you. Unless he's got a piece of paper somewhere. That's why I wanted to see you immediately.'

'Thanks for seeing me by myself,' McLaren smiled.

'And if the director doesn't believe him,' Mallory went on, 'I wanted to talk with you today, to see if we can keep this story off the streets.'

'Oh, hell . . . he'll tell the press?' McLaren asked innocently.

'Tomorrow morning Dick Carson's likely to have it all over town. He told me if the director won't believe it, he'll take it to the newspapers.'

'Involving McLaren and the K G B too?'

'Everything,' Mallory nodded. 'The lot, Mac.'

Mallory had a frozen image of McLaren at the end of his cast: leaning slightly forward, thigh-deep in water, right hand straight, left hand keeping balance and the long, looping line flicking through the still air. Then McLaren laughed.

'Mallory, the saviour of the CIA,' he said. 'Let's talk

about Mallory. The problem with him is he's a little stupid.' McLaren turned and his eyes were like cold, wet stones. The stream suddenly seemed much colder.

'Why?' Mallory asked quietly.

'We got Carson a week ago,' McLaren said matter-of-factly as he worked with a hook. 'You could say the KGB wants this matter buttoned up, once and for ever.'

Mallory had finally broken through. Here was proof that his analysis was correct. 'So what about Mallory?' he said, knowing already.

'I think Mallory gets killed too,' McLaren said gently. 'By the CIA.'

'By the CIA?'

'Oh, yes, just like Harper and Carson were killed by the CIA. That's what everybody will figure, if it's done right.' The KGB agent sent the fly unerringly through the air on to clear water. 'Then I'll get protection, proving they were after me, too. Self defence.'

The audacity of McLaren's plan was so enormous that Mallory wondered if he really meant it. As the red fly hit the water a trout struck in a flash of light, silver and dark green. It came out of the water, smacked on the stream's surface, sank and then rose once more into the air. McLaren's rod bent with another short struggle and the rod whipped from side to side.

'Then McLaren comes out of it clean as a hound's tooth,' the double agent said as he gingerly extracted the hook. The fish was in the creel when he turned once more to Mallory. 'Why did you really come?'

'I'm not sure – I just don't know,' Mallory said. 'I came to find out for sure, I guess.'

McLaren seemed unconcerned. 'Unless there is something that I don't know, unless somebody's got a piece of paper that somebody signed or some damn thing. . . .'

'I just wanted to be sure it squares with the facts, Mac. Now I know, I can fill in the details.'

'The director won't believe you, any more than he'd have believed Carson.'

'You used a free press to destroy the CIA,' Mallory said. 'I'll use it to turn the tables – and destroy you. It might even save the CIA.'

'When?'

'Tonight,' Mallory lied. 'Tomorrow. As soon as I can.'

'Too late, John,' McLaren said. 'I've got a guy covering you.'

Between them flowed the stream. Mallory stood with his legs slightly apart as water flowed around his waders, frothing against the rubber. There were gurgles where the stream washed up over rocks.

'Well, I guess we still don't know what's in store. You've got someone for me; and I've got Yazov for you.'

'Yazov works for us, John. He got Carson.'

'I know, Mac. Right now, he thinks I don't know about any of that. He thinks I'm just concerned to see he gets the money for the Sofia job. It's all very complicated.'

McLaren's face clouded. 'What are you trying to tell me?'

'It's just like when they let the missile go off *Kresta*. They haven't told you everything, Mac.'

'I have to admit, the missile was not my idea. The missile I didn't like.'

'Nobody told you, Mac. Just like they didn't tell you about Yazov. I think everybody on Fireplay is going to be hit; the KGB don't trust anybody, not even you. With you gone, nobody ever finds out.'

'That's pure guesswork.'

'They have all the cards. And you're going into retirement. It's a natural.'

'Think so, kid? Well, let's see about that.' McLaren smiled and spoke into the creel in which, as the CIA agent realized, there was a walkie-talkie.

'You can take him now, kid,' McLaren said.

31

Mallory thought he had given Yazov six hours' start. Instead, Yazov had left Montreal the previous afternoon, booked into a motel outside Stanstead and crossed the same day from Canada into Vermont on foot, walking the five miles to McLaren's fishing cabin for reconnaissance purposes, because he trusted nobody.

Dressed in red shirt and corduroys, like any hunter or fisherman, he carried a false passport but no gun licence. No licence would explain his strange weapon; if he was stopped, he would kill.

The Bulgarian had a detailed map, prepared by Mallory, showing the way to McLaren's cabin, a good compass, soft boots and a knapsack of food and ammunition. In a breast pocket were photographs of McLaren and the fishing cabin, all of which Yazov had studied carefully. He picked his way through pine and spruce which grew in the woods and bordered the fields, and once he stopped to wash down some cheese and bread with strong coffee. He had not felt in such good form for a long time.

To find McLaren's cabin was not easy since there were others in the area and the streams, woods and trees had no distinctive features. Still, searching doggedly, he spotted McLaren fishing in the stream in the late afternoon, and studied him through binoculars from under cover. The photographs confirmed it was McLaren.

Even as he watched him, McLaren stopped for the day,

rth and dust in his nose. His face itched as tiny insects
ttled on his skin, and at times he wanted to sneeze.
Nevertheless, in the end, he thought it was worth it because
e was sixty-five yards away when the guard sank into a
mall depression alongside a large maple. All Yazov could
see was the back of his blond head through longish grass.
It was a good place that overlooked the stream in which
McLaren was fishing.

Removing the cap to the top of his steel tube, Yazov
slid out the gun and silently pushed and screwed the metal
parts into place. Within four minutes, he held a weapon
into which was dragged a clip of ammunition.

Up ahead, the boyish head bobbed. Yazov put his eye to
the sniperscope's rubber eyepiece and focused gently.
Muscles flexed in the back of the guard's head in a way that
made Yazov think he was munching an apple or some kind
of fruit.

The Bulgarian inched forward through the long grass and
paused. When he moved again a woodpecker started in the
maple, wings crashing in the branches. The noises alerted
the boyish guard; in the sniperscope, Yazov saw muscles in
his neck go rigid.

The guard turned very slowly. Yazov slipped off the
safety catch and eased his right index finger on the trigger.
Ahead, the guard raised himself slightly, exposing his chest.
In his left hand he held a green, half-eaten apple and his
eyes tried to penetrate the thickish long grass. A bullet from
the silenced muzzle of Yazov's weapon hit the boy with a
light smack and flung him back against the maple's trunk.
He slid down the bark into the depression and was dead by
the time Yazov reached him. The Bulgarian moved the body
gently aside.

Below, McLaren was making skilful casts into the stream.
For a while, all Yazov did was watch him wade very slowly
and patiently in the quietly flowing stream, testing very
inch of the water's surface, changing flies half-a-dozen
times. But in the end, McLaren caught trout.

waded out of the stream and climbed the bank
gered to pack away his fishing kit, a man appear
a khaki shirt, jeans and carrying a hunting rifle
men talked above the stream before McLaren
guard on.

For a time, Yazov wondered if the CIA were b
another ambush. It pleased him that he had been
After some consideration the assassin guessed N
would have some kind of guard, for he was careful t
looked after himself.

Forty minutes later Yazov recrossed the border
twilight and easily found his motel by its flashing neor

Next morning he rose early so as to be near the
when McLaren's guard took cover: there were too many
places around the stream where men could hide. It was
Bulgarian's guess that the guard had taken the fishing cab.
nearest McLaren. For that reason he was in hiding close to
both cabins, having worked slowly through the last few
hundred yards and taken care not to snap dead branches.
The first thin plumes of smoke rose from McLaren's cabin;
minutes later, smoke came from the guard's cabin too.

McLaren came out carrying two rods, waders and a creel
for fish. Yazov watched him talk into the creel, and then the
door to the guard's cabin opened and he came out, carrying
a black walkie-talkie with a thin, silver aerial sprouting
from the top of its slim casing. The man waved to McLaren
and went back inside while the fisherman walked to th
stream.

Five minutes later, the guard reappeared, munching
sandwich. The walkie-talkie was slung around his shoulder
In his left hand he carried a rifle: a Savage 99F 5-shot repeat
with a Weatherby sniperscope.

The man finished munching, wiped his hand against
jeans and made for higher ground and a place from where
could easily cover McLaren in the stream.

Carefully circling around with him, the Bulgarian craw
over a hundred yards through tall grass with the smel

Some time that morning Yazov had inserted into his weapon a clip of mercury-tipped bullets. He squinted down the telescopic sight a dozen times. He could have killed McLaren anytime; instead, he knew he had to wait for Mallory. From where he lay, the fisherman was over 400 yards away in the stream. McLaren's head and shoulders filled the sniperscope as he fished with his back to Yazov; sometimes he half turned and Yazov saw the lean face, unsmiling in repose.

At last Mallory came. Yazov watched him slip down the slope, pull on waders and enter the stream. As the two men talked, only soft crackles came from the walkie-talkie. Yazov twiddled the receiver's knobs, but he could only pick up disjointed scraps of conversation. Mallory's mouth moved silently, but the tone of McLaren's voice carried softly, though it trailed away when he turned.

Mallory stood in the stream with his legs slightly apart, hands in his pockets, head bent to one side. McLaren fished unconcerned.

Then came McLaren's voice clear and loud over the receiver, as he spoke into the creel. 'You can take him now, kid. . . .'

The assassin had Mallory's back, a little below the neck under the cross-hairs. He saw clearly the ridge of the spinal bones through the shirt. Holding the gun steady, the assassin fired.

The bullet exploded in Mallory's spine, three inches below his neck, blowing out the bone there along with cloth and flesh. Mallory pitched into the stream on his face with a splash. Tumbling and turning in the water, he drifted lifelessly in the current.

With a triumphant smile on his face McLaren waved up at the maple tree. 'That's a fine shot . . .'

He was still half laughing when Yazov's bullet struck. The top of his head sprayed open like a punctured aerosol of red paint, throwing fragments of skull on to the slowly flowing stream. They made tiny ripples. McLaren slumped into the stream on his back and the water dragged him twenty yards before lodging him against a rock.

Gradually, the stream prised the dead fisherman loose to carry him along a series of small rapids. He bumped swiftly in the rushing, white water before he sank into a clear, quiet pool.

With his back against the maple's trunk, Yazov munched a half-eaten apple. Sun streamed into his closed eyes, making a bright orange glow under his eyelids. He thought there were some brilliant minds in the KGB able to play a game very hard and with icy calm. McLaren, Harper, Carson and Mallory were all dead: everybody on the CIA's Fireplay Committee was wiped out. In between, it had taken the opportunity of purging the Bulgarian Secret Service.

Yazov wondered whether the KGB would keep its bargain with him. He thought they would because they were practical men, but he would not rely on anything. He flung the apple core towards the stream, saw it bounce and disappear. A minute later he left as cautiously as he had come. Within forty-eight hours he was back in Paris.

Mallory's long handwritten report on Fireplay, airmailed from Montreal, thudded on to a desk in the *New York Times*. It came wrapped in brown paper. Inside, the notepads were held together by a broad elastic band. 'The decision to publish,' the managing editor said later, 'was taken almost the moment it came into our hands.'

The *Times* sent three of its star journalists to set up headquarters in a suite on the eleventh floor of the New York Hilton. It imposed strict security. A direct telephone line from the Hilton suite to Washington was used by reporters to check Mallory's facts. All local calls were made from phone booths.

The main story was written by a CIA specialist, Andrew Greenfield. It was set in type by a small, trusted composing crew. Its headline started simply: CIA VICTIM OF MASSIVE,

The security precautions taken by the *New York Times* were unavailing. Mallory's five xeroxed copies arrived in the post at other newspapers, and they in turn forwarded details to newspapers throughout the country which took their news services, while agencies circulated it to the radio and television stations.

Ivan Yazov booked into the Hotel Monaco near the Sorbonne, a fourth-floor room with a radio and a strong chain to the door. Through the wooden louvres of his window the Bulgarian watched a queue of Parisians filing into a cinema.

Yazov smoked a lot, drank red wine. Late that night he put a chair up against the door, checked the chain, latch and lock, then also locked the windows and louvres. With his bed pushed into a new position, he lay in the hot, stuffy dark. Still later, through the locked window, he heard the cinema crowd go home.

The Lüger under his pillow, Yazov was dozing off when he though he heard a scrape at the door. He was suddenly awake and stayed like that until the hour before dawn, when, very tired, he slept. The porter knocked at seven. Yazov moved the bed back into place, cautiously let him in with a breakfast of croissants, coffee, fresh cream, butter, and jam.

The news in French made the Bulgarian stiffen. Very quickly he dressed and hurried down the hotel's four flights into the street to look for a copy of the *International Herald Tribune*. Mallory's story took up most of the front page.

Yazov read the news standing up, near the news stand. Turning to the inside pages, he read more about himself, Brzina Street and Zürich. The story even carried Mallory's own prediction that he would be shot along with McLaren.

Yazov looked casually around before walking to a corner

table in a secluded pavement café, where he could sit and think while he drank strong, black coffee and Pernod. Now the KGB had no alternative: whatever the bargain, they would have to kill him quickly. Maybe they would have killed him anyway – later when he thought he was safe. Now there was no time left.

The Bulgarian was so preoccupied with his thoughts that he forgot to pay his bill. The waiter chased after him along the pavement and remained blissfully unaware that the sound of his feet thudding on the pavement had almost cost him his life.

As it was, the waiter's pursuit caused Yazov to exercise more caution than ever. KGB agents were probably already stationed outside the United States Embassy. Every agent they could possibly muster would be after him, covering airports and embassies. Fortunately, Yazov reflected, even the KGB could not cover everything.

Making up his mind, he took a taxi to Rue de Berri and the offices of the *International Herald Tribune*. As he walked into the foyer, a man with high cheek bones stood up from a seat. Yazov recognized strong Slavic features, and out of the corner of his eye he saw a group of people entering an automatic lift. He dashed towards the open doors at the same moment that the man put his hand in his coat pocket and ran after him. Luck was with Yazov. A briefcase lay on the floor and the killer stumbled over it. Someone, perhaps the owner of the case, went to his assistance and the two men seemed almost to be wrestling as the lift doors closed.

Yazov wasted no time. He entered the first office he came to when the lift stopped and started speaking very calmly and persuasively. He asked for asylum in the United States and was already telling his story to the *International Herald Tribune* by the time the officials arrived from the embassy.

He left for Orly Airport wearing a bullet-proof vest in a black, armoured car that stopped only once: ten paces from a United States Air Force jet far from the terminal buildings.

32

Extract from Newsweek, 20 October, 1976

SPY SHIP FOR HIRE

The CIA is seeking assignments for *Pacific Klondike*, the $250 000 000 ship built by the late Felix Townsend to recover the Soviet submarine in the Pacific earlier this year. The spy agency wants to lease the craft for private scientific and engineering jobs, with no military or intelligence connections.

A major problem is that oceanologists have never forgiven the CIA for sending the ship to pick up the Russian sub and using as a 'cover' the story that the vessel was engaged in deep-sea mining.

That mission, these potential customers charge, has given their industry a bad name.